"To all of my family past, present and future.

The two legged and the four legged."

Especially for Becky who lay faithfully at my feet whilst I wrote every word.

Rest in peace my Angel.

"Let us never forget them but learn from their silent wisdom."

“Langfell Hall: February 2015

Preface.

“Hi auntie Emm, is it alright for Laura and I to join you?” Sarah asked her great aunt.

“The men folk have taken themselves to the Pub in the village for some male bonding, or so they tell us! In fact Gavin wants to get his own back after Nidge thrashed him at pool the other night.”

Emma laughed and looked up fondly at her two great nieces saying with a smile,

“So you thought you’d keep the old girl company for a while!”

“Well we do have a kind of favour to ask and it may have been your seventieth birthday yesterday but you know quite well none of us think of you as old, we wouldn’t dare! It’s a wonder you didn’t join us this afternoon on the back lawn! We were like kids again playing in the snow and we even built an igloo and a snowman!”

“I know,” chuckled Emma, “I watched you from my window and I’ll have you know I’ve done plenty of that throughout my years but I so enjoyed watching you all having fun in the snow! My heart was in my mouth though Sarah when I saw you on that sledge in your condition. At least you have got that husband of yours well trained. He would make a good carthorse the way he was pulling the sledge back and forth as if it were empty!"

"Well Nidge is big enough and strong enough I might as well put him to good use," replied Sarah with a laugh, "and the midwife did say I had to keep active! Might as well have some fun at the same time!"

"Well, what's this favour you want to ask me?"

"Well as you know aunt Emm, Laura is on her first ever visit to the UK and staying with us for a couple of months to get to know her Yorkshire relatives before she starts her history degree at York University. Laura was wondering how the family ended up acquiring Langfell Hall in the first place and how they managed to make it what it is today. I know a little of the history but we need your superior knowledge to fill in the blanks!"

"Hmmm...superior eh?" laughed Emma "I would be pleased to and I am so happy that the two of you are interested in finding out about your family roots. It's a fascinating story with lots of twists and turns as I found out myself when I started tracing our family tree. It was made easier because fortunately most of our forebearers kept diaries and wrote letters that enables us to get a clearer picture of what life was like for them back in those days."

“Right Sarah, put another log on the fire and then I think a glass of red for Laura and I would be lovely and help yourself to a glass of juice.”

Emma grinned at her as Sarah pulled an expression of mock disappointment as she left the room.

Emma was so pleased that Sarah was getting on well with her cousin Laura. Out of all her great nieces and nephews Laura was the one she knew the least about yet worried about the most.

Laura lived in Canada with her mother who was a top shelf Lawyer who was totally immersed in her work and her father played no role in her life. She had spent her formative years in the company of her nanny and in her later years away at boarding school and college.

Emma had met Laura only the once when she was about ten years old whilst she was staying with her grandfather, Emma’s cousin Philp, during the school holidays. She remembered that Laura as a ten-year-old had been extremely quiet, shy, and too well behaved for Emma’s liking. She still seemed too reserved but she hoped that spending time with them would bring her out of her shell. Certainly, as Emma had looked out of her window that afternoon, Laura had looked more animated and relaxed than when she first arrived.

Laura took in the comfortable and tasteful surroundings of auntie Emma’s apartment. It wasn’t decorated like an old person’s home and although some of the furnishings were obviously antique they didn’t overpower the room or make it look dowdy. The very pale blue and cream paintwork worked well with the richer colours of the rugs and curtains.

“Aunt Emm, I would love to have the ability to harmonise the old and the new together as well as you have.” said Laura just as Sarah arrived with the drinks.

“Well, if you think about it Laura it’s just like the relationship between people. To create the right balance in life it helps if the old and young communicate with each other without judgement and with open minds. If we listen openly we can learn from each other to our mutual benefit and it helps narrow the generation gap.”

“Right girls, raise your glasses as we are about to journey back to Langfell Hall as it was in 1867, so if you are sitting comfortably, then I’ll begin!”

Chapter One.

Langfell Hall circa 1867.

Bessie had lived on the Langfell estate all of her life and loved the place dearly. In her eyes Langfell was the bonniest dale in Yorkshire. Her family were tenant farmers at Meadow Bank farm which was one of the two farms on the estate. Meadow Bank was situated on the far west corner of the estate overlooking the lake. The farm buildings nestled at the foot of the Fell. Here the slopes of Langfell raised gently behind the farm creating perfect pasture for the dairy cattle and the crops that were the main source of income for the family. At the end of the pasture the ground rose steeply to form the Lang fell.

Langfell Hall estate sat on the east bank of the river Ribble with the actual village on the opposite bank. The approach to the Hall was through an impressive wrought iron gate that led to the north Gate house and from there on to the main house via a long driveway that followed the meandering river on the right and thick woodland on the left for about a mile or so before the woodland thinned out and passed a picturesque cottage at the edge of the wood. Shortly after the cottage the drive forked with the left fork sweeping to a large clearing where the Hall stood in splendour. The right fork continued onwards passing around the back of the Hall and the woodland lake and finally coming to its end at another Gate house. A farm track carrying on to the left provided access to both farms on the estate, the stables and the workers cottages. As the road turned right a bridge spanned the river and the road south of Langfell village was reached.

Langfell was a typical Dales village and although in the shadow of the Fell its beauty stood out for all to see. It consisted of an ancient church, a school, a village square where several shops and a Coaching Inn surrounded the green. The small Mill, owned by the estate, and the estate workers cottages stood to the north of the village and the railway line swept between the back of the village and the high slopes of the Garth fell where a lead mine was situated and the miner's cottages were dotted about on the steep slopes of the fell.

Bessie had worked at Langfell Hall since she left school several years previously and her post of chamber maid required that she live at the Hall. At that time she shared a room in the attic with Tess the kitchen maid. She and Tess had attended the village school together and were good friends. Bessie remembered how excited they were at being accepted for their posts at the hall. Neither of them wanted to move away from the area and although they might not want to admit it, they were both home birds at heart.

At that time the Dowager, Lady Elspeth ruled the Hall with a rod of iron. Lady Elspeth was a stickler for correct protocol and only addressed staff by their surnames. She would not tolerate staff slacking in their duties by chatting or laughing. Her lady's maid, Mavis, would report to her any misdemeanours from the rest of the staff. A real snitch! The staff had to walk on eggshells when the Family were around.

However, Sir John, who was Lady Elspeth's only son was easier going. He would always acknowledge the staff if he met them in the corridors or the grounds of the estate. He also made a point of thanking staff as they performed their duties despite the frowning of the Dowager. Staff were staff and there to serve a purpose in her eyes.

It was common knowledge to everyone at the Hall that the Dowager was desperate for Sir John to marry. He wasn't getting any younger after all. She saw it as his duty to provide a son and heir.

Parties and social gatherings were organised with all the local ladies deemed to be suitable invited. Sir John was always polite and courteous to them and some even became friends to him but none became special. As time went on the Dowager, in desperation, accepted invitations on his behalf from further afield. His older cousin had a large estate near Harrogate and would hold several large social gatherings throughout the year. These gatherings attracted the gentry from as far afield as Bath and London.

Sir John had attended several of them but had not met one lady that interested him. He was becoming tired of his mother's insistence and told her so. He was not going to enter in to a loveless marriage just to provide an heir to the estate. He said he would continue running the estate and the Mill in the village to the best of his abilities as his father had before him, but if in the end, the estate was passed on to one of his cousins, she would always be well provided for.

Lady Elspeth was upset by his decision and also by the way he had spoken to her. She wasn't used to anyone speaking to her in that way and especially telling her what she didn't want to hear!

Shortly after she received yet another invitation from his cousin to attend a social gathering at his home near Harrogate. She managed to persuade Sir John to go for one last time and after that she promised she would not mention it again.

Sir John met Lady Celeste that night and were married seven months later.

Lady Celeste was the very last female that Lady Elspeth would have wished for her son to marry. She was an American lady and had no time for the social etiquette of the British aristocracy. She thought the class system was foolish, demeaning and a waste of time.

It wasn't very long before Lady Elspeth and her maid retired to the Dowager house at the west gate of the estate.

The atmosphere at the house changed overnight. The staff became more relaxed and the new mistress earned their respect and loyalty by treating them as individuals.

Morale was uplifted and the job seemed less monotonous as Lady Celeste ran it her way.

It was at this time that Bessie was promoted to lady's maid to Lady Celeste. Bessie had finished her duties in the bedroom one morning and was having a quick cuppa in the kitchen whilst leafing through a brochure of patterns for gowns in between sips of her tea when the kitchen door suddenly flew open and Lady Celeste entered. The staff were by now used to her popping in and out and weren't alarmed by her sudden entrance although they did make sure they were occupied with work. She moved over to Bessie to see what she was reading and after a quick look she asked Bessie "Oh, so you are interested in making clothes then?"

"Yes Ma'am, I like trying my hand at making some of the gowns. It's been kind of a hobby of mine ever since my Granny taught me how to make clothes for my dolls. Of course I couldn't afford the material to make something like these so I have to make do with a plainer affair" she said as she motioned towards the pages in front of her. "It gives me ideas of the latest trends in fashion and I still make clothes for my childhood dolls and they are the best dressed in the dale" she laughed and Lady Celeste laughed with her.

"When you have finished here Bessie would you come and join me in the drawing room?"

Bessie was a little nervous as she tapped on the drawing room door.

"Come in Bessie," she heard through the slightly open door.

"Please take a seat Bessie, I have a proposition to put to you."

Bessie sat down on a single hard back chair next to the door whilst wondering what on earth the Lady of the house could want from her.

"Bessie, I would like you to be my lady's maid if you would consider it? You seem to have a greater knowledge of fashion than I do. I have also noticed the different ways you dress your hair. I confess that I know truly little about such niceties as I was brought up on a large ranch in Colorado and my mother died when I was very young. The only female company I knew was an elderly Mexican housekeeper. My father and much older half-brothers worked tirelessly on the ranch and rarely did we venture out to civilisation. It was only recently that I came to Britain and found myself launched in to society. I don't give a damn about myself but I don't want to be an embarrassment to Sir John and so it is clear to me that I shall have to make more of an effort in my appearance for Sir John's sake!"

Bessie could not believe it! It was not only a promotion for her but a dream come true and she readily agreed to the proposition. It was to be the start of a close relationship that would develop between her and her Mistress over the coming years.

Several years later.....

Bessie was sitting in her workroom at the Hall. It had been specially furnished and equipped with every single item she might require to create the gowns and other garments for Lady Celeste's wardrobe.

She loved the bright airiness of this space on the first floor of the house and situated on the south west corner of the building. It always caught the early morning sun from one of the two picture windows at each corner of the room. As the sun passed overhead the other window received the light and so the room always seemed well lit. The window on the west overlooked the two walled gardens one of which was dedicated to growing vegetables and herbs for use by the kitchens.

The other garden was her favourite though for it held every flower known to man. From spring onwards the colours were spectacular and now in the middle of August with her window thrown open to the elements the scent drifting in to the room was intoxicating. It could not have been a better place to work.

She was working on a gown that Lady Celeste required for the wedding of one of Sir Johns nieces. This was the estate at Harrogate owned by one of Sir Johns cousins. It was on the other side of Harrogate which was about thirty miles or so from Langfell. It was about five times larger than Langfell and the House had over forty bedrooms although none of the staff from Langfell who had visited had actually counted them.

Lady Celeste had told her that she always felt like the proverbial poor relation when visiting there. Bessie knew that she said this tongue in cheek because she knew quite well that nothing would intimidate Lady Celeste!

The gown she was making was made from the finest silk in a deep lilac colour with pleated inserts of dove grey. The colour choice could not have been more perfect to suit Lady Celeste's colouring of dark almost black hair and dusky complexion. She was going to look spectacular as usual! Bessie was sure she would be the envy of all the ladies hereabouts, especially when worn with the dove grey bolero jacket that Bessie had already finished.

Lady Celeste's clothes had become a topic of conversation at many of the coffee mornings and afternoon teas she attended throughout the county. Bessie was immensely proud that her creations caused such a stir but then she did have the best of models to do them justice.

She could hear Lady Celeste now, laughing and singing in the nursery next door. She spent as much time as she could with her two young boys. Master James at three years old was already protective of his younger brother David who was approaching his first birthday. She could hear the children giggling and laughing making the most of their time with their mother. Occasionally Lady Celeste would take them out for the day in the pony and trap around the local countryside and stop in the village to buy them treats from the shop. This allowed Nanny to spend some quality time with her friends Martha the cook and Celia the house keeper. They would sit around the kitchen table and catch up with the latest gossip from the house and village. Bessie was sure that the odd glass of sherry was imbibed by the friends as all three ladies always developed a rosy glow to their cheeks on these particular days!

Watson the butler, however, did not really approve of the Lady of the House driving the trap herself. He had been trained in a Royal household, a fact he never tired of telling everyone, and was a stickler for correct protocol and liked everything to be done according to tradition. Lady Celeste was quick to point out that she had been brought up on a ranch and could handle horses and her infectious personality soon broke through his dignified manner. He had been put in his place without even realising it. Although Watson would be the last person to admit it, he had a real soft spot for Lady Celeste.

Suddenly, out of the corner of her eye, Bessie caught the movement of the vegetable garden gate swinging open and there was her beloved Jack carrying a large basket full to the brim with vegetables he was about to deliver to the kitchen. She smiled as she watched him make his way across the yard. Although it had taken her a while to realise and accept her love for him, there was no doubt in her mind now that marrying Jack was the best thing she had ever done.

Aided by the warmth of the sun and the edifying scent of the flowers drifting through the open window, she was soon lost in her own thoughts and was transported back to the day that she and Jack met for the first time.

Chapter Two.

Jack had been employed as a coachman on Sir John's cousins' estate near Harrogate and whenever they visited Langfell, Jack found himself accommodated in the rooms above the stable with Sid his fellow coachman. The staff at the Hall looked forward to these visits from the two coachmen as not only did they catch up with the gossip from the big estate but also because Jack had a way about him that would have them crying with laughter. Many an evening was spent around the kitchen fire listening to Jacks stories.

Arthur and Sam, the two stable lads at Langfell, held Jack in high regard for his knowledge and way with horses was second to none. They said he had the gift of being able to communicate with the horses, a true horse whisperer. Apparently he was in great demand for his expertise at some of the top racing stables in the county and Jack joked that he could make the horses run faster!

Bessie though, thought he was a bit of a loud mouth and far too sure of himself for her liking! To make matters worse he would always refer to her as bonnie Bessie which embarrassed her greatly and he always seemed to take great pleasure in seeing her cheeks glow red. She asked him in no uncertain terms not to call her by that name again but he did it all the more! Sometimes though, she had to admit to herself that just like the others she enjoyed some of his stories. Usually though, when she knew he was about to visit she would make herself scarce with some excuse or other but this did not always work for he would seek her out or get one of the maids to talk her in to joining them. Not only did the rest of the staff think he was the bee's knees but he had ingratiated himself with her own family at the farm.

On one of the visits to Langfell he was called to home farm where a horse was having a difficult labour. His natural ability helped save the life of their best work horse and the life of the foal too. Arthur and Sam, the two stable lads, were glad when Jack calmly stepped forward and they watched in earnest and took in every move as he gently calmed the mother down and eased the foal in to a birthing position.

Bessie's brothers Ed and Bill became friends with Jack and would try to join in with the evening's entertainment around the kitchen fire whenever they could. Some of the older female staff would tease Bessie about Jacks interest in her. Cook in particular thought she was crazy not to encourage his advances. Such a fine handsome young man in his livery of dark green with gold braiding. Bessie agreed that he did look smart but was adamant that he was too bolshie for her!

This situation carried on for a year or more and Bessie thought that if she continued to knock him back he would eventually lose interest in her and that would be the end of it. Jack however was not so easily put off and eventually Bessie got used to his antics. She decided that if she couldn't beat him she would join him and so, to the great delight of the staff, this heralded the start of their bantering matches and because each one was determined to have the last word they could go on late in to the night. They were equal sparring partners and eventually became good friends.

One afternoon she was taking a short stroll by the lakeside when she came upon Jack sitting by the boat house. He was holding his head in his hands and did not see her approach. He looked so anguished that she immediately sat beside him and took his shaking hand in to hers.

He explained to her that he had been called to a local farm on the way over from Harrogate that morning to help with a young mare who had given birth a few days before.

All had seemed well at first but that morning she began to fit and froth at the mouth. The mare was very distressed and in great pain and in her distress she had trampled on the foal and severely injured it. When Jack arrived he entered the stable to calm the mother but he immediately knew that there was nothing he could do for either of them. He had to put them out of their misery as quickly and humanely as possible. This was the first time he had to perform this deed himself and he was devastated. He felt so guilty and powerless because he could do nothing to save them.

Bessie held him whilst he cried in her arms and tried to offer him words of comfort. Eventually his sobs subsided and he gave her a weak smile. He thanked her for understanding and gave her hand a squeeze before slowly making his way back to the stables.

As she watched him walk away she thought that perhaps this loud, bolshie man had a much softer exterior to the one he portrayed to others.

He returned to Harrogate with the family the next day without saying goodbye.

Chapter Three.

Two months later the family were due to visit again and Bessie realised she was really looking forward to seeing Jack. She was missing his banter but also because of their last encounter at the lake she wanted to make sure he was alright. She found herself preening in front of the mirror and pinching her cheeks before she entered the kitchen that evening. However, to her disappointment Jack was not there and she found only Sid amongst the others having his usual mug of strong tea. To hide her disappointment she said "Oh, I thought it was quiet in here! Where's your partner in crime tonight Sid?"

Sid told her that Jack had been involved in a bad accident. Her heart stopped, she felt light headed and Sid noticed her look of anguish and pale face as did the others.

"He will be alright love," he quickly continued "he's sustained a broken pelvis, a couple of broken ribs and a bad break to his left leg. He's still in hospital and will be for some time but the Doctors are confident he will make a full recovery in time but he could be left with a permanent limp."

Although Bessie felt bad for Jack's condition she was relieved by the Doctors prognosis and at least he was alive.

Sid went on to describe the accident. Jack had been called to one of the racing stables bordering the estate over in Harrogate to see if he could give advice to the young groom on how to quieten a young, spirited stallion. Unfortunately, as he entered the stall, two of the stable dogs began to fight in the opening. The snarling and growling of the two dogs spooked the stallion who reared up on to his hind legs and knocked Jack to the ground as he turned to shut the dogs out. He was trampled by the frightened horse whilst laying there but the young groom plucked up the courage to drag Jack out of the stable saving his life.

The groom told Sid, "The bugger was laying there in a lot of pain but all he was bothered about was calming me and the bloody horse down. I have to admit I was shitting me self until help came."

Even now, from his hospital bed, Sid told them that Jack was determined he would return and work with this horse.

"If it were me I'd give it a wide berth, one time would be enough for me but you know what he's like! Silly bugger."

Bessie felt so proud of Jack and her sigh of relief didn't go unnoticed by the older female staff who looked at one another and grinned. Bessie was realising that her feelings towards Jack had changed to something more than friendship.

It had begun, she realised, when she witnessed the more vulnerable side of him down by the lake. She just hoped he felt the same about her.

It was to be over four months later before the family came to visit Langfell Hall again. At the news of the visit Bessie waited their arrival with anticipation. Would Jack be with them? If he were would the accident have changed him? Most importantly would his feelings for her before the accident have changed.

The family weren't due to arrive until later that evening and Bessie had been on tender hooks all day and found it hard to concentrate on her duties. Even Lady Celeste had noticed and asked her on more than one occasion if she felt unwell.

However as news of their arrival spread through the house and she was just about to push open the kitchen door she heard Jack's voice "Then the silly old beggar went flying and ended up on his arse in the mud. He'll not be doing that again in a hurry!" The company inside roared with laughter as he ended one of his stories. At least he sounded like the old Jack.

She took a deep breath and grinning she entered the kitchen.

"Well look who's decided to grace us with her company," Jack said with a broad grin "My bonnie Bessie as I live and breathe and bonnier than ever if I may be so bold!"

"Just as I was getting used to the peace and quiet," Bessie countered, "the bad penny has turned up again and as bolshie as ever if I may be so bold!"

Neither could hide the grins on their faces and it was so obvious to those present that they were so pleased to see each other again. Unnoticed by the rest of the staff cook and Sid exchanged a knowing wink.

"Did yer miss me bonnie lass? I heard that you were pining dreadfully. In fact the news you were pining for me picked me up no end as I lay there in that hospital bed. It spurred me on to get well so my bonnie lass could stop fretting over me!"

"Pining for your company? That's a laugh! More like hoping for a long respite from your constant jibes at my expense" she said as she took a seat next to the fire warming her hands from the heat.

"Well," said Cook "despite what this young madam says we are all pleased to see you mended and back round our table again. Everyone, and I mean everyone" as she pointedly looked at Bessie "was worried sick when we heard of your accident. Praise to the Lord that you are back with us again. Right I think it's time for a night cap and then an early night for everyone. It's been a long day so Tess get the milk warmed my dear and Bessie you give everyone a mug."

Bessie collected the mugs from the large dresser and as she was distributing them she could feel Jacks eyes following her every move. As she handed him his mug he gave her hand a little squeeze and she knew then everything was alright between them.

The next afternoon cook informed them that the stable lads could not break away from their tasks and get to the kitchen for their afternoon break. She enquired if anybody would be willing to take a sandwich down to them and Bessie jumped at the chance.

When she entered the stable with her basket of goodies she was taken aback as Jack was sitting there alone with no sign of the others. She realised she had been set up but instead of being annoyed at their ploy she was glad to have some time with Jack on his own. She thought it was time to be honest with him.

Smiling, he patted the straw bale that he was sitting on and motioned for her to take a seat. He was surprised she readily took up his offer.

"Well budge up then," she said and she saw Jack's face was a picture.

They both began to speak at once and started laughing.

"You first." laughed Bessie.

Jack proceeded to tell her how much he thought of her. He knew from the moment he first set eyes on her nearly two years ago. He said he knew she didn't feel the same but he kept hoping that over time she might come to feel the same way. One thing he had learned from his accident was that life is too short and could be taken away with the blink of an eye. He took a deep breath "So I've decided to take the bull by its horns and tell you my feelings."

Bessie was so taken aback by his honesty she couldn't speak but when she saw the flicker of fear in his eyes the tears began to pour down her face.

"I'm so sorry lass," Jack said as he started to rise "the last thing I wanted to do was upset you and I wouldn't hurt you for the world. I guess that's my answer and friends only from this point on."

Bessie heard the crack in his voice, "Don't be daft ya silly beggar" she said through her tears as she threw her arms around his neck and kissed him long and hard on the mouth. "That's my answer!"

They laughed all the way through their shared lunch and afterwards Jack insisted on carrying the basket back to the kitchen. They would tell the others their news.

Jack had never felt so proud as he crossed the yard with the basket in one hand and the hand of Bessie in the other. When they entered in to the kitchen hand in hand there was no need to tell anyone and a loud cheer erupted from the others as they had all seen it coming for a long time.

For the rest of the day and in to the evening Bessie had a permanent smile on her face as she carried on with her duties. Lady Celeste noticed immediately but did not mention it although she was pleased to see Bessie back to her old self with a spring in her step.

That evening Jack and Sid were later than usual in joining them in the kitchen. The staff that were present had already split in to groups to pass the rest of the evening.

There was a domino match on the go in the corner and cook and Tess were knitting by the fire. Watson and Celia were continuing a long-standing game of chess. Celia had decided to let Watson win tonight. Bessie was just about to get a book to read when Jack and Sid entered the kitchen. She intuitively knew something wasn't quite right. Jack had none of his usual bravado and he quietly asked if she would care to take a stroll with him outside. She was puzzled by this change in his demeanour but collected her wrap and stepped through the door that he held open for her.

They walked silently along the footpath leading to the lake. They entered the boat house and Jack lit the lantern. Sitting in the golden light Jack took hold of her hand.

"What's wrong Jack?" she asked, "you are scaring me."

Jack said that if they were to be a proper couple, and he sincerely hoped they were, he didn't want any secrets between them.

Bessie breathed a sigh of relief "But whatever is the matter?"

Jack squeezed her hand as he started to explain to her in the best way he could.

He knew, or could guess, how most of her life story was so far. She had been born and brought up in this dale. She had attended the village school and then entered in to service at the Hall. She had always been surrounded by the love of her family and friends and had not experienced life outside the safety of the estate as such.

"Yes," Bessie agreed, "that's been my life in a nutshell more or less but what's wrong with that?"

"Nothing at all," he answered, "you know exactly who you are and where you come from and your life is on a sound footing. I can't say the same Bessie. My life has been totally different. You don't know anything about me and who my friends are or what family I may have. You don't know anything about my background or my life so far and you don't know what makes me......me. Don't get me wrong, mostly I've had a good and happy life but because of my unfortunate beginnings I carry a deep-rooted shame. If I'm honest it is something I will never come to terms with. I experience emotions of fear and abandonment, loss and guilt that I don't understand. I have kept those fears hidden from even the closest to me. I have done deeds that I am not proud of and have never told anyone before but I need to tell you Bessie because of my feelings for you. I hope you will understand a little why I am the person I am and hope with all of my heart that your feelings for me will not change."

Hand in hand over the next few evenings, either in the boat house or sitting on the seat overlooking the lake, Jack related to Bessie the events of his life so far.

Chapter Four.

Jack's story.............

Nervously Jack began to explain to Bessie that he found it difficult to talk about some aspects of his past because some of the memories he would prefer to forget. He had very little memory of his early childhood, just snippets of vague images in his mind that when he tried to grasp or make sense of them they would vanish in to thin air. One such instance was of being held gently in the warm arms of someone and had experienced an overwhelming feeling of being loved and safe. The colour blue enveloped him and the faint scent of roses lingered in the air.

He had spent his early years in an orphanage in York. He had been taken there after he had been found crying and in distress sitting on the steps of York Minster. Lantern Len had found him early one morning when he was carrying out his daily round of extinguishing the gas lamps of the town. Len had picked him up and tried to comfort the wee boy as he took him to the nearest constabulary a few streets away. From there a kindly Policeman had delivered him to a church run orphanage on the outskirts of York.

It was not unusual for children to arrive at the orphanage this way but what was unusual in Jack's case was that he had obviously been well cared for and was wearing good quality clothes as opposed to the usual half nourished waifs and strays that turned up at the orphanage door in bedraggled clothes.

He had a note pinned to his little jacket bearing one word "Jack". Matron and her staff wondered why the little mite had been left in this way. They were hopeful that some distressed parent would come to claim the child before too long. This was not to be and as each month passed they eventually abandoned the hope that he would be reunited with his family.

The staff gave him the name of Jack Minster. He had only vague memories of his earlier years at the orphanage. He was kept in a large room with lots of other young children and babies. He seemed to remember the constant sound of babies crying and the constant smell of urine. The female staff were always busy feeding them or trying to keep them clean but they never had time to comfort the babies or play with the toddlers. They were not cruel but no real kindness or love was given to him or the other young children in their care. He remembered being left in his bed for most of the day confined in that small space by the cold metal rails. He soon learned that it did no good to cry so he just laid quietly staring in to space. Occasionally a small toy would be placed in to their cots but they didn't know how to play with it.

When he was about four years old he was moved in to another dormitory with slightly older boys. He was terrified at first but then became fascinated at the sight of these other children who were able to communicate with each other and play together. Jacks' vocabulary was very limited at that point but he soon started to learn from the other boys.

On fine days the children were allowed to play outside in the yard for a short time. He would never forget the first time he felt the warm sun on his face. One of his memories that was particularly clear was when an older boy taught himself and a couple of other young ones to play with a ball by either throwing it to each other or kicking it against the wall and trying to catch it on the rebound.

This became the norm where the older boys showed the younger ones how to carry out basic activities such as washing, dressing, taking themselves to the privy, making their own beds and putting the soiled linen in to the correct baskets for the older boys to take to the laundry.

When he was six years old he was moved to another dormitory and here he was expected to work for half of the day six days a week. His tasks varied from scrubbing floors, sweeping the yard, helping in the laundry or the kitchen, fetching and carrying the water from the tap in the yard, filling the coal buckets, cleaning out the fireplaces, cleaning the outside privies and worst of all emptying and cleaning the chamber pots!

He was now allowed to spend the other half of the day attending classes in the large school room. Here he began his basic lessons of reading, writing, and arithmetic. Jack loved attending the lessons as it stimulated his mind and he rose to the challenge of learning new skills and he soon excelled in all subjects.

On Sunday mornings the children were marched in line to attend church. He didn't mind this so much as it gave him the chance to experience the noise, smells and colours of the streets of York. He had never seen such beautiful colours because inside the orphanage the predominant colour was grey. Walls, ceilings and even the clothing of the staff and the other children were grey. Even the food looked grey! So these weekly trips to church and being outside became quite a treat for him.

He wasn't too keen on the church services though as he found them boring so his mind would drift to the sounds of the street outside. He got on well with the other boys but did not have any good friends. He kept to himself. A lot of the boys talked about the families they had before entering the orphanage but Jack had no experience of this and could not join in.

One day one of the boys asked him about his own family and he couldn't avoid answering. Instead of telling the truth he lied and made up a story. This became the start of him making up stories of his life, partly to fit in with the other boys and partly because he was so ashamed of being abandoned like a pile of rubbish.

One evening two new boys were shown in to the dormitory. They were brothers, Archie the eldest was a couple of years older than Jack and Tom was about the same age as himself. Tom's bed was next to Jacks but

Archie was put further along the long room with the older boys.

At first Tom didn't want anything to do with Jack or the other boys. Jack knew that Tom was crying himself to sleep most nights but didn't say anything. Tom was also given a school desk to share with Jack and he too enjoyed the lessons. He was a little ahead of Jack as he had attended school before he entered the orphanage and they soon became good friends. Tom would help Jack with his lessons and he soon caught up. Jack showed Tom the daily routine and how to fit in. They had a shared interest in reading and would read whatever books they could get hold of and shared views on how good it was.... or wasn't!

Archie would join them for a chat most evenings and also to make sure his younger brother was alright. He was pleased that Tom had made such good friends with Jack.

Jack came to learn that the boys' mother had died and their father had become ill and unable to work. Their sister had been taken away somewhere and the boys had been brought to the orphanage. As the boys talked about their mother, father and sister, Jack was made aware that he couldn't comprehend sharing his life with others that loved and understood him. He realised how empty his own life was. Jack had felt sad when he heard their story but part of him envied them. At least they had the experience of being part of a family even if it was just for a short time. It was better than having no family at all.

One evening, a few months after the boys had arrived, Jack and Tom were told to gather their belongings together for they would be leaving the next morning. Archie was devastated at the thought of being separated from his younger brother and marched down to the Matrons office to find out what was going on.

She explained to Archie that a Lady of good repute had approached the orphanage to foster two boys of the same age.

She owned a haberdashery shop in Knaresborough and required help to deliver goods to her customers. She gave absolute assurance that the boys would be well cared for and be able to attend the local school. Her credentials seemed genuine and she came across as a caring lady. She was informed that one of the boys still had a father who hoped to take the boy back home at some point when his health and his finances improved. She understood this arrangement perfectly but thought that in the mean time she could offer him a better and more normal life until such time that he could return to his family.

Archie was assured by this explanation from the Matron and thought Tom might be alright after all. At least he was with Jack and he knew that Jack would look after him as he did at the orphanage.

Archie was crying inside but he knew he had to be strong for Tom and not show any distress for Tom to worry about. He took a deep breath and returned to the dormitory where he told the boys what Matron had said to him. He said it would be a more comfortable life and would be a good opportunity to learn a trade and live more normally. They listened as Archie spoke and although he was upset he tried not to let them see it. Tom was scared but both Jack and Archie persuaded him it was a new adventure and he could always go back home once their father was better.

The next morning the two boys were taken in to Matron's office where a very stout but well-dressed lady sat in a chair next to the fire. She smiled warmly at them. Matron introduced the lady as Mrs. Gooding who would be their guardian from now on and explained the situation to the boys. It was much the same as she had explained to Archie the previous evening.

As they left the office Archie was waiting to say goodbye to them. He hugged Tom close to him and told him he would be alright. He turned to Jack and held out his hand and Jack grasped it before pulling Archie close to whisper he would look after Tom.

A grand coach was waiting outside the gates to take them to their new home. They both thought that maybe their fortune had changed after all as they climbed in to the comfort of the coach. Early in to the journey Mrs. Gooding produced a flask and offered them a drink of milk. They thanked her and drank the liquid which tasted quite sweet. Presently they both became weary and fell sound asleep.

Much later when the boys woke up it was dark outside and the coach was passing through the streets of a big city. It pulled down a back lane and in to a yard enclosed by high buildings. Jack was confused and asked where they were. Mrs Gooding laughed and answered, "The great City of Leeds my boys," and when she saw the incomprehension on Jacks face she laughed even more.

The door of the coach flew open and Tom and Jack were grabbed by their collars and hauled out of the coach by a big brute of a man who hauled them across the yard and pushed them through a door where they fell down a flight of stairs in to the darkness below. Jack reached out to find Tom and pulled him close.

Once his eyes had got used to the dark he saw that they were in some kind of cellar. From the dim light coming through a small dirty window at ceiling height he saw other figures crouched in the corners of the cellar. Jack knew their situation was not good and he made a promise to himself that he would get Tom and himself out of there no matter what. He took hold of Toms hand and realised his friend was shaking. He gave it a big squeeze and told Tom not to worry because he would make things alright. He didn't know how but he vowed to himself that he would.

They were to discover that they had been taken by a ruthless gang of thieves led by Mrs. Gooding who gave the gang a respectable front. They discovered that there were four other boys in the freezing cold and filthy cellar that was to become their home. The stench was almost unbearable from the overflowing bucket of excrement and unwashed bodies. They were fed on scraps and left-over food and had to drink from a bucket that was brought in once a day, that is when the thugs remembered to.

The only time they could leave the cellar was when they were expected to work on the streets on busy market days. They were taught to cause a distraction in the street so that the older boys could pick the pockets of the unsuspecting public or to crawl beneath the tarpaulin of the many supply wagons to pilfer whatever was onboard. Often the younger boys had to feign playing a game of dice on a street corner until one of the older boys dropped a bag of ill-gotten gains to them. They would then carry it off to one of the men that were strategically placed up and down the street. One of the men was a supposedly blind beggar sitting on the steps of the town hall.

At first Jack had refused to cooperate and Tom followed suit but after a few hard beatings and starved of their meagre food for a few days they had no choice but to take part. Both boys were terrified of being caught as the thugs had told them that the penalty was life in prison or death depending on the contraband. Jack was always looking for a possible way of escape but when they were out on the streets their every move was being watched by the thugs standing in the shadows. One of the other boys had tried to run off but he couldn't outrun the men and that night he was thrashed in front of the other boys to within an inch of his life. They then carried him out of the cellar and they never saw him again.

They had endured this life for about two months when one night they were both dragged from the cellar and thrown in to the back of a cart. They soon left the lights of the city in to the dark countryside. Three thugs sat in front of the cart without speaking. Jack felt Tom trembling at his side and he reached out his arm to comfort him. Neither boy knew what would become of them that night.

Chapter Five.

The cart trundled on for several miles until the driver pulled in to a wooded clearing at the side of a lane. Two of the men jumped from the cart and reached for a couple of sacks under the seats. They dragged Jack and Tom out of the back of the cart and silently indicated to them to keep quiet. Each man steered a boy up a wooded lane and into the woods. The boys were led through the trees until they came to the back of a large house that stood in darkness. The men dragged the boys to a small window and one of them pulled out a large knife and inserted it in to the edge of the window frame and there was a slight clicking noise as the catch was released. The men held their breath for any sound from within and once they were satisfied that all was well they told Jack that he was to climb through the window where he would find himself in the scullery and from there he had to make his way to the kitchen and open the back door so the men could enter the house.

Jack was terrified and shook his head in refusal but the man grabbed Tom from behind and ran his knife over Tom's throat. Tom's neck darkened with a trickle of blood as the thug stifled Toms scream with a hand over his mouth. Tom's eyes were wide with terror and he was trembling badly. Jack gasped. The man continued to hold the knife at Toms throat and motioned to Jack with a nod of his head to get through the window.

Jack scrambled through the window and found himself in a small dark room but managed to feel his way to the kitchen. There was more light in there because of the large window and the glow from the remnants of the fire. The kitchen still retained some heat of the day and the smell of whatever had been cooking was delicious.

Jack's mind was racing but he had to think of a plan as it was maybe a chance of them making an escape. Instead of going directly to open the back door for the men he opened another door and his hunch was correct for he was now in a large larder full of food. He snatched two large slices of fruit cake, two small loaves and ripped off a chunk of ham from the joint lying on a silver platter. He wrapped them up in a cloth hanging by the fire and then made his way to the door.

The men pushed passed him and one of them whispered in a gruff voice for him to get back to the cart and wait for their return.

Jack stepped outside of the doorway and grabbed Tom by the arm and whispered, "Come on Tom we have to run as fast as we can."

He steered Tom away from the house and up the hill through the woods and in the opposite direction to the cart. He knew they would have to make as much distance as they could before the men returned to the cart to find them gone. They literally ran as if their lives depended on it, upwards and upwards through the woodland their feet cut with brambles and rocks. Eventually they reached the top of the hill where the woods thinned out and from there they could make out the dim lights in the distance of the City of Leeds.

They stopped to rest for a few minutes and Jack told Tom his plan. They had to get back to the city of York. If they travelled in the opposite direction from Leeds and kept to the fields and woods and travelled only at night there was a good chance that they would avoid the thugs that would surely be looking out for them. They had to avoid being found at all costs. Tom didn't say a word but he nodded that he understood and agreed.

The boys continued their escape. They crept along the plateau of the hill but made slow progress over the rough moorland. Hindered by ditches, bogs and streams they soldiered on. Their feet and shins were sore and bleeding but they dare not stop. Late in to the night they heard the sound of a cart below them and they dropped to the ground and froze. However the cover of darkness prevented them from being seen and the cart trundled slowly on.

When the first rays of daylight appeared over the distant horizon they could just make out the shadow of a solitary building just below them. They would hide out there during the daylight hours. As they approached the barn they could hear the ripples of a stream. They sat on its bank scooping up the clear cold water in to their parched mouths and then let the water run over their broken feet and shins but they soon became chilled although the water did ease their discomfort for a while.

“That’s better,” Jack said to Tom who silently nodded his head.

Jack looked at Tom out of the corner of his eye. He noticed that the cut on his neck had dried up with congealed blood but Tom was staring in to space. Jack realised that something wasn’t right and he realised that he had not heard Tom utter a word since that thug had run the knife along Tom’s throat. Jack was frightened but did not want Tom to see his fear. He dipped the sleeve of his shirt in to the water and gently cleaned the dried blood from his friend’s neck. Thankfully the cut was superficial but he wondered if it might still leave Tom with a permanent scar.

The boys managed to enter the barn through a gap between the doors that were tied together with a piece of rope. The barn was empty apart from a pile of sacks in one corner. They huddled under the sacks and shared the food that Jack had taken from the house earlier. Cuddling together for warmth the boys fell in to a deep exhaustive sleep.

When Jack woke up it was late afternoon. Tom was still sleeping soundly on the sacks by his side. He quietly crept out of the barn without waking him. Keeping in the protective cover of the barn and low to the ground he crept up the stream bed that meandered down from the top of the hill. From this vantage point he could see that the shoulder of the hill stretched far ahead more or less shadowing the lane below. If they kept to this high ground they would stand a better chance of being undiscovered. Patches of tall grass provided them with a screen from the road below and hopefully they would make better progress than the night before.

He carefully made his way back to the barn picking a handful of juicy blackberries on the way down. Tom was still sleeping. Jack was worried about Tom who had never uttered a word since the thug held the knife to his throat. He didn't know what to do about it and thought it best not to make an issue of it hoping Tom would speak again in his own time. He put it to the back of his mind and settled down next to his friend and soon fell asleep.

They woke up to the darkest of night. They felt refreshed after their long sleep and after splashing their faces and quenching their thirst in the stream they strode out in to the night. Using the light of the moon they managed to navigate across the plateau of the hill. Occasionally they stopped for a drink or fed from the berries in the hedgerows, always hidden by the blanket of thick grass. Eventually they reached the edge of the plateau where the ground gently sloped to the bottom of the hill. Jack pondered what to do. Should they stay where they were until the following night before they ventured down the hill because he wasn't sure how much cover of darkness they had left. He felt Tom shiver next to him so he decided they would keep moving.

As they reached the low ground Jack heard the rippling of water. He peered into the darkness and could just make out the shadow of a pack horse bridge not too far away. They headed down to the shelter of the bridge that spanned the narrow river and lay down to rest in amongst the high stems of a reed bed. Jack thought that they had made good progress that night but both were limping badly. They would stay there for the day. The lane over the bridge didn't look like a main thoroughfare judging by the size of the bridge. They should be safe here he thought.

The two boys tried to sleep under the bridge that day but kept getting roused by the clattering of carts as they crossed over the bridge and the shouts of men as they bid one another good day as they passed. So much for being quiet! Each time this happened they would tense and hold their breath until the noise subsided. They kept hidden until well after nightfall and then once more they set off into the darkness.

Their feet were damaged and Jack decided to keep to the lanes as the walking would be easier. They could always leap over the dyke if anyone came in to view. They were certainly covering more ground but both boys were still limping badly. They passed by fields of crops and managed to dig up some potatoes with their hands and after washing them in a stream they gobbled them up. The hedgerows still held an abundance of berries that they ate as they walked along.

They crept past several small sleepy hamlets keeping a low profile as they walked. In one of them Jack spied a white sheet left out on the washing line. He crept forward and snatched the sheet away. The sheet was almost threadbare so he didn't feel too bad as he tore the sheet in to long strips. He used the strips of sheet to bind their feet. The going became a little easier and they trekked on until the break of day where they took shelter under a tree in thick woodland. Unfortunately, the weather took a turn for the worse and it rained non-stop all day.

They huddled together as best they could but neither of them managed to sleep. It was still raining when they set off into the night once more. They plodded along for several hours with their heads bowed in silence. Fortunately the rain stopped but it did little to help as they were already wet through to the skin and were cold and hungry. They were also very frightened.

The bindings on their feet became soggy and caked in mud and offered little protection. Tom began to shiver uncontrollably but Jack forged on to keep Tom moving for he knew they would become even colder if they stopped. They must have walked a good few miles in this state when Jack suddenly noticed the faint glow of a fire up ahead amongst the trees. He pointed it out to Tom and indicated to Tom to keep close behind him whilst he crept forward to a large boulder at the edge of the clearing where the glow seemed to be coming from. As they reached the boulder Jack peeped over the rim. He saw a man warming himself by the fire stirring a pot that emitted the most delicious smell of food. Jack's mouth began to water as he took in the scene. There was a brightly painted wagon parked close by and two tethered horses grazed contently. The boys watched the scene for a few minutes then suddenly without turning to them they heard the man say.

"Good morning gentlemen, would you care to join me in a bowl of stew?"

Jack started and quickly looked behind to see who the man had spoken to but there was nobody there.

The man continued to stir the pot for a few more minutes still with his back to them.

“It’s a shame for this stew to go to waste gentlemen and it’s much warmer here beside this fire than it is behind that rock but I understand if you don’t want to join me. It’s a pity because I was looking forward to a good old chin wag as it can be lonely on the road.”

Jack realised that the man was speaking to them and wondered what they should do. He looked at Tom who was pale and shivering and made up his mind. He took hold of Toms hand and walked forward into the firelight.

Chapter Six.

As the boys moved towards the warmth of the fire the stranger got to his feet. Jack noticed that a little brown and white dog had been lying at the man's feet.

"Good morning gentlemen, I'm pleased that you have decided to join our company. This here is Pod and over there is Shannon and her daughter Sheeba who are two of the finest ladies in the land. I go by the name of Joe or gypsy Joe hereabouts. Get yourselves warm by the fire for this stew won't be a minute."

Jack and Tom crept closer to the fire, its warmth drawing their chilled bodies as close as they dare. He left them and disappeared into the wagon returning moments later with a couple of blankets that he draped over their shoulders. He disappeared again and this time produced a basket containing bowls, spoons and three mugs. In silence he filled the mugs from a large metal teapot that was warming on the stones surrounding the fire. He gave a mug to each boy.

" C'mon" he encouraged them, "drink up whilst it's still hot."

The boys began to sip the brew slowly. It was certainly hot and a little bitter too. Jack was wary, this could be some concoction to make them sleep again just like Mrs. Gooding gave them. He took tiny little sips but Tom on the other hand was gulping it down. To Jacks relief Joe filled his own mug from the teapot and joined them.

"I'm so glad gents to have your company for breakfast. It makes a good start to the day," he said as he offered each one of them a bowl and began to fill it with stew from the pan on the fire.

He reached into the basket and retrieved thick slices of buttered bread for them all to dip in their stew. Both boys ate ravenously until the bowls were scraped empty. Joe refilled them. This was a true feast for the boys and Jack thought he had never tasted food this good in his whole life!

Joe sat opposite them with his bowl on his lap and poured himself another brew from the teapot. The little dog stood up and then rearranged himself across Jack's feet.

"Pod's a good judge of character," Joe commented "you've made a good friend already young Sir."

Joe was different to any adult Jack had ever met before with his strange way of addressing them and treating them with respect as if they were doing him a great favour instead of the other way round. Jack found it difficult to age Joe. He was lean and strong looking but his tanned face was weathered like a much older man. Although it was quite cold Joe only wore a waistcoat over his collarless shirt. A cap covered his head and his thick dark curly hair. Around his neck was a red neckerchief that he wore at a jaunty angle. He had a kindly face Jack thought but the way he looked at you with his deep-set dark eyes made Jack wary. It was as if those eyes could read your innermost secrets. Then Joe smiled at them and he noticed the gap between his front teeth but the smile was endearing and Jack relaxed a little.

"Well gentlemen," Joe said, "may I ask which direction your journey is taking you this fine day?"

"We're on our way to York." Jack replied without thinking.

"Well I never! That's exactly the way I'm heading young gents although with your fine young legs you'll probably get there afore me. It's a good few days of walking you have ahead of you I reckon. Myself, I have to take the long way round. I get work from the more remote farms and hamlets along the way. It'll be more likely a week or more before I reach the outskirts of the big city. However, if you are in no rush gentlemen I would be glad of your company on the way if you would do me the honour?"

Jack didn't need to be asked twice. "Yes please Sir" Jack answered for both of them.

"Nay, I'm no Sir, just plain Joe to you gents and you've fair made my day."

Joe collected all the dirty bowls and cutlery and left the boys huddled by the fire whilst he entered the wagon. He returned to them presently and told them that he had taken the liberty of preparing them a bowl of hot water for them inside the wagon to have a wash and bathe their feet if they so wished. He beckoned them inside and although they were reluctant to leave the warmth of the fire they followed him inside the wagon. A small pot-bellied stove gave out a welcoming glow and warmed the wagon and made it cosy. A lamp illuminated a bowl of soapy water and a towel that stood on a wooden dresser.

"Welcome to my humble abode young gents and please make yourself at home."

He indicated to two shirts that were folded neatly on a bed at the rear of the wagon.

"Please make use of those shirts while your clothes dry on the rail above the stove." he reached into a drawer and gave them a little jar containing a yellow paste.

"If you put this on your clean feet it'll work wonders. Just throw out those dirty bindings when you have finished and I'll burn them on the fire. I have several jobs to do yet for my two ladies before we can be on our way or they'll take the huff if they feel there being neglected."

For an instant Jack didn't know what Joe was on about but then smiled as it dawned on him that the ladies were the two horses.

Joe left them to sort themselves out whilst the boys undressed and washed before bathing their feet. The warm water felt good and eased the pain a little. Jack took in their surroundings. The bed was covered in a brightly coloured patterned quilt that looked so inviting.

There was shelving at the back of the stove containing an array of cooking utensils including a large kettle. There was a cupboard or drawer in every available space but they didn't encroach in to the living area. A fiddle hung over the bed next to a picture of a young woman with a little girl.

When the boys had finished their ablutions Jack opened the top half of the wagon door to throw out the filthy bindings. Joe was harnessing one of the horses between the shafts of the wagon.

"You alright there young gent?" he asked, "I'll get rid of the used water in a minute."

Shortly afterwards Joe opened the door of the wagon to see the two boys' sitting side by side on the bed. He noticed that the smaller boy was still shivering. He opened a cupboard and took out a small bottle containing a brown liquid and poured out a little in to a glass and offered it to the boy.

"This should make you feel better little gent," as he offered the glass to Tom. Tom took the glass and swallowed the liquid down in one gulp.

"Feel free to use the bed and get a bit of shuteye young gents. We'll be on the road shortly."

He picked up the basin containing the filthy water and left. The boys curled together under the warmth of the quilt. They felt the lurch of the wagon as it moved on its way and soon fell asleep as the wagon rocked gently side to side.

Jack woke with a start. It took him a few moments to realise where he was. Tom was still sleeping soundly with only the occasional spasm of a shiver Jack noted with relief. He settled down once again in to the softness of the bed. Suddenly he heard a loud scraping noise coming from outside accompanied by gruff male voices shouting to each other. He held his breath and waited. He could just about make out the words above the scraping noise.

"Well I can't thank thee enough for work yer did on me mower last year Joe. Made it cut through grass like a razor! Cudna believe it! Glad yer managed to call by agin cos t'old shears need a sharpen amongst wife's kitchen knives I brought for yer. By't way, she sends this to yer from baking she did this morn."

"You've a grand missus there Seb and the best baker for miles and bonnie with it too. You're a lucky man Seb!"

Seb guffawed, "Nay lad any beauty she had is long gone if she ever had it at all, but I'll grant ye she's a grand baker. Oh I better nay forget she asked for another jar of yon salve says it werks wonders on er and she sess it has got healing qualities. I sess she should try it on 'er face then."

"Nay Seb be careful or she'll be after you with one of those knives I'm sharpening' for thee."

"Nay I'll be alreet" said Seb, "she knows I'm in jest. She's a good un. Hey up, 'ere comes George from Nether field. He'll be ere to collect yon tools ye did earlier."

"How do George, how ist thee?

Jack could hear another voice join in the conversation.

"Fair to middling lads. Yon rain last neet put paid to getting crops in fer winter."

Nah" Seb assured him "We'll be reet fer a couple a week yet. Them strong lads a yours will get crops inside in a flash. I'm 'oping sum a Joe's folk will be along shortly ta gi me a 'and. It's a gud feeling when all't crops are safe int barn."

"Aye yer reet" agreed George "Hey up! Look at Joes wee dog cumming up lane an yon rabbit it's got. It's as big as hisself. Just look how proud he is strutting up lane! Well Joe that's yer supper sorted!"

Joe agreed "And that's the second one this morning, the others in the pot! Pod here keeps me well supplied with grub. I'll eat like a king tonight. He's just like your lady wives keeping the two of you well fed by the look of you both."

"I'll swap yer anytime Joe," said George "cud do wi a gud dog round farm ta keep rats and bunnies at bay. Wife's nay gud at that!"

They all laughed. "Now Joe, lets settle up. I can't stand round callin' all day an don't forget the salve."

There was a brief spell of silence then Seb bid both men good day.

"He's a character yon Seb" said George "worships the ground his missus walks on he does. Always bin just the two of em up there. Hard workers both of em and gud neighbours. I see tha's finished my lot of stuff an add on a couple of jars of yon salve and I'll be on me way. Oh, old Seth at Upper Wood asked if ya cud call. He's in need of yer skills! He can't get darn to thee as coo stood on his foot and e's fair crippled. 'Eere's a bag a veg from missus, it'll go nicely wi that rabbit stew! Thanks agin lad and watch yersen, a couple of rough looking buggers passed by a couple a days ago lookin' for a couple of runaway bairns. A likely story! Wunt gi em time a day."

Jack who had been enjoying listening to the men bantering stiffened at this last statement. Could it be Mrs. Gooding's thugs looking for them? Just as he was beginning to feel safe too. What would Joe think about it. Suddenly there was the clatter of a cart and the sound of horses' hooves stopping at the side of the wagon. Jack slid back under the quilt.

"A thought I might av missed ya Joe! 'ad to set out early this mornin to tek sum stuff up to Helmscroft. Is it possible for yer to sort mi mower blades? Yon Seb sess thee sharpened 'is up a treat. Ast thee got time lad? I knows it will tek yer a good part of day so yer can camp darn in bottom meadow. Tha knows where I mean, tha's bin there afore. I'll bring darn sum bran an oats fer 'orses an the grass darn there is still gud. Missus will 'ave summat for thee an all."

"No bother" said Joe "twas wondering where to camp tonight. I'll get those blades done tomorrow as I've got to call in at old Seths yet but I'll be in thy field by early evening. Just leave the stuff by the bridge."

"By yer a grand lad Joe! I'll be getting on then."

Jack crept to the door of the wagon and tried to peek out. Tom began to stir.

"Well gents, I bet you want to answer the call of nature by now. Yon bush over there will accommodate that. Don't worry it's safe to show your faces!"

Again it took Jack a second to realise Joe was calling out to them. He gradually opened the door to see Joe grinning at him.

"Good afternoon fine Sir, we've got some lovely looking scones to devour so I'll get the kettle on."

Jack laughed, everything was going to be fine for now.

The boys thoroughly enjoyed the home baked scones that the farmer's wife had sent for Joe. He had spread them with butter and blackberry jam which was yet another kind gift. A second brew of tea washed it all down nicely.

Tom was beginning to look a little better but when Joe heard him cough he advised Tom to take another dose of lincture and to stay in bed for the rest of the day. He had a little work to finish off where they were but once everyone had collected their items they would be on their way to visit a farm at the top of the distant hill. Joe told them that this was how he made his living. He sharpened all manner of farming, gardening and household implements.

He would usually set himself up at the side of the road in a hamlet central to the surrounding farms and crofts so his customers could drop off their tools and collect them later. On the more remote farms he worked on site. Most of his customers were thankful for Joes visits as it saved them from travelling further afield to the city which would take them a full day and away from their other tasks.

He advised the boys to bathe their feet and apply the salve again. He asked Jack to keep the stove stoked up, to chop up the vegetables and add them to the rabbit stew that was simmering in the pot and to see to their clothes that were now bone dry. Tom snuggled back down to sleep again while Jack tended to the chores that Joe had given him. He heard more conversations outside as more of Joes customers came to collect their sharpened implements.

A second man also told Joe that he had been approached by a couple of rough looking men who were looking for two runaway boys. When he had questioned them they told him that the boys had run away from their home in Leeds after a misunderstanding. The boys' mother was distraught and they thought the boys may try to make their way to York where their Granny lived. The men were offering a reward to anyone who could give them good information.

When Jack heard this his mind raced in panic as there was now no doubt it was the Gooding's thugs that were looking for them. What should they do? His first reaction was to wake Tom and make a run for it but it was broad daylight and they wouldn't stand a chance. No, he thought, it would be better to bide their time with Joe and then make off when Joe was asleep tonight. He just hoped that in the meantime the thugs didn't find Joe's wagon. He began to wonder what Joe was thinking about all of this. Surely Joe was suspicious. Jack sat and waited until Joe had bid all of his customers farewell and wishing them good fortune.

Joe popped his head through the door and told Jack that he was going to take the horses down to the river for a drink and then they would be off. Joe hesitated for a second before saying it might be better if you and Tom kept out of site until tonight.

"We'll have a talk then," he said as he looked deep in to Jacks eyes. Jack nodded. He knows Jack thought as Joe closed the door, he knows.

The wagon climbed slowly up a rough steep track for what seemed like hours before finally coming to a halt at the top of the hill at the edge of a farmyard.

This must be Seth's place Jack thought. Tom was still sleeping soundly which was good but Jack was bored and a little restless. He positioned himself so he could peek between the drawn curtains to watch the goings on outside. Joe lifted the big stone wheel from its metal brackets that were set to one side of the wagon door. He dropped it in to a frame he had retrieved from the big wooden chest that was held up under the back of the wagon. He had just brought a stool out when Jack noticed an old man limping badly across the yard towards Joe. He carried a pale in one hand and was leaning heavily on a stick in the other hand. The yard was cluttered with all sorts of what looked like junk to Jack. Hens scratched between the gaps in the cobbles that were strewn with weeds and sheep muck.

"It's reet grand of thee Joe to cum all tha way up 'ere out of yer way" said Seth as he sat himself down on a large stone to watch Joe work. "We cudna manage another season wi sum of this stuff," as he indicated to a pile of metal implements in the pale. "Yon shears cudna cut through slice a bread."

No problem at all" Joe told him "I always enjoy a catch up with you and your missus, speaking of which, here she comes," Joe nodded his head towards the cottage where an old woman had just left leaving the door open as she hobbled across the yard.

Jack couldn't believe his eyes! Hobbling across the yard came Seth's wife. She had long grey hair that trailed down her back and across her shoulders that she topped off with a man's flat cap perched on the top of her head. Her brown weather worn face was so wrinkled Jack couldn't tell if her eyes were open or closed. Her cheeks hung and flapped as she made her way across the yard. She was wearing an old brown jumper that had seen better days and Jack thought it had more holes in it than wool! Her legs were shod in men's work trousers tied up with string and her feet were clad in a massive pair of hob nailed boots that clattered over the cobbles like horse's hooves. Every other step a boot would fly out moving the hens out of her way. She was carrying a basket covered in blue cloth and two collie dogs were at her heel and they too had the odd lunge at the hens.

"'ello Joe!" she bellowed "grand of thee to cum up to us. I've got a few bits for ya. No, no Joe" as she lifted up her hand to stop Joe responding, "don't start with that silver tongue of thine telling me I'm best baker int dale as tha knows me bakings shite so instead I've got a couple of loaves, not today's mind you, not 'ad time wi this silly bugger being crippled an all that but I've put in a bit of good pork drippin' to 'elp it go darn easier. There's a couple of slabs of rice puddin' an all wi sum rhubarb jam in't middle. I know ya like that an we had a good crop a rhubarb this year. We were havin' it stewed for weeks on end and me an Seth 'ere could shite through eye of a needle! I've put in one of me 'aggises cos I know ya like it sliced wi yer breakfast. It'll put 'airs on tha chest it's that spicy! Seth ere won't touch the stuff that's why he's as bald as a coot! I see yuv got yon cleaver to sharpen cos its so blunt ya cud 'ave it upright on seat of cart and ride it bare arse to York an back in comfort."

Joe guffawed with laughter.

“Ast silly bugger ‘ere telt thee e got ‘is foot trapped under Daisy’s foot? Nowt broke but ‘is toes as black as devil’s armpit. Daisy’s fine though that’s main thing. Speaking of which gis us yer milk can and I’ll fill it to tek away wi yer an ya can keep ‘old of basket till next time.”

Joe opened the wagon door to get the milk can. He grinned at the look of disbelief on Jacks face as he put a finger to his lips to motion Jack to not say anything.

She clattered back over the yard with the milk can in one hand and her foot flying out at the hens with the two collies still at heel and they too had the odd lunge at a hen. Not a good place to be a hen Jack thought.

“You are lucky Seth with a missus like yon.” said Joe.

“Aye lad she’s a reet ‘eart of gold is that one. She luv’s the sheep an every animal ‘ere an she treats them like ‘er own bairns. I’d a reet job in’t winter when yon snow storm swept country. Had to bar door ta stop her going up’t ‘ill wi lads. It were bad but lads got all sheep darn to safety bar seven. Nearly lost one dog as well but she took reet bad wi seven that were gone. There’s nowt she dunt ‘now about sheep an training dogs an she niver lifted a ‘and to any of em. ‘Ere she cums wi yer milk lad.”

“’Ope yer not yakking lads’ ear off Seth” she said as she placed the milk can on the wagon step.

“I’ll ‘ave sum of yer salve an all lad. Them round ‘ere think it’s sum kind a magic potion silly buggers! I’m a sheep woman born an bred, raised on’t teet of an old yow me Pa used to say, an wi eight kids in't family e cudda bin tellin' truth. I knaw fine it's lanolin from washed fleece. Can't mistek yon stink. Good stuff though. Meks me laugh them fancy wimen paying a King's ransom for same stuff wi a bit o scent added."

"Have ya 'erd lad that a couple 'o runaway bairns are supposed to be rand 'ere? Folk 'ave bin offered gud coin for information. Summat not reet if ya ask me. Gladys darn at Thorpe End ses she 'ad a best white sheet teken off line tother neet. Reckon's it cud be them. Best white sheet me arse! Everyone 'nows she gets cast offs from big 'ouse where her daughter works, so thread bare ya can see reet through em. Only gud enuff to wipe yer arse on. Don't suppose yuv seen owt Joe? Nay.... why am I askin thee! Mouth as tite as an 'ens arse that's thee but a gud lad non the less. Well gents, yer 'olding me back with all yer callin, I've got werk ta see ta an all. Si thee next year lad. I knaw lad" as Joe opened his mouth to bid her farewell "May gud fortune follow me and you an all lad."

She clattered back across the yard lashing out at the hens which she never managed to hit. As she reached the door of the cottage she turned around and shouted back.

"Hey Joe, did tha knaw yon curtains on tha wagon are twitching by thee sen?"

Joe looked up with surprise on his face.

"Aye" she said "tha shud knaw that a sparrow can't tek a shite round 'ere wi out I 'now abart it. Yal be wantin' another couple slabs a rice pudding then."

She went through the door to fetch it.

"Don't worry lad" said Seth "she'll say nowt, she knaws 'ow to 'old her tongue reet enuff. She's a gud un is yon an she's missing lad's summat shockin'. They working up norf just now on big sheep farm meking extra spence up there. They'll be back afore winter sets in. I better be off lad, money's in't cup. Tek care of thee sen lad an I'll see ya in't spring."

Seth made his way slowly to the cottage reaching the door just as his missus was coming out with a couple of extra paper wrapped parcels. She clattered over to Joe and patted his back then placed the wrapped food on to the step of the wagon.

Thanks missus Seth" said Joe acknowledging her kindness "I'll call up here next spring. No need for you to come down to the hamlet with your tools, it'll save your legs.

"Nay, no need ta go ta yon trouble." she answered.

"It'll be no trouble at all, I'm just making sure I get my haggis and rice slabs and to see the most beautiful lady in the dale!" She laughed out loud and patted Joe's head.

As she turned to go back to the cottage, from his vantage point Jack could see the twinkle in her eye and the wide grin on her face as she made her way across the yard giving the hens yet another fright.

Chapter Seven.

Jack heard Joe packing away his equipment. He felt really bad for nearly giving the game away by peeping out of the window and not keeping out of sight as Joe had asked. From what he had heard of the conversation he was sure that Seth and his wife would not tell anyone that someone was hiding in Joe's wagon. It could have easily been another story if it had been someone else that had seen him at the window. He had risked the safety of Tom and himself just because he was bored. He had no idea how Joe would react but he thought he was probably very angry.

Another thought passed through his mind. What if Joe didn't want anyone to know that the boys were with him because he wanted to claim the reward money for himself. All of his instincts were telling him that he was wrong but at eight years old and living in an orphanage all of his life what did he know of the ways of men? His experience with Mrs. Gooding had taught him not to trust strangers and although Joe appeared to be kind he was still a stranger to them. No, the idea he had of taking off at nightfall still seemed to be the best plan.

Tom woke up as Joe entered the wagon to put away the food Seth's wife had given him.

"How are you feeling now little gent?" he asked of Tom who smiled and gave him the thumbs up.

“We’ll be setting off now. We should be at the site where we can camp for the night within the hour. Keep your heads down lads.” He gave Jack a long look loaded with meaning and left.

Tom seemed much better and his face had a little colour and there wasn’t any sign of the cough that had troubled him earlier. Jack poured them a mug of milk each and gave Tom a couple of oatcakes that he found in a tin on the dresser. Jack wondered what to tell Tom about his plan to escape but as he watched Tom contentedly sipping the milk and nibbling the oatcakes he didn’t have the heart to tell him as he knew it would frighten him. He would leave it for now.

When the cart finally came to a stop Joe opened the door telling them it was alright to come out. The boys discovered they were in an amazing place.

They were in a small clearing with thick woodland on three sides and a high rocky gorge in front of them. A stream cascaded from the top of the gorge to follow its path down the dale. There was a small pack horse bridge spanning the water further downstream. It was breathtakingly beautiful. Jack noticed Toms eyes light up for a second as he turned slowly to take in their surroundings.

Even Pod seemed excited at being there and chased around the clearing taking in all the new scents and leaving some of his own on several trees before splashing in to the water and lapping up a long drink.

“Well lads, do you like your new home for the next two nights? It’s safe enough here for you to be outside. Only the birds and the sky above will know we are here. The farm is over the other side of the gorge so nobody will bother us. This is one of my favourite places to stay.”

“I can see why,” Jack said, “it’s beautiful. You said we are to stay here for two nights Joe. Is that right?”

“Yes” said Joe, “I’ll be working all day tomorrow on the farmers mower blades and the rest of the tools he’s left by the bridge. The following day is Saturday market and there will be a lot of traffic on the roads so I think it is better to wait until Sunday before we make a move again.” He gave Jack a knowing look.

“That sounds like a good plan Joe” He was relieved. They had another night and a day before they had to leave and it would give Tom more time to recover.

“Right Jack, me and you are going to set up the camp, and you little gent, wrap yourself up in a blanket and sit outside in the sun. Pod will keep you company.”

“Right Jack, our first job is to see to the ladies. I’ll show you how to unhitch them from the wagon.”

Jack tentatively approached Shannon who was in the shafts.

“She’s as gentle as a puppy Jack, give her nose a gentle rub.”

He reached out and gently touched Shannon's nose. The horse nuzzled in to his neck and rubbed her face in to his shoulder. He instantly felt relaxed and stroked her neck before rubbing his face against her neck. He was trembling as he experienced a strong feeling of belonging that he had never experienced before. It was as if Shannon could sense his fear and confusion and was trying to comfort him. He didn't know why he felt this way but the sense of joy he was feeling was amazing. He began to have hope that everything would be alright.

Joe watched Jack's interaction with the horse and smiled to himself. It reminded Joe of his own reaction when his father took him to meet his first horse. Although he was much younger then than Jack he could see the same connection in Jacks eyes.

Joe showed him how to unhitch Shannon from the shafts then asked Jack to lead her down to the water for a drink. Joe followed him with Sheba who he had untethered from the back of the wagon. The horses drank their fill then Joe and Jack tethered them on a long rope under the trees in the clearing.

"Next job Jack is to collect everything that the farmer left for me by the bridge."

There was a box of assorted tools, several long blades, a bag of mash and a basket wrapped in cloth waiting for them. It might take two trips Joe had said but it didn't take them too long to get everything back and safely stacked in the clearing.

“Time for a brew now Jack and whilst the kettle is on we’ll mix the mash for the ladies and feed Pod. After that Jack you can collect the wood for the stove and the campfire and I’ll get our grub ready.”

As Jack was collecting the wood he wondered why Joe had not said anything about him being seen at the window. He still felt bad about it. Maybe Joe didn’t want to say anything in front of Tom. He made his mind up to apologise to Joe later.

As twilight dawned the three of them were sitting around the camp fire tucking in to bowls of stew and thick slices of bread and dripping. Pod sat looking pleadingly at Toms dish. Tom picked out a small piece of meat and blew gently on it to cool it before offering it to Pod. Joe laughed but reckoned he deserved it as he was the one that provided the meal after all. Tom smiled at Joe and yawned.

“Back to bed for you young gent when we’ve finished the brew.”

“Joe, where are you going to sleep?” asked Jack.

“Me and Pod will kip down under the wagon. We’ve done it lots of times before and there’s no sign of rain, besides the heat from the stove above makes it quite cosy under there.”

The three of them sat for a while gently sipping their brew. Jack was getting used to the bitter taste by now and quite enjoyed it. Joe disappeared into the wagon and came out grinning.

“Nearly forgot the slices of rice pudding gents. You are in for a treat and we have to eat it up as it won’t keep,” he said as he dished out the slabs of rice.

“This is really good Joe, I’ve never had rice like this before.”

“I think it’s made thick like this so the farmers can take it out to the fields with them for their packing up,” Joe told them.

“That’s a really good idea,” said Jack, “This is so good I could eat it every day.”

“Wait until you taste the haggis in the morning and speaking of food, go fetch the basket that was left at the bridge. Let’s see what the farmer’s wife has sent down for us. Usually she’s really generous.”

Jack took the cover off the basket and lifted out two boxes of eggs, two loaves of bread, a pat of butter, a chunk of cheese, two slices of thick ham and a fruit pie.

“That lot will keep us from starving and we still have the rest of the stew left,” said Joe who noticed Tom yawning again.

“Come on young gent, I’ll fill the basin with hot water and you can get those feet done and then off to bed.”

Jack walked across to the horses and stroked their noses and nuzzled his face in to their manes. He felt all the tension he had been holding back for days overwhelm him and tears began to roll down his face. He couldn't stop sobbing and his whole body trembled in anguish. The horses nuzzled in to each of his shoulders as if they were offering comfort to the little boy.

This was the scene that confronted Joe as he left the wagon. He strode quickly over to Jack and held him tightly in his arms.

"Now lad, it's time to let it all out." Joe said in a gentle voice.

"I'm sorry Joe." Jack spluttered in between sobs.

"Nay lad you've nowt to be sorry about. Come on let's get you by the fire and you can tell me all about it."

Jack told Joe everything that had happened to them at the hands of the Gooding gang and how they had made their escape. He told him about the treks through the night and being terrified of being found. He told Joe of his promise to Toms older brother Archie that he would look after Tom and how it was his fault that Tom couldn't speak anymore. He had let Tom and Archie down and then that afternoon he had put them at risk again by peeping out of the window.

"That's quite the weight you've been carrying on those young shoulders Jack," Joe said gently, "but you are wrong, none of it is your fault."

"But if I hadn't refused to climb through the window then Tom wouldn't have had the knife slice his throat! He wouldn't have been so scared and he would still be able to speak."

"You don't know that Jack," Joe told him "These things are never as straight forward as they seem. Often it's a build-up of fear over several days or weeks and the way you were treated it's no surprise. Eventually, and God willing, Tom will find his voice again and be able to tell you himself but it was not your fault in any way, shape or form lad. Do you understand me Jack?"

Jack nodded his head.

"It's down to your quick-thinking lad that you managed to get away and remain undetected for so long. You're a little hero Jack if you ask me and I don't want you worrying over something that's not your fault."

Jack took a deep breath. He felt exhausted but much calmer.

"It was my fault though Joe for looking out of the window when you asked us to keep out of sight."

"Aye well that might be so Jack but Seth's wife is such a spectacle is she not, that it would be hard to resist her charms," he grinned at Jack who grinned back.

"She was pleased Joe when you called her beautiful."

“To me Jack she is beautiful. Forget what she looks like on the outside, it’s what’s in her heart that counts and there’s no doubt it’s a heart of gold. In my eyes Jack that makes her more beautiful than all the fancy ladies of this world and I care to venture she has not once connected with those hens!”

Jack nodded thoughtfully.

“Whilst we are having this heart to heart there is something that I have to confess to you.”

Jack looked at Joe in puzzlement.

“I was approached by those Gooding thugs a couple of days before we met. Like the others I was offered a reward for any information or if I picked you up I was to deliver you to the west gate at York where someone is watching out for you arriving there.”

“Oh no!” said Jack, “what are we going to do?”

“Don’t you worry Jack, I’ll think of something. Meantime we have a busy day ahead of us tomorrow so we had better get some shut eye. We’ll leave the pots soaking in that pale for now. You go and sort out your feet and I’ll get Pod when I’ve done here.”

Shortly afterwards when Joe entered the wagon to retrieve Pod he found the boys fast asleep with Pod in the middle. Pod looked up and saw Joe but just snuggled further down in the bed. Joe smiled and shook his head. He quietly crept out of the wagon and closed the door.

Chapter Eight.

It was some time before Joe could get to sleep. What Jack had told him kept going round and around in his head. He hadn't realised just how bad the boys had been treated. It was lucky that they got away when they did. He had no doubt that the boys would have become expendable to the gang following the burglary and as they were witnesses to the deed, a shallow grave may have been their fate. Joe was angry that people could prey on children this way and it just proved to him that evil did exist in this world. He had never seen a young boy as upset as Jack had been earlier. Someone so young shouldn't be carrying such a weight on their shoulders. He just hoped that it wouldn't leave any lasting damage to the boy. He would try to alleviate some of that weight whilst they were in his care and he hoped to go some way of getting them back to just being boys again. He would do all he could to get them safely back to the Orphanage in York.

He seemed to have just dropped off to sleep when the sound of screaming abruptly woke him up. He scrambled out from under the wagon and dashed inside.

Jack was holding Tom in his arms and was trying to comfort him. Tom was gasping for breath and clinging tightly to Jack. Joe lit the lantern and spoke gently to Tom telling him he must open his eyes and see that everything around him was alright and he was safe. Tom began to relax. It was just a bad dream Joe told him. Nothing to worry about but as they were all wide awake why not have a mug of warm milk and finish the rice pudding off? Both boys smiled and nodded in agreement.

Joe couldn't help but smile the next morning at the picture that greeted him as he entered the wagon to start preparing breakfast. The two boys were still fast asleep each one clinging to his side of the bed whilst Pod lay outstretched in the middle with space to spare! Pod opened one eye and quickly closed it again ignoring Joe's presence.

He chuckled to himself as he said "Come on sleepy heads, lots to do today while the sun is shining. Go give your faces a splash in the stream and that will soon wake you up."

Pod jumped over the boys and was out of the wagon as quick as a flash happy to find new smells. The boys followed in his wake. It was a little chilly but a beautiful bright sunny morning with the certain promise that it would warm up as the day progressed.

Whilst Joe was cooking breakfast he outlined to the boys what their duties were for the day. He would be busy working so he was relying on them to do all the chores around the camp. Their first task was to see to the ladies and feed Pod and then to clean the breakfast pots and last night's dishes and put everything away. He wanted a washing line strung between two trees and all the dirty clothes and linen washed in a basin of hot water, rinsed in the stream and pegged on the line to dry. The quilt on the bed needed to be thrown over a branch to air. The stove needed a clean out, the rugs taken outside and given a good shake, the floor swept and washed along with all the surfaces, the jars dusted on the dresser and the windows cleaned.

"That's just for starters, now can you remember all that? You'll also have to keep the stove going, prepare the campfire for tonight and gather enough wood to fill the store under the wagon. Now do you think you can manage all that lads?"

Tom nodded and Jack cheekily answered., "No bother at all and we'll nip up to the farm and milk the cows as well!"

Joe laughed and smiled inwardly for they were beginning to open up a little.

"Now who wants to try a slice of this haggis but I'll tell thee it's not to everyone's taste!"

Both boys thought they should at least try some and they loved it. They were sitting outside with a brew with the sun on their faces and Jack thought if it weren't for their situation he would be enjoying this. He knew Joe was keeping them busy to keep their minds off their predicament and by the look on Toms face he thought it was working. Tom was looking much better and more relaxed and as he sat sipping his tea he began to stroke the top of Pods head who responded by rolling over on his back for a tummy scratch.

By midday the boys had completed most of their tasks. The inside of the wagon was like a new pin and the washing was blowing gently in the breeze. The ladies were grazing contently in the clearing and now Pod was fast asleep at Toms feet. Jack prepared slices of bread and butter and cheese that he was going to spread with chutney from one of the numerous jars on the dresser. All were gifts from the farmers wives along with assorted jams and pickles.

Joe had been working steadily all morning and was making good progress with the mower blades. The kettle was simmering on the stove almost ready for Jack to make a brew.

“Grubs up!” shouted Jack as he carried the plates outside. Pod leapt to attention expectantly. Joe went down to the stream to freshen up and Tom joined Jack with the food.

” My, my lads! That looks good, couldn’t have done better myself. You’ve both done well this morning and I wouldn’t be as far on with my jobs if I had to break off to do the chores. We make a good team!”

The boys spent the afternoon collecting a mountain of wood for the fire. Joe finished the blades then collected a bar of soap and a towel and went to have a refreshing wash under the water falling from the gorge above to the stream below.

“Time for another brew lads,” he said as he shook out his wet hair back in camp.

“Cut a few slices of that fruit pie lads!” He laughed to see the boys still in their nightshirts.

“You better see if your clothes are dry, those shirts could do with a wash whilst the weathers fine. It might be an idea for you Jack to have a shower as well. Tom you stick to the basin of warm water for now.”

The icy water falling on Jack’s head took his breath away at first but as he soaped his hair under the torrent his body became used to the temperature and he soon found it refreshing. Dressed in his clean but threadbare clothes he felt amazing. Tom was also wearing his clothes when Jack returned to camp. Who would have guessed that they were the same two boys that had landed at Joe’s door just two days before. Joe feigned surprise when he saw them both.

“Excuse me gents! Have you seen two ragamuffins round here?”

Pod wondered over and gave them a good sniff and satisfied that they were the same two boys he flopped back down to sleep again. Joe explained that the farmer would be collecting his tools any time now and maybe they should stay inside until he had been and the boys readily agreed.

The farmer arrived at the camp about an hour after Joe had spoken. He was delighted with the work Joe had done.

"By lad, I dint think they were as good as this when they were new! It will mek the job a bit easier an I'll spread the word. You'll be busier than ever next year lad. Ya dunt have to rush off from 'ere lad, stay as long as thee wants."

"Much appreciated" Joe acknowledged, "but I'll be away in the morning."

"Of course lad, I understand. I'm just glad ye had time to sort mi blades out. Now, the wife has sent ya sum more victuals, they were left ower from market today, 'ope they'll be of sum use to thee."

"Please convey my heartfelt thanks to your good lady sir," said Joe "are you wanting a lift with yon blades on to the back of your cart sir? I've got the buckets and basket you left by the bridge yesterday. That was really good of you, a fair feast it was and if the horses could speak they'd be saying the same. It's not everyone thinks of the beasts."

"I 'now more than most lad that if ye luk after the beasts they'll luk after thee. Well, I better settle up an be on mi way. Still got coos to sort out an it's bin a long day. Have a gud journey tomorro' an we'll sithee next year."

"You will indeed sir and good fortune to you and yours."

A few minutes passed before Joe entered the wagon with the gifts of food. It would be safe now as he started emptying the bag.

“Well! Look at this boys, two custard tarts, two loaves, another pat of butter and a pot of cream. It’ll be another feast tonight lads that’s for sure.”

The stew was almost ready so he instructed the boys to see to the ladies but to not give them so much mash tonight as they had not been working.

“I’ll get the campfire lit as the daylight is fading already.”

Another grand meal was enjoyed by them all sitting around the campfire. It was such a peaceful place to be.

“Why can’t we stay here another night Joe? asked Jack “the farmer said he wouldn’t mind.”

“No he wouldn’t mind but I will be happier to reach the lanes north of York as soon as possible to put some distance between us and the main highway. The quickest way to do that is to actually travel on the highway for a couple of hours and then branch off on the north road again, that will get us on to the back lanes again. The hamlets and crofts I visit are scattered around that area so I can continue working. Tomorrow is the Sabath so the main highway will be quieter without the usual hauliers, pedlars and tradesmen on the go. The only people we might encounter are the regular church goers making their way to worship.”

“Why are we heading north of York?” asked Jack.

“We’ll be safer up there Jack and if we skirt round the top of York and approach York from the east it’s less likely anyone will be looking out for you. They mentioned the west gate to me so best keep away from there. It will take us longer but that’s in your favour as well as the longer you stay undetected the more the thugs will think you have perished on the moors and will let their guard down.”

“That’s a brilliant plan Joe,” said Jack and Tom nodded in agreement.

“An early night is called for tonight boys, we’ve all had a busy day and we need an early start in the morning. I think we’ll settle the camp for the night and get some shut eye.”

The next morning dawned bright and sunny again for the time of year. After a quick breakfast it didn’t take the three of them long to pack up the camp. The only evidence that they had been there was the ash that remained in the ring of stones in the camp fire. This would eventually disperse in the wind leaving the area ready for the next group of travellers that passed that way.

They weren’t long into the journey before Joe indicated to the boys by tapping on the small window above the bed that they were soon to join the main highway and they should keep their heads down. They were making good progress with just the smattering of other carts on the road.

It wasn't long before Joe spied a stationary cart on the verge up ahead. He turned to look through the back window to warn the boys to be cautious but could not see the boys at all until he noticed the two humps under the quilt where he surmised the two lads were hiding. Good he thought, better to be careful than careless. He proceeded warily and as he approached the cart he could see two rough looking men who seemed to be scrutinising each passing vehicle.

Joe nonchalantly raised his hand in greeting as he passed them. He heard Pod beside him growl from the back of his throat. Joe's calm demeanour belied his thumping heart.

"Lovely day gents" he hailed and one of the men raised his hand in acknowledgement. In his other hand he held a pie ready to take a bite and his mate was already in the process of devouring his pie. Thus distracted they took little notice of Joe as he passed by with no incident.

Joe pondered about this. The men were certainly not worshippers on their way to church but of course there could be an innocent explanation for them being there. If there was, Joe couldn't think what it could be. The only reason seemed to be that they were connected to the Gooding gang and in that case they were still actively looking out for the boys. It would seem they had just had a very close shave. Saved by a couple of pies Joe smiled to himself.

They continued their journey for another couple of hours with the main highway now far behind. Joe pulled the wagon on to the verge next to a wide shallow stream and dismounted.

"Time for a brew, boys," he said as he entered the door, "best if you two stay put whilst I see to the ladies and let Pod have a run. Sheba has done well this morning but I'll let Shannon take over this afternoon."

"I'll get the kettle on then," said Jack, "and rustle up some grub whilst you are doing that Joe. We can finish off the fruit pie and cream!"

The afternoon saw them again making steady progress. The boys were allowed to sit looking out of the back window, which was half obscured by Jack's back yet they still managed to catch some of the passing scenery.

They hadn't met another vehicle since lunch and only sighted a couple of distant crofts. The lanes began a steady ascent as the pastures gave way to rough grassland. The wagon continued the steady climb for another hour or so before reaching the summit of the moor. Here the lane levelled off for a while winding its way around rocky outcrops.

After negotiating a particularly tight bend the lane began to make its descent steadily through an outcrop of boulders. There was no sign of habitation as far as the eye could see, just vast swathes of cotton grass and peat hags far in to the distance.

Slowly Joe manoeuvred the wagon off the lane on to a rough grass track keeping in the shadow of a large outcrop of rocks until they reached the far side. Here the rocks had formed a large semi-circle with a natural lake in its midst. The wagon came to a halt here and Joe jumped down and called for the boys to join him.

"What do you think lads? Is this a good place to camp? You'll be safe up here and we can spend a couple of nights if you want? There's trout to be caught in the lake and with the rest of the food we shan't starve. We'll tether the ladies down by that copse of willow by the stream. There's fresh grass down there."

It's perfect" said Jack as he took in the surroundings, "just perfect Joe."

"There's not much of the day left boys so the two of you set up camp and see to the ladies. There's still some cereal left to make up a mash for the girls and they deserve it after all the miles we've covered today."

Joe strode off to cut a nice straight piece of willow to fashion into a fishing rod. The boys set about making up the camp and as they led the ladies down to the lake for a drink they came across the remnants of an old campfire. It was sat in a natural horse shoe indentation of grassy turf that offered shelter from the wind on three sides. The circle of stones had a large flat one to one side and Jack told Tom it would be perfect for keeping a pot warm by the fire.

"It's a good job we stocked up on wood yesterday Tom, there doesn't seem to be much around here," Tom nodded and took hold of Jacks hand and led him to the back of the wagon to show him a stash of peat.

"Of course Tom, the peat! Well done, we can burn the peat!"

Tom pointed to the lake where Joe was casting his line. Pod was busy making his way round the site marking his territory once again. Tom smiled at Jack and gave him the thumbs up sign.

"You are right Tom. I think we will be alright with Joe and Pod on our side."

The light of the day was just beginning to fade as Joe returned carrying two nice sized trout.

"Well done boys for setting up camp. I'll get these beauties in the frying pan, they'll only take minutes to cook."

Jack and Tom had never tasted trout before and were in for a special treat. All three plates were licked clean much to Pod's disgust who had been hanging around in anticipation. He was placated with a piece of custard tart that was on the menu for pudding.

Later that night, after all the chores had been completed, the three of them were sitting round the fire in silence and gazing in to the flames with the mugs of the last brew of the day cupped in their hands. Jack decided to broach a subject that he had been pondering over for some time.

“Joe, how did you know that me and Tom were hiding behind that boulder on the morning we met? You didn’t turn around, you just seemed to know we were there.”

Joe laughed, “have you been wondering about that all this time?”

Jack and Tom nodded.

“Well I don’t have the gift of sight if that’s what you think although many of my folk are blessed with that gift. In fact lads, my own mother has the ability to see in to a person’s past or future and sometimes even gets messages from those that have passed over. She never called it a gift though as it sometimes could be a curse depending on how you look at it. The only gift I possess is a strong intuition. As for the morning we met it didn’t take much to work out. I had already been given the information that there were supposedly two runaway boys in the area by the two rogues that were looking out for you. I just thought if you had any sense you would keep away from the main roads and be following similar terrain to myself. It had rained hard all that day and in to the night and I knew you would be very cold and hungry and maybe desperate enough to approach someone for help. So that night, as you saw, I got a good fire going with dry wood that would burn fiercely and brightly on the off chance that my hunch would pay off and then I waited.”

Jack and Tom were enthralled with this.

“I had just about given up for the night when the ladies became restless and Pods ears pricked up. I knew then that somebody was not very far away so I put another log on the fire and continued to wait. The ladies continued to be restless and Pod gave a little growl from the back of his throat, both clear signs that danger may be around as they perceived it. Then when I heard a twig break and the scuffling of leaves amongst the trees I knew someone was nearby. That's when I shouted the greeting and hoped it was two boys in the darkness and not a couple of highwaymen ready to slit my throat! Well you know what happened next. Sorry to disappoint you if you thought I had super human powers lads. I just have the sense to observe and trust in my animal's behaviour. Humans can learn so much if they just took the time to watch how animals communicate to one another."

"I'm not disappointed," Jack said "it's really interesting. Can we learn how to do it Joe?"

"Anyone can lads if you have the desire and commitment to do so, but not tonight, it's time for some shut eye. Tomorrow you can start your observations of Pod here."

Pod wagged his tail as if he had heard every word. Perhaps he had.

Jack looked out of the window early the next morning. There was a low mist surrounding the countryside below them. It looked really spooky he thought as he jumped down the steps of the wagon on his way to see to the horses. We could be on a different planet he thought. He could only just make out the trees on the other side of the water. He was glad he didn't have to cross the moor, it's no wonder people got lost if it was like this.

Joe strode out of the mist giving him a scare. He saw the brief look of fear on Jack's face and reassured him it was only himself.

"I was just thinking how spooky it was when you appeared from nowhere like a lost soul doomed to walk the moor forever," grinned Jack.

"Nay lad, I know I'm not a pretty sight in the morning but I didn't think I was that bad!"

"Don't count on it." Jack replied with a grin.

"The cheek of it," responded Joe, but he was glad to see the boy more relaxed. "I've already sorted out the ladies and am just about to get kettle on."

Jack shivered and thought it sounded like a good idea for it was much colder that morning with the mist everywhere. Joe explained the mist could come down with no warning up there and catch folk out if they weren't prepared for it.

"It's not going to last Jack, it'll burn away as soon as the sun gets up. By that time we'll have finished the morning chores. I think we'll have breakfast in the warmth of the wagon this morning."

True enough a couple of hours later the mist had cleared and the sun was beating down on them. The three of them were sitting on the shore of the lake in anticipation of catching a fish. Joe had equipped the boys with a willow rod each and a length of fine thread that had one of Joe's handmade hooks tied to the end. The boys had dug for worms on the side of the bank under Pod's supervision. Then Joe showed Jack how to bait the hook and he was ready. Tom had watched this procedure with disgust. He shook his head and pulled a face when it was his turn to bait the hook so Joe did it for him.

The three of them sat in silence passing the time hoping to provide a meal for later. Tom was the first to catch a good-sized trout and he couldn't hide his excitement as he dragged it to the shore safely! Joe gave him a big pat on the back and then showed the boys how to gut and clean the fish. Tom wasn't keen on that process either. Not long after Tom's luck was in again with a trout slightly bigger than the first.

"Well done Tom!" said Joe as he duly dispatched the fish and cleaned it for him, "you're a natural at this."

Tom had a broad grin on his face.

By mid-afternoon they had five trout on the bank, one each for Joe and Jack and a third for Tom.

"We've got more than enough boys. No point in taking anymore as they won't keep and we need to leave some for those who follow us. We'll get back for a brew and the last of the pies will put us on before we eat these beauties tonight."

The sun continued to beat down and by the afternoon it was really hot. Joe said they would move the ladies in to the shade of the rocks and give them a good grooming and then they could all go for a swim to cool down.

The horses stood patiently as the boys meticulously groomed their coats. Joe helping when the boys couldn't quite reach the horses backs. The boys were hot and sweating by the time they had finished.

"I think you two could do with a dip as well! You both stink to high heaven! Get a bar of soap each and strip off and get a good soak in the water. This might be the last chance you get before the weather turns cooler. Wash your shirts at the same time."

While the boys were away fetching the soap and towels Joe stripped off his shirt and jumped on to Shannon's back riding her in to the shallow lake. Sheba was led behind on her lead rope. They swam to the far side of the water and then he turned them around and swam back. The horses were just emerging from the lake when the boys returned with Pod at their heels who had been taking shelter under the wagon all morning.

Joe laughed as he heard the shrieks from Jack as he entered the cold water only to increase in volume as Pod joined them. Tom was holding Pod by the scruff of his neck as he rubbed soap in to his wiry coat. Pod soon wriggled free and made a hasty retreat.

Joe noticed the weal marks on the boys backs and his blood ran cold. He wasn't a violent man but he would make an exception if he ever got hold of the people that had done this to the boys. He watched them playing and laughing in the water. Children were resilient that's for sure but he worried about them non the less. Especially Tom. He was more relaxed now and even showed pleasure when he spent time with the animals but he still hadn't uttered a word. Joe wondered what the future held for the boy.

That night as they were sipping their brew after the feast of fresh trout, Jack asked of Joe,

"Joe, why do you always wish people good fortune when you are saying goodbye to them?"

"Let's see if I can explain. As you know I carry out a service of sharpening tools and what not for folk and in return they pay me a good price for that service. Both parties are happy with the transaction but when the lady of the house takes some of her precious time to bake a little extra or share with me produce they would normally sell at market it makes me feel good about myself. Makes me feel that I am appreciated. The best thing you can do for another being is to make them feel good towards themselves. The most precious gift you can give to a person is the gift of your own time. Whether that time is spent baking, making produce, chopping wood or even just listening to another person the gift of time you give them not only benefits them but is returned to you and you then feel good about yourself too. It's a two-way exchange of good energy. When I wish someone good fortune this is what I am wishing for them to feel good about themselves as they have made me feel good by offering me their gifts. I suppose most people think I am wishing for them to have more money but money can also bring its own problems. It may make some happy for a short while but it doesn't last. Most people after such a windfall either spend it too quickly and want more or worry they are going to lose it all and hoard it instead. By wishing someone good fortune to feel good about themselves that can be life changing because when we feel good about ourselves it automatically makes us feel happier and healthier no matter how much money we have. That's the best possible outcome anyone could wish for."

The boys looked studious for a minute or two.

"I think I understand now" said Jack "I kind of felt good about myself when I helped someone else or read stories to the boys who are not so good at reading themselves but I have never thought they may be feeling good just because I am reading to them but they are always pleased and thank me. Is that the same thing Joe?"

"Exactly" said Joe. Tom grinned and nodded his head. Pod yawned and scratched behind his ear.

"Time for some shut eye lads."

The next couple of days passed without incident with the three of them taking a share of packing up and setting up camp which was now done in half the time. They were still travelling in a northerly direction stopping for Joe to do his work at several crofts and hamlets along the way. Joe was still well known in this area and the residents watched for Joe passing through. They brought out their various implements to the wagon for Joe to work on and the usual gifts of foodstuffs which were always gratefully received. They managed to camp in secluded places that allowed the boys to leave the confines of the wagon.

On the second night as they dined on sausages and eggs on the banks of a shallow river Joe announced to them that he thought it was now safe enough for them to not have to stay out of sight all day. He explained to them that they were now far enough north to be out of the area that anyone would be looking for them in and also there had been no mention from any of his customers about a missing pair of boys.

"What do you think boys?"

"Well Joe you've not been wrong up to now. I'm sure we can trust your judgement and to be honest it's really boring sitting in the wagon all day." Jack replied.

"Right boys from tomorrow you can ride up front with me. I've still got a couple of regular places to stop at and I'll introduce you as my nephews if that's ok with you young gents?"

"That's fine with us Uncle Joe!" Jack laughed.

The next day saw the boys riding behind Shannon at Joe's side and hailing "good morning" to the few other travellers on the road. Jack couldn't remember ever being any happier. He felt so proud sitting next to Joe. Tom also seemed really content and even lifted his hand in greeting as they passed by the locals.

At the first hamlet they stopped at the boys proved a big attraction, especially with the farmers wives. Jack was polite and courteous and managed to swerve any awkward questions away from Tom who just gave them one of his winning smiles. Needless to say when the wives returned to pick up their sharpened implements they were even more generous with their gifts of food.

Joe was due to visit one of the larger dairy farms before the end of the day. He told the boys the farmers name was Alex and his wife Martha usually invited him into their kitchen to eat with them. As they were making their way up the long farm track the heavens opened and a deluge of rain battered the wagon. In minutes the track turned into a mire of mud. By the time they entered the farmyard they were soaked to the skin.

A large man appeared from one of the buildings and called out to Joe whilst gesturing with his arms to pull the wagon in to one of the big barns behind him that he was already opening the doors to.

“Ye can set up in ‘ere outa rain lad.”

They entered the large space empty apart from a couple of straw floored pens at the far end of the building.

“Thank you farmer Alex.” Joe shouted above the noise of the rain hammering down on the roof.

"Meks sense lad" farmer Alex replied, "this is goin' ta last late inta night an you'll not get darn lane till mornin'. Settle thee sen in an who have we 'ere then Joe?" Joe introduced the two boys, "well very pleased to meet ye young sirs. I'll tek ye ta meet me wife an she'll get thee dried out. I'll be back in a jiffy Joe to gi ye a hand with 'osses."

The boys raced across the yard on the heels of farmer Alex. They entered a large warm kitchen where a small stout lady with a cheerful face was stirring a pot on the range.

"These two drowned rats are Joe's nephews Martha" he told her, "They cud do wi dryin' art."

"Oh my poor wee bairns cum an get thee sen next ta fire. I'll see what a can find for thee to wear while we get yon sodden clothes dry."

She disappeared through the door at the back of the kitchen while Jack and Tom stood as near to the fire as they could get with the steam rising from their clothes causing the mirror over the mantle to mist over.

Martha returned with a bundle of clothes and a couple of drying cloths, "Get ye sens in't scullery ower there an strip off ya wet stuff an put these on, they'll be a bit big but better an nowt."

The boys did as they were told and emerged back in to the kitchen carrying their wet things.

“Reet little farmers ya luk wi yon overalls! ‘eres sum ‘ot milk for thee then ya can go up to mistle ta gi lads a ‘and wi coos if ya wants.”

Joe and Alex stabled the horses and rubbed them down then Alex went to finish his work in the milking parlour whilst Joe changed in to dry clothes and got stuck in to the pile of tools and implements waiting for him in the corner of the barn. An hour or more passed before Joe was finished. He packed the equipment away and washed his hands and face in the old pot sink. He wondered what was keeping the boys but reckoned they were glued to the fire place drying out their wet clothes but he hoped they weren’t getting in Martha’s way. It was still raining but not as heavy when he ran across the yard and in to the kitchen. Martha was busy setting up the table for the evening meal. She turned and smiled at Joe.

“It’s luvvly to see ya agin Joe, ‘ope you and yours are still well? What grand boys ye nephews are. They’ve gone up to mistle ta gi lads a ‘and.”

Joe noticed the boys clothes drying over the rail of the fire.

“Thanks Martha, it’s really good of you to help them but I hope that they haven’t been too much trouble?”

“No trouble at all lad” she answered, “got em all sorted out wi sum of our Glens old clothes, in fact they may as well keep em as they dunt fit our Glen any more. ‘Ees shot up like a beanstalk this past year.”

Suddenly the door burst open and Alex, Glen and two farm hands and the two boys raced in to get out of the rain. Joe was amused at the sight of the boys in overalls.

"Get yer sens cleaned up," Martha told the newcomers, "Meal will be on table in a minute."

The workers emerged from the scullery with faces and hands scrubbed clean and took their seats at the table.

"Has anyone seen my nephews round here?" asked Joe, "you can't miss them they look like two ragged urchins!"

Everyone laughed and Jack rolled his eyes.

"They bin a reet gud 'elp" Alex told Joe, "Gud little werkers the both of em. Ya can leave em 'ere Joe if tha wants."

"Careful Alex I may just be tempted to do that!"

All went quiet as the meal was served and everyone tucked in to the beef stew, creamy mash and Yorkshire puddings followed by jam roly poly and custard. Afterwards the conversation around the table was mostly about farming matters but Jacks ears pricked up when Martha asked Joe what he did in the winter months.

"Boys," Joe said, "it's maybe a good idea for you to clear up and wash the dishes as a thank you to these kind folk's hospitality."

The boys stood up and started clearing away the dishes and carrying them in to the scullery. Glen carried the kettle of hot water through for them before refilling it and putting it on the range for a brew later. Blast thought Jack, just as the conversation was getting interesting we get turfed out. He left the door to the scullery ajar so he could listen to the conversation. Tom realised what Jack was doing and gave him the thumbs up sign. Both boys washed the dishes as quietly as they could whilst straining to hear what was being said.

Joe began to describe the place he called his home up north. It was here where Joe's family and extended family lived during the winter months. It was a stretch of land about one and a half miles long by one quarter of a mile wide and was situated between a dense pine forest to the west and a bank of undulating sand dunes to the east. At each end of this strip of land a river emptied in to the sea. From the top of the dunes you could see Holy Island in the distance when it wasn't shrouded in mist. The land had been part of a large estate whose owner had granted permission for generations of Joe's family to winter there in return for their help in ploughing and planting in the spring on several of the farms on the estate.

One year when Joe's grandfather was just a young man tragedy struck. The young son and heir to the estate was walking his beloved spaniel on the beach. He was throwing sticks into the waves for the dog to retrieve when the tide turned and the dog began to struggle to get back to shore. Without thinking he ran into the sea to rescue his dog but he also got into difficulties by the strong pull of the waves. This whole scene was witnessed by a group of village women who were collecting shell fish further along the shore. One of the younger women ran and raised the alarm by shouting down to the camp at the foot of the dunes. Ted, Joes grandfathers' elder brother who was a strong swimmer ran to help. He dived in to the waves and managed to reach the boy. He battled the strong current dragging the boy back to shore. Both young men lay gasping for breath on the beach then Ted heard the dog yelping in fear and he returned to the sea to save the dog who by now was much further out to sea. He reached the dog but unfortunately couldn't make it back to shore and both boy and dog were taken by the sea.

As a result of this tragedy the Laird gifted the wintering grounds to Joe's family as a mark of gratitude for his son's life. To this day, two generations after the event, it's become a tradition that both families gather on the beach on the eleventh of December in remembrance. Joes' family to honour the bravery of their ancestor and the family from the Big House to give thanks for the life of theirs without such they would not have been born.

"So that's how it came about we are landowners and are always drawn back there."

"What a fascinating but sad story," said Alex, "dus any of your family stay there permanently Joe?"

"Oh yes," said Joe, "my Mam is there all the time now, she looks after grandad and my great uncle. They still have their own wagons though. Neither will entertain moving in to a house. My grandad was from a large family of sons and had lots of brothers but only his youngest is still with us now. I've got lots of uncles and cousins some of whom have built homes on our land and live there all of the time. Others, like my immediate family still travel to make a living through summer but prefer to stay in their wagons over winter. My older brother though works on the estate as a gamekeeper, the classic case of poacher turned gamekeeper! Two of my cousins work with the local blacksmith and another two have got a herring boat moored in the local harbour. It's good to get back after months on the road. With all the wagons parked in the shelter of the dunes it's fine to fall asleep to the sound of the waves crashing on the beach."

"It sounds a beautiful spot," said Martha, "I dunt think I'd want ta leave".

"The funny thing is," said Joe," by the end of the winter I get itchy feet and can't wait to get back on the road again."

"Well lad," said Alex, "I think thee hast best a both worlds and ya very lucky."

"I'll not argue with that," agreed Joe.

"Better see 'ow the two young fellas are getting' on" said Martha rising from the table, "it's very quiet in there."

The boys quickly moved back from the door and pretended to be putting away the last of the dishes.

“Well look at that!” she exclaimed as she entered the scullery. Everything was clean and tidy with the pile of crockery neatly stacked ready to be put away.

“What a gud job you’ve dun boys! Wud ya like a mug o warm milk as a nightcap, yav deserved it.”

Joe and the boys bid the family goodnight when they had finished their drinks. Joe told them that he wanted to be up early as he still had a couple of things to finish off before they made tracks.

” You’ll probably ‘ere me an t’lads getting ready for’t milkin’”, Alex said, “we’ll be up an about around five o’clock.”

“Can we help again?” asked Jack.

“Aye lads thee can if tha’s up! Com’n join us.”

As they were leaving for bed Martha reminded them that breakfast was at seven thirty sharp! The rain had stopped as they crossed the yard. Joe hoped that the farm track would be passable tomorrow as he planned to start heading south east to York. He estimated that it would take them a couple of days to reach the outskirts where he would drop off the boys. He wanted to time it to coincide with the Saturday market to allow the boys to mingle amongst the usual crowds as they entered through the gates.

He had been trying not to think about the boys leaving. He would miss them dreadfully. Who would have thought that the two little scallywags had broken down the barriers he had built to protect himself from being hurt again. It's a strange world right enough he thought to himself.

When they entered the wagon Pod was looking so forlorn at being confined to barracks. He held his head in his paws and his hound dog expression would have melted the hardest of hearts.

"Let's have a game of fetch" said Joe and Pod's ears pricked up instantly. The boys found a stick and began to throw it across the barn. His tail wagged ten to the dozen and his woes were instantly forgotten.

The boys were woken by the lowing of the cows as they were herded through the farm yard on the way to be milked. They jumped out of bed and threw on the overalls that Martha had given them the day before.

"By you two are keen." Joe said as they jumped out of the wagon. He had been up for a while and was on the last of the tools to be sharpened.

"Good to see that you remembered your offer to help. Take heed of what Alex and the boys tell you and try not to get in their way! I'll finish off here and prepare the wagon for our journey now away and enjoy yourselves."

The boys scampered out of the barn and into the darkness of the yard. Joe got finished sooner than he thought so he took Pod for a walk up the fields. Well Pod, he told the dog, we'll be in new territory today and plenty of new smells for you but I'll be in the dark regarding a safe place to camp for the ladies. He didn't want to tether them at the roadside. Pod looked at him as if he understood every word. I know Pod, we'll just have to see what the day brings, it's no good worrying about what might not happen.

Joe was already in the kitchen when the door burst open and the party of workers entered. Jack was chatting with Glen and the two of them had certainly hit it off by the look of things.

"Get thee senns cleaned up lads!", Martha instructed them "I'm just abart to serve up't porridge. Get it while its 'ot."

Jack and Tom had never tasted porridge like this before. At the orphanage the porridge was grey, watery and tasteless with no sign of fresh cream or a sprinkling of sugar.

"This is the best porridge I've ever had Martha."

"Thank ye Jack, I'm glad you are enjoying it an get anuther bowl full. Save some space for buttered toast an jam for afters!"

It wasn't long after breakfast that they were packed up and ready to leave.

"Thank you all once again for your hospitality. You've made me and the boys so welcome. It's always a pleasure to call here on my travels and I wish you both good fortune." Joe said to Alex and Martha as they were about to leave.

"It's always a pleasure lad, nae bother at all but, aye, you'd better be on tha way. There's nay many weeks left now afore weather changes an you'll need to be 'ome afore then. So God speed an 'ave a safe journey."

Martha and Alex waved them off as they made their way down the track.

"I wunder if we'll see yung uns agin." said Martha,

"'Ope so, grand little werkers the pair of em." answered Alex.

Chapter Nine.

The wagon had been underway for some time with the boys sitting up front with Joe again and Pod nestled between them. Joe told them that they were now heading south towards York. He would be leaving them in two days' time. Jack went quiet for quite a while and seemed agitated.

Suddenly he said "Joe, do we have to go back to York? Can we not stay with you and go to your home up north? We'll help with any chores and try not to be a bother to anyone."

Joe's heart ached as he replied "Don't think it hasn't crossed my mind Jack. I know my family would welcome the two of you with open arms but there's a couple of factors against this happening. Firstly and the main reason is that there is still a chance that Toms father will recover from his illness and be in a position to take Tom back home. How do you think he would feel finding out that Tom had vanished without a trace because nobody would know you had been taken to Leeds and had managed to run away? Secondly, if you don't go back to the orphanage and tell them what happened and how you were treated the Police won't be able to bring the Gooding gang to justice. How many more children would end up in their clutches? It's up to you to decide Jack but that's what I think."

It didn’t take Jack long to come to the same conclusion. He remembered promising Archie that he would look after Tom.

“You’re right Joe. I hadn’t thought it through properly. We have to go back and face up to our responsibilities.”

“Well said young man, I’m proud of you,” responded Joe.

They were now travelling down lanes that Joe was not familiar with, passing through hamlets instead of stopping for Joe to see any customers and therefore making much better progress. They stopped for lunch and to give the horses a rest at the side of a stream by woodland before continuing the journey in to the unknown.

It was late afternoon before they came across a suitable place to camp on the edge of a small village green. There was a stream running through the centre of the green and a large duck pond under the shelter of a grand old oak tree. The only problem was that it was bordered on three sides with cottages and a church amidst woodland on the far side. Joe would have preferred somewhere more secluded but the day was drawing in and they could travel further and only find worse places. Besides, the horses had done well and needed to rest. Joe knew it was common land and they wouldn’t require permission to camp there. He pulled the wagon on to the green by the side of the stream. He told the boys that they would cook on the stove and not build a camp fire here as it might annoy the villagers.

“How about you two boys take Pod for a run through the woods at the back of the church and I’ll see to the ladies.”

Jack and Tom made their way through the village to the path that led to the back of the church. Jack thought what a pretty village, the cottages were all well maintained with lovely gardens. Pod raced off in to the wood, his tail wagging at all the fresh smells. The path continued a good way through the wood until eventually stopping at a ford in the river. Well this was as far as they could go thought Jack and decided they had better get back to the wagon. Jack told Tom he had seen some juicy blackberry bushes up near the church and thought they should go back and fetch a basket to pick some.

Joe had already watered and tethered the ladies when they got back and the kettle was simmering away on the stove. The three of them were just finishing their brew when they heard the clatter of a horse and cart pulling up in the lane opposite them. There was the sound of men shouting as they approached the wagon.

Oh no, Joe thought, and turned to Jack and Tom “You two stay inside and bolt the door. Do not come out no matter what!”

Jack jumped up and bolted the door of the wagon as Joe left. He took hold of Toms hand and both boys watched Joe approach the group of men through the window.

“What can I do for you fine gents?” Joe asked them in a calm manner yet his heart was beating like a sledgehammer.

“Clear off! That’s what tha can do! We don’t want yor kind round ‘ere,” replied the leader aggressively, “now itch up an get out o ‘ere afore we mek ya.”

Joe almost laughed out loud in relief, this was a situation he had dealt with lots of times in the past.

“I’m so sorry,” said Joe, “I thought this was common ground and I wouldn’t need to ask permission to camp here for one night.”

“Aye, that’s what law sess,” argued the leader, “but we’ll tek law into our own ‘ands if tha dunt pack up an bugger off under thar own steam,” he raised his stick high to add weight to his words.

By now a small crowd of locals had emerged from the cottages to see what was going on. Fuelled by this attention the man continued, “This is a decent village wi ‘ard werking decent folk an we dunt want idle thieving dirty bastards like thee amongst us.”

“Well Sir, I can assure you that I certainly do not fit your description in any way! I have an honest trade providing a service to the outlying hamlets and crofts north west of here and have done for fifteen years or more. Known thereabouts as Honest Joe. Keep coming back year after year because of the welcome I receive. You’ll not find kinder, friendlier folk than Yorkshire folk, salt of the earth they are. Only last night farmer Alex bade us shelter in his barn out of yon storm then took us in his home to share an evening meal. Most obliging folk you could ever meet are Yorkshire folk. I tell everybody."

"He's telling the truth," stated an old lady at the front of the crowd who had stepped forward, "I've heard our Gabbie from up that way mention his name. They luk forward ta is visits every year, 'elps em out no end."

"I understand why you are so concerned Sir" Joe addressed the ring leader, "I'm a stranger to you. I don't want to cause any ill feeling to any good Yorkshireman. I'll be on my way, though it's a shame as those ladies grazing there have covered a lot of miles today and my two young nephews in the wagon who are too frightened to come out need their grub. Not to worry, hopefully we can find another site before darkness."

"Jack, it's alright lad you're safe to come out now."

Jack sheepishly opened the door and left the wagon, "I'm sorry lad you'll have to wait a bit longer for your grub. If you make a start hitching the ladies I'll join you in a minute."

A ladies voice in the crowd was overheard saying to her friend, "Luk at poor mite, 'ees frightened ta death."

Joe turned back to face the man who had now lowered the stick and was calming down now that Joe was doing his bidding.

"If you don't mind me asking Sir, is that your horse hitched to that cart over there?"

"What's it ta thee?" the man answered.

"Has he been restless and off his food lately?" Joe replied.

"Aye Dad ee has," said one of the young stick bearers.

"I can't help but notice,", Joe continued, "he's leaning a bit and the shoe on his left back foot is well worn whilst his other three look like new. It will put a lot of strain on the tendon on that leg, see the swelling around his knee? That will cause him a lot of pain and if left untreated it could cause permanent lameness and his untimely death."

I wonder why the Smithy allowed this to happen Joe pondered out loud.

Again the younger man responded, "Remember Dad wen Todd was in ta get all 'is shoes replaced an smithy got called awa afore ee cud finish an ee asked ya to wait but ya dint 'ave time so ee telt ya ta cum bak later that day. That were a couple a month's ago naw Dad."

"Alreet, alreet 'od yer tung!" his father said as he turned to glare at him, "I'll get 'im ta smithy in the morn."

"May I also say Sir, it may be too late if he has to travel any distance. With your permission Sir, I have spare shoes I carry all the time for the ladies here and I know how to fit them. I could fit one on Todd here for the time being so you can get him to the smithy for a proper fit without doing him any further damage."

"Ya can try but I dunt think thee'll manage. Ee 'ates bin shod," answered the man with the wind clearly taken out of his sails now.

Joe collected all the equipment he would need and approached Todd. He gently made acquaintance with the horse before approaching the affected foot. To the amazement of the crowd he managed the procedure without a problem and nary a sound from Todd.

"That should be alright now", said Joe, "I've got some liniment you can have. Apply it twice daily and it will take out the heat and reduce the swelling in that knee. I'll just get it for you Sir and then we'll be on our way."

"Well mebbe I've bin too 'asty lad," the man told him, "No arm ya stayin' for't night I suppose."

The old lady in the crowd scoffed, "That's awful big o ya Bill Grady! Yon lad 'ere just saved thee 'osses life near enuff an that's all yuv got ta say for yassen! Ya allus too quick ta judge t'other folk. Let this be a lesson ta ya. Naw get thee sen 'ome for ya mek a bigger show of yasen."

Joe gave the man his liniment and the man and his gang left without another word.

“Thank you Ma’am”, Joe turned to the old lady doffing his cap.

“Nay lad, thank thee! Best show I’ve sin for a long while! Yon Bill’s allus full o ‘is self-importance. Ees not a bad fella but ‘ees bin in military ya see. Ee thinks ee ‘as to speak for rest of us. I’m reet glad ta meet ya lad, Iv sin wi me own eyes now what ar Gabbie’s bin on about! She sess ya a reet ‘ansome fella wi a silver tung. Cud charm birds owt a tree! She’s reet an all. Ya’ll know ‘er, as a sheep farm on tops, once sin niver forgotten. She’s mi late ‘usbands sister.”

“Not Seth’s wife by chance?” asked Joe.

“The one an only,” replied the woman.

Joe and Jack laughed as Jack put a name to Mrs. Seth.

“Aye Gabbie be name an gabby be nature,” the old woman laughed with them, “Now lad” she said to Jack “bring yon basket an cum wi me.”

Jack followed the lady to her cottage. “Reet lad! Wi better liv up to Joe’s expectations of us Yorkshire folk,” she grinned as she put a loaf in to the basket followed by three duck eggs and a blackberry pie that she had left to cool on the window sill, “now away wi ya lad an if I’m reet tha’ll be plenty more cumming ya way afore nights out.”

Later, as the three of them were eating their evening meal, one by one several of the locals knocked on the wagon and each one bearing a gift of food.

“There’s enough here to last a week and we haven’t even opened the box that Martha gave us this morning!” Joe grinned.

“Joe, I was frightened there was going to be a fight back there. That man said some horrible things to you.”

“Nay lad, getting angry and fighting would have solved nothing. I would have ended up with a bloody nose or maybe worse and we would still have been chucked off the site. It’s always better to deflate a situation than to aggravate it by letting tempers control your behaviour. Unfortunately, it’s a situation that me and my folk find ourselves in more often than we would like.”

“Why is that Joe? You’ve been nothing but kind to us. I’m sure your family would be just the same.”

“There’s good folk and bad folk in all walks of life Jack and it’s the bad folk who spoil it for the rest of us and it’s the same no matter what background you come from. People like that man earlier don’t give us credit for being individuals. He doesn’t know anything about our customs and beliefs and judges us all the same and thinks we are all vagabonds. Let’s hope from now on he might have a more open mind about me and my folk.”

“Aye” Jack said, “I think you might just have given him something to think about Joe.”

“Well if so Jack it’s all been worth it. Now open that box and let’s see what Martha has been kind enough to share with us.”

Jack hardly had time to open the box before Pod was at his side, tail wagging in expectation.

The following morning dawned bright and sunny and unseasonably warm for the time of year and promising a lovely day ahead. Appropriate Joe thought, for his last day with the boys. He was determined that his dread of saying goodbye to them the following morning was not going to overshadow this day.

They were hitched and ready to go before most of the village had risen out of their beds. Although the route was unfamiliar to Joe the scenery held the same drystone walls dividing the fields making a patchwork pattern on the landscape. The same narrow lanes threading up and down dale as they followed the contours of the land sometimes bordered by the stone walls or thick hedgerow or dense woodland. Every crest of a hill opening up to a new vista to gaze upon.

Joe found he was quite enjoying the anticipation of what lay round the next bend or the crest of a hill. They only met the odd local from time to time just going about their daily business, always getting a wave of the hand in acknowledgement.

They had been travelling for a couple of hours when an old, ruined castle came in sight. It was set back a couple of hundred yards from the road and surrounded on three sides with dense woodland.

“Good place to stop for a bite to eat do you think?” Joe asked the boys. They agreed immediately. It looked to them like a good place to explore. Pulling into what would have been the castle courtyard Joe brought the wagon to a halt.

"I can see that you two are eager to investigate so on you go, take Pod with you and I'll get a brew on. No climbing on yon walls though, they might not be safe!"

The boys jumped from the wagon and ran off in excitement. The kettle had boiled and the tea was in the pot and yet there was no sign of the boys returning. Joe was just thinking that he would have to go and look for them when they arrived back full of smiles and faces flushed with excitement.

"It's brilliant!" Jack said, "there's loads of rooms still intact! Two of them look like they were old kitchens and they had massive stone ranges and hooks hanging from the roofs! There was a long room with enormous fire places and high chimneys at each end. There's a winding stone staircase that would have led up to the bedrooms but all the upper floors are caved in. We even found the entrance to what could have been a dungeon but we didn't dare go down there! At the back of the castle there's a big circular pond surrounded by a stone wall about four feet tall with a gap of about six feet where steps go down to the water. I think this could have been the well!"

"Sounds likely," said Joe, "those old walls could probably tell a story or two. Does the water look alright for the ladies to drink?"

“No it’s all green and a bit smelly,” answered Jack.

“We’ll have to stop at the next stream we come to then,” said Joe “anyone want a slice of blackberry pie with their brew?”

They were only minutes in to their journey following their break at the castle when they came across a river. They followed its bank looking for a suitable access point for the horses until they came across a small cluster of cottages where a grassy track between two buildings led to a ford. Perfect observed Joe as he pulled the wagon in to a clearing.

“I’ll get the ladies unhitched,” just as at that moment the door to the nearest cottage opened and two young boys about the same age as Jack and Tom ran out carrying a ball. A small dog that could have been a twin to Pod scampered at their feet. They stopped suddenly when they saw the wagon and then inquisitively approached.

Pod was down like a shot to investigate the young dog his tail erect he circled around his twin sniffing its rear end. The little dog made a submissive gesture by lying on its back with paws in the air. This was good enough for Pod who then wagged his tail in greeting. The dog then jumped up and ran across the green beckoning Pod to chase him. Thus began an hilarious game of cat and mouse with both dogs seemingly taking it in turns to be the pursuer. They ran, tumbled and leaped in to the air and wrestled on the ground resting briefly to catch their breath before they set off again. All four boys began laughing together at the antics of the dogs.

“Do you fancy a game o footie” one of the boys asked Jack and Tom, “I’m Sid and this is me brother Davie.”

“That’ll be great,” answered Jack who introduced Tom and himself to the boys.

Of course when the boys began to play both dogs decided to join in the game and ran off with the ball and generally got in the way and spoiling the game!

Joe chuckled to himself as he led the ladies down to the river. It was heart-warming to see Jack and Tom playing without seemingly a care in the world after what they had been through. He passed an old man sitting on a bench outside one of the cottages flanking the lane to the ford.

“How do,” the man said in a greeting to Joe as he gestured his hand towards the boys,” Oh to be young agin” he laughed with a toothless grin. Joe grinned in acknowledgement and continued down to the river. On his way back he stopped to pass the time of day with the old chap who seemed to be glad of a bit of company. Joe was happy that he did because he was a mine of local knowledge. He had been a haulier in his day and he knew the lanes like the back of his hands. Joe told him that they were on their way to York and did he know a good place to camp that night.

He knew the ideal place, a place he often used to pull in for a break to have his midday meal. It was a disused quarry with a stream running through a grassy area and ideal for the horses. It had a view right across the Vale of

York. Joe thought it sounded perfect and got instructions on how to get them there. They remained seated for a while watching the antics on the green between the boys and the dogs until all the candidates seemed to run out of steam and tire.

"Time to be off," said Joe, "thank you for your company and advice Sir."

"A pleasure lad, it's been nice speaking to thee," the man waved him off.

The boys said their farewells and Sid and Davie waved the wagon off until it went out of sight. It took a couple of hours twisting and turning on the narrow lanes before they reached the quarry. It was just as the old man had described to Joe and it didn't take long to set up camp. There was no shortage of decent sized stones to build a campfire and the stream was crystal clear. Pod did his usual scouting around and proudly returned with the offering of a rabbit.

"We've got more food than we know what to do with," Joe chuckled, "let's have a feast tonight boys and how would you like to sleep under the stars for a change? It will be warm enough with a good fire and a cosy blanket."

"Yes please!" answered Jack, "it'll be like a proper adventure won't it Tom?" Tom's eyes lit up as he nodded.

The boys took off to climb the side of the quarry with Pod at their heels while Joe prepared their feast. The human adventurers returned with grazed knees and faces smudged with mud and grinning from ear to ear.

"You can see York Minster from the top of the quarry," Jack told Joe.

"Aye I've no doubt" said Joe, "we're not far off now."

He felt a rush of sadness. To hide his feelings he told the boys to get cleaned up in the stream his voice gruffer than he intended but the boys didn't seem to notice. When darkness fell the three of them were huddled around the fire nestled amidst their warm blankets. Pod had decided to share Tom's makeshift bed with him.

Earlier they had enjoyed their feast of duck eggs scrambled with the last of the cheese, fried sliced potatoes with onions and garden greens followed by the last of the blackberry pie and cream. It was indeed a feast.

The night was clear and bright. A multitude of stars twinkled in the darkness above them and Joe pointed out the North star to them. It's always the brightest star he told the boys and went on to explain how sailors used it to navigate their way around the world.

"What are the stars made of Joe?" Jack asked him.

"Well there are men called astronomers who study the stars and they reckon that each star is actually another distant planet."

"But there's millions of them," said Jack.

“Aye, and maybe lots more that are too far away to see with our eyes. The astronomers use very strong telescopes to enable them to study the night skies. Some people believe that each star is the shining soul of a person that’s passed away. They use their Light to watch over loved ones left behind. I like that explanation the best,” said Joe.

“Yes so do I,” agreed Jack and they heard Tom sigh as if he also gained comfort from this explanation. Joe continued to tell the boys that his folk believed that the stars were gypsies, scattered in the sight of God.

“That’s lovely” Jack told Joe, “And I feel that to be true.”

It wasn’t long before the boys were fast asleep. Joe watched them sleeping in the firelight and he knew he was really going to miss them. He knew he would have to be strong in the morning when finally saying goodbye to them.

He owed these youngsters more than they would ever know. Caring for them had opened a door inside that he thought he had firmly bolted after the death of his beautiful wife and their two-year-old daughter seven years ago. They had perished with a severe lung disease during a particularly severe winter. He never wanted to experience such devastating pain like that again as long as he lived. Up to now he had avoided close relationships with other people and at the time he had pushed his family and friends away too. He refused to travel with them, preferring his own company. He realised now how selfish he had been for his family and friends were hurting too. His loss was also their loss but he had been too wrapped up in his own grief to see theirs. Now, thanks to the boys he was able to see this more clearly. He had to stop running away from his grief and accept it for what it was. He felt strong enough now to acknowledge that he needed his family and friends around him. He felt that meeting the boys was meant to be in some way. Life was strange he thought as his eyes closed and he joined the boys in a deep sleep.

The boys awoke with the sound of Joe preparing breakfast. The kettle had boiled and sausages were sizzling in the pan over the fire. Three plates held a thick slice of bread and butter.

Wake up sleepy heads! I'm about to crack the eggs in to the pan and with this hot fat it will only be minutes before grub is served". The boys emerged from their nests and stretched before they washed their faces in the stream and came back to find breakfast ready.

The atmosphere in camp was subdued as they packed up camp for the last time together. It continued as they made their journey down the lane to meet the main road in to York. Joe attempted to lift the mood by pointing out various objects of interest but his heart wasn't in it and the two boys remained locked in their own thoughts.

Far too soon they reached the junction on the road where Joe would have to leave them. Joe pulled the wagon on to the grass verge and they all jumped down.

"It's time to say our farewells boys" Joe told them, "I want you to know beyond a shadow of a doubt how proud I am of you both for deciding to return to face your responsibilities. I've enjoyed every moment of our time together and only wish it could have been much longer. In just a little while you'll be safely back at the orphanage away from the clutches of those villains for good. No more hiding or being suspicious of strangers. You are both brave, clever and generous of spirit and are going to grow in to fine young men. I'm going to miss you terribly."

Joe had to stop as his voice began to crack.

"We are going to miss you Joe," Jack told him as his chin trembled and he was fighting back tears, "we can't thank you enough for all you've done for us Joe. We'll always remember our time together and the things you taught us. I hope with all my heart that one day we'll get to meet again."

He couldn't hold back the tears any longer and both boys ran in to Joe's arms and clung tightly to him. Tears streamed down Joe's face has he held on to the boys. So much for being strong he thought. Tom gently pulled away from Joe and knelt down to Pod. The young boys body wracked with sobs and tears streaming down his face as Pod gently licked them away.

Joe's reserve almost wavered to witness so much anguish coming from the young boy. He wanted to bundle the boys back on to the wagon and head north but instead he took a deep breath and reached for the basket that the boys were to carry in to York to help them blend in with the other folk going to market. He gently wiped away their tears and handed them the basket.

"Time to be off gents," he said smiling warmly at them, "I wish good fortune to follow you every day of your lives."

He climbed back on to the wagon and as he pulled away he heard Jack shout "And the very same to you Joe!"

The boys watched solemnly as Joe's wagon disappeared out of sight. Then Jack looked deep in to Toms reddened eyes and told him to be brave. They had a job to do and couldn't let Joe down. Tom nodded sadly and Jack took hold of his hand tightly and they began walking towards their goal.

When the East gate in to York came in to view Jack became nervous. What if someone was still watching out for them? He then noticed a family a little way in front of them who were just about to join the throng of people slowing down to pass through the gate.

Quick! He instructed Tom as he manoeuvred them through the crowd until they reached the family. Walking close behind the parents and children it looked to any onlookers as if they were all one family. Once they were through the gates safely they continued to shadow the family until they reached the market square. From here they knew they were close to York Minster and would then know their way back to the orphanage.

The boys reached their destination without mishap. When they entered the yard that led to the large double doors of the building they turned to one another and in unison gave a big sigh of relief.

“We’ve done it Tom, we’ve done it!” Jack said in triumph.

Matron could not believe her eyes when she answered the knock on her office door and saw the two of them standing there hand in hand. She listened intently to their story becoming increasingly concerned as the story unfolded. When Jack had finished relating everything to her she immediately sat down and began to compose a note that she despatched with a staff member to deliver to the nearest constabulary. She then called for Archie to join them.

Archie was bewildered at being called to Matron’s office and even more so when he saw his brother and Jack sitting in her good chairs by the fire. He took in the state of the boys and the scar on Tom’s neck.

“What’s happened to you?” he said angrily. Jack once again related the story for Archies benefit. Archie experienced a multitude of emotions as he silently listened to Jack and Tom’s story eventually feeling a massive sense of relief that the boys were safely back. It wasn’t long before two Constables entered Matron’s office. One was in uniform and the other in regular clothes. The one in regular clothes introduced himself as Robbie and informed them that he was in charge of the investigation. The man in uniform was Sergeant John Derwent and would write everything down as Jack related the story for the third time but now in much more detail.

"You are both very brave and very lucky," Robbie told them. "You have given us enough details that we can arrest these villains and bring them to justice. Is there anything you would like to aske before we put the wheels in motion?"

"Yes" said Archie, "will the boys have to go to court and face them again?"

"Very unlikely," Robbie answered, "what will happen is we will arrest a couple of them, we know their names, descriptions and where to find them thanks to the boys and when they realise they may get a leaner sentence by cooperating they'll spill the beans on the rest of the gang. That's how it usually works but don't worry Sergeant Derwent here will keep you informed. We just ask of you not to tell anyone else what happened to you for now until we have caught the lot. Thanks to you two boys the streets will become a safer place for a while. You should be both proud of yourselves."

After the Police had left Matron sent for a tray of food to be brought to her office for all three boys. She left them alone while she went to carry on with her other duties.

“Thank goodness that Joe turned out to be alright!” said Archie. “The best!” replied Jack.

“And so are you Jack for looking after our Tom! I’ll never forget how brave you’ve been.”

“Nay Archie, I’m sorry Tom had to go through what he did and now he can’t speak.”

“That’s not your fault Jack.” Archie assured him.

“Never the less I promise I’ll do all I can to help Tom. I think he’s been the bravest out of the two of us.” Tom shook his head vehemently and pointed to Jack.

Life at the orphanage continued as before. Jack found some reassurance in the monotony of the routine as it made him feel secure and safe knowing what to expect as each day unfolded. His only worry was Tom who seemed to have withdrawn back in to himself since they left Joe. It made him wonder if it was the right thing to do to return after all. Jack thought of Joe often as he lay in his bed and silently thanked him for being such a wonderful friend to them both. He really missed him because Joe had been the only father figure he had known. Joe was the only adult that he truly respected and trusted.

Jack was as good as his word. He looked out for Tom all through the day. The other boys knew better than to tease or make fun of Toms muteness as one look from Jack changed their minds. Knowing how much Tom used to enjoy Jack reading adventure stories to him Jack asked the teacher if he could borrow books from the school room and he would read the stories to Tom on an evening. Some of the other boys would join them sitting around Tom's bed as Jack's portrayal of the characters would bring them to life. Sometimes they would be sailors on the high seas exploring distant lands or finding treasures on a faraway island. Other times Jack would be asked by one of the boys to tell them one of his own stories from his life before he came to the orphanage. These made-up stories never failed to have the boys laughing out loud or gasping in amazement!

One night as Jack laid in bed after telling one of these stories he began to feel guilty. He didn't mind telling these stories to amuse the other boys but he felt he was being dishonest with Tom and Archie. From the beginning of their friendship Tom had looked up to him not knowing that his so-called adventures and experiences with his family were all fictional. He and Tom had overcome a real-life drama together and it didn't seem right to pretend to his two friends anymore. He came to a decision.

"Tom" he whispered, "are you still awake?" Tom turned towards him, "Tom I have to tell you something," as he took a deep breath then hurriedly told Tom he had made up all the stories about his family.

"None of them were true Tom. The truth is I don't have any family, I've never had a family and I've been here since I was a baby. I don't know why I make the stories up Tom but I want you and Archie to know the truth. I don't know what it's like to have a brother Tom but I guess it's something like the feelings I have towards you and Archie. I'm sorry for lying to you."

Tom was silent for a moment and then reached across and squeezed Jack's hand.

"Thank you." Jack whispered.

The year wore on. Christmas came and went with the usual sparse activities. It was late January when Jack, Tom and Archie were summoned to Matron's office. Sergeant John Derwent was there and told the boys that it was all over. All of the villains had been arrested and sentenced to either transportation or the gallows. The gang not only operated in Leeds but in Bradford and Manchester too. Thanks to the boy's bravery more than thirty children had been rescued and either reunited with their families or taken back in to care. Jack felt a weight lift from his shoulders and he knew this was proof that they had done the right thing by returning.

It was the middle of February on a cold wintery night and the snow was falling heavily outside and the windows in the dormitory were rattling in their frames. Tell us a story Jack said one of the boys. The one where you and your Pa nearly got caught poaching rabbits on that estate and you got the backside of your breeks torn out by the guard dog! A small crowd of boys gathered around Jack's bed. Tom looked on with interest and a smile. Jack began to relate this particular story embellishing it as he went along. Thanks to his gift of storytelling and emphasising with gestures to exaggerate a point the boys were soon rolling with laughter! Tom also began laughing. He laughed and laughed with tears streaming down his cheeks. The boys were now laughing at Tom's infectious laugh and soon everyone in the dormitory was laughing hilariously!

Tom turned to Jack and winked "That's a great story Jack!"

There was a second of stunned silence and then an almighty cheer erupted just as Archie entered the room.

"What's going on?" he asked the room in puzzlement.

"Not a lot," said Tom as he ran across the room into Archies arms. Then once more a deafening cheer exploded around the room.

Chapter Ten.

Jack was so glad that Tom was back to his old self. It made the days pass more quickly with Tom chattering away at his side whilst they carried out their daily chores. Better still, the two of them were back to discussing the merits or otherwise of the books they read in the schoolroom and had started to take it in turns to read to the other boys most evenings.

Life in the orphanage had definitely taken a turn for the better as life settled down to normal. It was towards the end of April with its longer warmer days that Jack was called in to Matron's office.

He was puzzled because he couldn't remember doing anything wrong. As he entered the office she gave him a warm smile as she said, "Jack, I've got some very good news for you! You've been accepted for a foster home by a good Christian family who run a hill farm up near Pateley Bridge. It's an excellent opportunity for you to have a proper home and learn skills in animal husbandry and agriculture, both of which will stand you in good stead for the future. The couple are a little older than is customary for foster parents but I'm sure you will be very happy there."

Jack was so shocked by this sudden change of events that he couldn't speak.

"Now I know what you are thinking Jack and it's understandable after what you went through at your last placement but I assure you this will not happen again. The rules are stricter now to ensure the safety of all our children."

"Bbb...but why can't I just stay here?" Jack stuttered.

"Believe me Jack," she answered, "this is the absolute best outcome I could have wished for you. It will seem a little scary at first but I am sure you will settle down there just fine. There will be a visit to the farm by an Inspector employed by the trustees of the orphanage to see how you are getting on in about two months' time. His job is to make sure yourself and your foster parents are happy with the arrangement. There are now new rules in place after what happened to you and Tom to make sure all is well for both parties involved. Now run along and I'll see you back here after breakfast in the morning. Have your belongings and bits and pieces packed ready to go."

Jack returned ashen faced back to the dormitory. The boys couldn't believe Jack's news but the good friends that Tom and Archie were didn't let Jack see how upset they were. Instead, they tried to reassure Jack that everything would be alright. The three of them made a pact that no matter what they would try and stay in touch so they could meet again in the future.

Jack was so nervous when he entered Matron's office the next morning. He hadn't slept a wink all night and dreading this very moment.

There was a very tall thin man with grey hair and beard standing by the window. He was dressed all in black with the neck of a white shirt showing beneath his jacket. He was clasping a black hat between his hands and he looked as uncomfortable as Jack.

"Good morning Jack," said Matron, "This gentleman is Mr. Smithson and he will be your guardian from now on."

"Good morning sir," Jack acknowledged politely.

"Morning lad," the man replied.

"Well I know you've got some distance to travel today so I'll not keep you. Mr. Smithson has been made aware of his responsibilities to you in his care and has agreed to carry them out to the letter. Everything has been signed and you are ready to go."

Matron gave Jack's hand a gentle squeeze and smiled as she said, "We will all miss you Jack but believe me it's for the best and I wish you both well for the future."

"Thank you," said Jack and Mr. Smithson nodded in acknowledgement.

Jack followed Mr. Smithson outside where a horse and cart stood waiting in the yard.

"This here is Esmerelda or Elda for short," said Mr. Smithson as he stroked the horse's nose. Jack stepped forward tentatively towards the giant horse, "Don't be afraid of her size lad, she's as gentle as a kitten."

Jack gently stroked the horses' velvety nose and rubbed her neck, Elda nuzzled his hand.

"Hello Elda," Jack said to her and he didn't know why but he felt instantly relaxed. It was as if Elda had told him everything was going to be alright in the same way Shannon had done when he first met her.

From is new vantage point sitting high at the front of the cart next to his guardian Jack enjoyed watching the people of York bustling through the streets intent on carrying out their daily business. His guardian didn't seem to notice the throng of people, instead he was gazing silently ahead concentrating on safely weaving through the many carts and carriages. Eventually the crowds became less and before too long they had left York behind. They were now surrounded with the green of the countryside listening to the gentle clip clop of Elda's hooves and the mild sway of the cart. Jack began to drop off to sleep, jerking awake with a start as he was about to fall over.

"Climb over to the back lad, there's a couple of blankets in the corner and make yourself comfortable."

Jack did as he was bid and was fast asleep in minutes. Sometime later he was roused from his sleep by the sound of a busy street to find the cart at the side of the road outside a large shop. Jack watched his guardian walk empty handed out of the door of the shop. What's going on thought Jack as he rubbed the sleep out of his eyes.

“You’re awake then. Jump up front if you want, we’ve not far to go now before we stop for a break. You’ve had a good long sleep. You must feel better for it?”

“Yes sir,” replied Jack as he clambered over to the front once more. It didn’t take them long to leave this town behind and reach the countryside. They travelled in silence for about half an hour or so when a hamlet came in to view.

“Here we are lad,” as he pulled the cart in to a narrow lane and stopped at the door of a small cottage.

The garden was the most beautiful garden he had ever seen. Even at this time of year it was abundant with every colour you could imagine. As they both climbed down from the cart a lady emerged from the cottage door.

“You’ve made good time then,” she said to his guardian, “Come on in then.”

Feeling a bit bewildered Jack entered in to a large warm kitchen that ran the full length of the front of the cottage. It had a range at one end flanked with two rocking chairs. The fire was blazing in the hearth and there was another smaller fireplace at the far end of the long room set ready to be lit. A huge oak dresser stood between the two areas and a long table and its chairs sat in the middle of the room. A spinning wheel with a stool and two soft easy chairs surrounded with baskets of wool sat by the range. The lady and his guardian had followed behind Jack as he entered and noticing the puzzled look on his face the lady asked if he was feeling alright.

"Am I going to live here?" Jack asked her.

"Mighty no lad, don't look so worried."

Turning to his guardian she said, "have you not explained anything to the lad?"

He told her that he had not had a chance as Jack had been asleep most of the time. She tutted at him and then turned to Jack.

"I'm Mistress Ruth and this is my brother Master Jacob. Now have a seat lad and I'll get us some refreshments and then I'll explain everything while we eat."

She returned with glasses of milk and pork pies and a large jar of pickles.

"I make a living by spinning wool and knitting children's clothes. I've been doing this for many a year," she told Jack, "I supply one of the big shops in Harrogate with the clothes I make and they then sell them on to the public. My husband used to collect the wool for me and deliver the end product to the Harrogate shop but unfortunately he passed away six months back. Jacob here has now taken over that task and visits me every five weeks or so. It's a fair distance between here and the farm so he usually stays overnight and returns the next day. Now that pie you are tucking in to is one of Mistress Graces's pies. She is Jacob's wife and your other guardian. Grace is a wonderful lady and hopefully you'll meet her before nightfall."

Things started to make sense now to Jack and he smiled gratefully at Mistress Ruth.

"My brother, as you will find out for yourself Jack, is a man of few words but he is the kindest most selfless man you'll ever meet. Now Jacob, if you go see to Elda, Jack and I will clear the dishes then you better be on your way."

Jack carried the dishes through to the scullery and as he helped Mistress Ruth with the dishes he watched through the window as Jacob fed and watered Elda in the field at the back of the cottage.

"You've got a lovely garden," he said to Ruth.

"Aye, well my Albert was the head gardener at the big House. He worked there all his life. He spent more time out gardening than anywhere else. He was at his happiest when his hands were in the earth. Jacob and Grace wanted me to move to the farm when he died but I have this cottage for my lifetime and I'm still able to make a living with my knitting so I decided to stay put. Besides, I love this place and like to be as independent as I can. I would be like a fish out of water up at the farm but I'm sure you are going to get on just fine up there."

As they were ready to leave Ruth handed Jack a package.

"Here you go Jack, it's just a pair of knitted socks but you'll be glad of them come winter. Hopefully, I'll see you again before too long. You might be able to come with Jacob when he visits."

"Thank you," said Jack "I'd like that," and he meant it.

This was the first time anyone had given him a present and he felt really touched. This day was turning out to be a lot of firsts for him he thought and it wasn't over yet.

Almost immediately after leaving Ruth they passed over a bridge that spanned a river and turned left on to a lane that followed the rivers flow.

"I'm sorry Jack," Jacob said, "I should have explained things to you. To tell you the truth this is all new to me as well and I really didn't know where to start. I can see now it wasn't fair on you so I will try to make things a bit clearer for you. Firstly, Mistress Grace and I have taken on your guardianship from the orphanage. This entails us paying a sum of money to the church that runs the orphanage and in return we get yourself as an apprentice for ten years. Hopefully, you'll learn every aspect of farming and at the end of that period you will be fully qualified to get a farm tenancy of your own, or hopefully, stay with us as a paid worker. During this period we provide you with food, lodgings and clothing. We'll have a visit from a representative of the trustees of the orphanage in a couple of months' time to see if all is well. If for any reason you don't want to stay with us you can return to the orphanage but I sincerely hope that won't be the case. We'll do all we can to make your stay with us a hospitable one. What do you think of that Jack?"

"I think that sounds fair," said Jack, "but I won't really be a part of your family will I?"

"In time Jack I hope that we will become a proper family but all three of us will need to work towards that goal. It may take time but that's what we should all work towards."

Jack nodded, satisfied with Jacob's answer, "What's the farm like and what will my chores be?"

"The farm is classed as a hill farm and as the name suggests it sits on the side of a hill. We rear sheep but also have twelve dairy cows, two pigs, a multitude of hens, several cats and my faithful companion Bob the sheep dog. Oh and we've got Elda here and her friend Matilda, Tilda for short. They help with ploughing the fields, pulling the hay carts and transporting us to the neighbouring towns. We've several fields, meadows, paddocks and barns, out buildings and stables and nearly forgot, a small orchard when the wind doesn't blow the fruit off the trees. Mistress Grace is quite famous in our area for her pie making! She used to sell them at the two local markets. They became so popular that some of the local trades people now sell them in their shops and the Inn keepers include them on their menus. As well as her pork pies she also supplies her customers with cheese and onion pasties, meat and potato pie, curd tarts, cheese, butter, eggs, pickles and jam! She's so busy but she does have help from two ladies, Nell and Flo who are sisters and live in the village. She delivers her goods twice a week, on Tuesdays and Fridays. She's a busy lady alright as she often helps with the milking and tending to the animals as well. Oh and of course she keeps the house and feeds us!"

"That sounds like a lot of work!" said Jack.

"Aye it is lad and I look after the care of all the animals, make sure the barns are mucked out, make repairs to the dykes and fences. I plough and sow the fields, cut the hay when it's ready, bring in the crops, shear and lamb the sheep..

"That sounds like a lot of work too." Jack said.

"Well it is when you say it in one mouthful but it is spread throughout the year. We do different things depending on the season. Just now we are coming to the end of the lambing season. We then move on to the ploughing then the sowing and planting. In the summer we shear the sheep and bring in the hay. In the autumn we take in the crops we sowed and in the winter the cows and horses are kept inside so their bedding as to be changed every day and the lack of daylight means less time to do the work! Just now the cows are kept outside in the pastures and are brought in for milking twice a day. Sheep at the moment are still in the fields near the farm where they spent the winter and most have already lambed. Once the lambs are weaned they'll be moved back on the hill that surrounds the farm until we bring them back down around November. When they are on the hill I ride one of the horses up there with Bob just to keep an eye on them. Throughout the year we take animals to the mart at Skipton and that's one our main sources of income. There's probably much more that I've forgotten to tell you but I hope you have a better idea now on what goes on at the farm."

"Crikey!" said Jack, "it sounds like a heck of a lot and I can't remember it all already!"

Jacob smiled "I suppose it is but we are well organised most of the time and of course we've been doing it for years lad."

"What jobs will I help with. I'd like to help as much as I can" said Jack.

"Well you will but I think at first it's best if you just tag along and watch and learn and then gradually you can take on some of the work as your own. Don't forget you'll be attending the village school from nine till two every week day so we'll have to work round that. There's one more thing I need to tell you. At the moment we have Mistress Grace's sister Maud, her husband Gerald and their daughter Agnes staying with us at the farm. They lost the tenancy on their farm three weeks ago. Gerald doesn't start his new job out Skipton way until five days' time. Maud is a nice lady but the other two well.....let's just say there's room for improvement. It's not what we had planned for your arrival but we couldn't see them out on the streets. It means we are a bit overcrowded at the moment in the house so we've had to make accommodation for yourself over the stable for now."

"That sounds alright," said Jack, "I'll be close to the horses and I've never had a place just for myself before. I'm sure I'll be fine."

"Unfortunately, Grace might not have as much time as she would like to spend with you with family being there. It's a shame as she was really looking forward to having you to herself for a while before you start school. It can't be helped I suppose unless.... erm we can maybe delay school for a few days. Yes.... that might work, let's see how it goes. All this talking has made me parched. Time for a brew I think."

He pulled the cart on to the grass verge and reached in to the cart for a basket that Ruth had given them before they left. The tea was strong like Joe used to make and for a moment Jack was transported back to sipping a brew around the campfire. Drinking the tea now, with Jacob, felt almost the same. Jack was feeling less anxious now he knew what to expect. He was determined to do his best and hoped he wouldn't let them down.

The journey continued. After a while Jacob asked him what it was like at the orphanage. It was now Jack's turn to talk to Jacob. He described what life was like in the orphanage, the lessons in the schoolroom and how the boys looked out for each other, the visits to the church and the Minster. He hesitated and then decided to tell Jacob about him and Tom and what happened to them. Jacob had already been informed of the incident in a condensed version by Matron but he remained silent as he wanted to hear the story in Jacks words.

"It sounds as if you have a couple of very good friends in Tom and Archie," Jacob said when Jack had finished, "you are going to miss them."

"We've promised to try and keep in touch. With your permission sir, I would like to send them my new address so that we could maybe write to each other. I could get the inspector to deliver it back to them after his visit."

"Oh I think we can do better than that," said Jacob, "what if once a month we post a letter for you? How does that sound?"

"Thank you sir, that sounds grand."

Another hour passed in to the journey. They had been sitting in silence for a while and the day was now beginning to cool down. Jacob noticed Jack shiver and told him to get in the back again and wrap himself up in the blankets again. Jack climbed over the back but instead of staying there he clambered back to the seat with the blankets and placed one around Jacob's shoulders and the other around his own.

This moment was to be the beginning of a very strong friendship that would develop between them.

Chapter Eleven.

"We're just approaching Pateley Bridge now," Jacob informed him as the cart began a long steep descent flanked on each side by houses, shops, a tea room and several public houses. Jacob had to apply the brake to the cart to negotiate the steepness of the road and it was smoking by the time they safely made it to the bottom where the gradient levelled off for a short distance before crossing a bridge over a river and then took a steep winding climb up the other side. When they reached the top of the hill the road opened to a vast moorland as far as the eye could see. Hills and crags stretched far in to the distance on both sides of the road.

"Not far now Jack" Jacob told him.

Daylight was fading fast as a couple of cottages appeared on the right of the road.

"We're on the outskirts of our village now," said Jacob as they passed a church and a school house. Jacob turned the cart in to a narrow lane that ran between the school house and a large Coaching Inn. A shop and several cottages surrounded a village green on the left of the lane with a cluster of cottages on the right. As they travelled further through the village more dwellings ran down the right of the lane whilst the river that ran behind the village now flowed down the left-hand side of the lane. After a few minutes they reached a track that crossed a stone bridge over the river.

"Here we are Jack," announced Jacob as they turned and crossed the bridge, "the lane we've just left carries on for another couple of miles until it ends at several miners' cottages at the foot of the hill where the mine is situated. The light you see ahead is our farm. Welcome to your new home Jack."

As they pulled in to the yard Jack could just make out several farm buildings looming in the dark. A collie dog ran out barking and danced excitedly around the cart. Jacob jumped down and started patting and rubbing the dog's coat.

"Come and say hello to Bob our sheepdog Jack."

Jack bent over to pat the dog and Bob rolled over on to his back for a belly rub. Jack laughed and obligingly gave it a rub. Just at that moment the cottage door flew open and a small plump lady ran out.

"Jack, this is Mistress Grace."

Grace walked over and took Jack in to her arms. "Welcome to Crag House farm Jack, your new home and I hope you will be happy here!"

"Thank you Ma'am," said Jack who was feeling a little emotional.

Just then a male voice shouted from the house "Are we going to eat tonight or what?"

Jack caught the look of annoyance that passed between Jacob and Grace.

"I'll sort out our Elda and be in later. Jack if you get your belongings and take them in to the house for now and Grace will look after you and introduce you to the others."

Jack entered in to a large kitchen with Grace.

"Oh so this is orphan willie is it then," said a ruddy faced man dressed in dirty overalls. A young blond girl giggled whilst an older thin lady looked abashed.

"I 'll have you know," said Grace as she pulled herself up to her full five feet two inches, "this is Jack and this is Jack's home from now on and he's an orphan no more! I think you should hold your tongue Gerald if you want a meal tonight so less of your nonsense please! Jack and Jacob have been travelling all day from first light and they are cold and hungry and tired! The last thing they want to do is to listen to your smart remarks."

"Alright, alright, I was only joking but I get the message," he stood up "I'm going to our room Maude, make sure to bring my meal up to me. I know when I'm not wanted."

Nobody said anything as he left through a door at the back of the kitchen.

“I’m so sorry Grace,” said Maude “you know what he’s like. Jack welcome to your new home and this is Agnes my daughter.”

“Pleased to meet you Agnes,” said Jack politely.

Agnes shrugged, “If you say so,” she replied before standing up and leaving the room.

“Grace, you sit by the fire with Jack and I’ll go get you both a cup of tea” said Maude smiling, “then I’ll finish off our meal.”

Jack and Grace were sitting by the fire sipping tea when Jacob entered the kitchen. He looked pleasantly surprised. Maude was laying the table for the meal, “There’s a brew in the pot Jacob so get warm by the fire and I’ll bring it over to you.”

Jacob raised his eyebrows at Grace who smiled sweetly, “I’ll tell you later,” she whispered to him.

The three of them shared a moment of unspoken unity.

Reluctantly Agnes joined them for the evening meal but remained silent and sullen. Jack couldn’t believe the feast that Grace and Maude brought to the table. A gigantic shepherd’s pie with melted cheese on top, a dish of carrots with melted butter and a basin of fresh green peas. Two smaller dishes contained mint sauce and fresh beetroot. Jacob looked at Grace proudly, she always managed to put on a good spread no matter how busy she had been through the day.

Jacob informed Jack that the vegetables were home grown and the sauce was home made. He then said a simple prayer of thanks for the food placed in front of them before beginning to eat. When Jack opened his eyes he noticed Agnes smirking again. He supposed that she wasn't used to offering thanks before she ate a meal.

Once the main course was finished the table was cleared and reset with more dishes and Grace appeared with a large jug of custard. As she served it she said, "I hope you like custard Jack?" with a knowing wink, "we have it quite often. It's a good way of using up the surplus milk."

Jack watched as the yellow creamy liquid was poured in to his dish and smiled, "I don't think I'll ever get tired of this even if I had it every day for the rest of my life!"

They all laughed at his enthusiasm except Agnes who just rolled her eyes. When the meal was finished Jacob announced that he was going to check on the sheep and he would be grateful if Agnes would give her mother a hand to clear away and wash the dishes so that Grace could settle Jack in to his accommodation above the stables. Agnes pulled a face but reluctantly began to clear the table. She knew better than to argue with Jacob.

Jack picked up his parcel of belongings and crossed the yard with Grace who was apologising for not having room in the house for him. Jack assured her it wasn't a problem and that Jacob had already explained the circumstances. They entered a building into a tack room where an assortment of leather and rope reins, bridles and harnesses hung neatly on hooks along the length of the wall. There were three well-worn saddles on makeshift stands. A shelf held grooming tools and every item required for the good care of the horses. A ladder reached up to the loft above. There were two windows set back in to the thick walls of the tack room and on each sill was a lantern shining out in to the darkness.

"Ah good," said Grace, "Jacob must have lit the lanterns when he settled Elda down earlier."

Hearing her name called Elda gave a nicker. Grace laughed, "You better say hello to her Jack and you can meet Tilda as well."

They entered through an opening in the wall in to the stables next door. There were four stalls, three of which were occupied. Jack recognised Elda in the first and he went quietly forward and gently whispered her praises as he stroked her neck and she rubbed the side of her face in to his shoulder.

"You've certainly made a hit with her Jack! Have you had any experience with horses before? Grace asked.

"Just a little bit," he answered.

"Well you've got the knack that's for sure."

They moved to the next stall, "This is Tilda," and Jack again moved gently forward and repeated the actions he had made with Elda and Tilda responded to him in the same way.

The third stall held Briney, "She belongs to Maude and Gerald," explained Grace.

This time as Jack approached the horse she became a little skittish.

"She's not as biddable as our two Jack, maybe it's best to leave her be just now," Grace advised. As Jack slowly backed away he got the feeling that the horse was frightened and not just being difficult.

The two of them returned to the tack room and taking one of the lanterns from the window sill they climbed up to the loft above, Grace a little more unwieldly than Jack. She laughed at her breathlessness, "I'm not as young as I was," she grinned.

In the warm glow of the lantern Jack saw a lovely cosy room. Thick stone walls recessed with deep windows with lanterns placed on each of the two sills. Grace lit one of them and a brighter light illuminated the space. There was a bed against one wall with a quilt made up of a multitude of colours. Next to the bed was a small table and next to that a wash stand equipped with a basin, soap and a pile of towels. Grace explained to him that he could fill a pale with water from the tap in the yard and get warm water from the range in the kitchen. He told Grace that he was used to washing in cold water as they very rarely had the luxury of hot water at the orphanage. She told him that there was usually plenty of hot water in the kitchen as the kettle was permanently on the stove and he mustn't be frightened of getting a pale full at any time. She pointed to a chamber pot under the bed. It's there if you need it, otherwise there are two outside lavvies behind the stable wall. The scrubbed wooden floor was covered with a thick colourful rug, a wooden chair sat by the far wall and in the far corner of the room was a large chest. Grace opened it and lifted out a bundle of clothes.

"Some of these may be on the large side," she said, "I can alter some to fit but the rest will have to do until we can get you sorted out properly."

"All these for me!" he was astounded "I've only ever had two lots of clothes at any one time and hand me downs at that. We had to keep them until we grew out of them or they wore out beyond repair. Our boots were so patched up and worn that we dreaded going outside if it was raining."

"Well some of this is also second hand," said Grace, "there's shoes and boots at the bottom of the chest. Anything that's too small put in one pile and anything needing altering put in another and we'll take it from there."

She reached in to the trunk and brought out three pairs of overalls, "I think these will do just fine for now, it's what you'll be wearing most of the time around the farm anyway. The main thing Jack is for you not to worry about anything. Rome wasn't built in a day and we can sort things out as we go along."

She turned to climb back down the ladder and grinned back at Jack, "It's a lot easier going down than up!" she laughed as she disappeared from sight.

Jack sat on the bed and marvelled at his room. He loved it! From the scrubbed floor with its colourful rug to the mirror standing against the wooden dividing wall and the furniture and the lamps were all for him! He loved that it was his own space but most of all he loved the sound and the smell of the horses below. Their presence seemed to touch him deep inside and calm his thoughts. He didn't feel alone.

He spent an enjoyable half hour trying on the clothes. Nothing was too small and only a handful would need altering. The boots at the bottom of the chest were a bit too big but he would grow in to them and he was used to that. As he placed them under the bed he picked out some clothes to wear the next day and placed them neatly on the chair. He donned one of the nightshirts, extinguished the lantern and climbed in to bed.

Moonlight streamed through the windows as he pondered over the day's events. So much had happened since leaving the orphanage that morning and he couldn't wait to tell Tom and Archie.

"Night night ladies!" he shouted as he rolled on his side in to a deep sleep.

Chapter Twelve.

Jack slept soundly. When he eventually woke it was still fairly dark outside. He knelt up on his bed to look out of the window. There was a slight lightening of the sky in the distance. He could just make out the dark silhouettes of the village at the bottom of the hill. He had no idea of the time and thought that maybe he should try to get back to sleep until someone came to fetch him but he was too excited to get back to sleep again.

He got up and dressed in his new clothes. He couldn't help but glance at his reflection in the mirror! He smiled at himself. He didn't look too bad in the work clothes he thought! He went in to the yard and as he was splashing water over his face Bob came to greet him. He hunched down to pet Bob and he rolled over in glee.

"I think we're the only ones up Bob," he said as Bob followed at Jacks heel whilst he investigated the farmyard. There were several buildings surrounding the yard and the first he entered was a large barn. It had metal rails about shoulder height running on both sides of the long walls with feeding troughs strategically placed along the walls. The stools, pales and churn in one corner were the giveaway signs that this was the milking parlour.

He entered another large barn. This had a loft above with ladders running up either side to where he could see stacks of hay. At ground level were similar stacks of straw and lots of wooden barrels. He peeked under the lid of a couple of barrels and found they contained some kind of grain. Pallets were set along the walls with sacks full of what looked like turnips and beets. A long wooden table held baskets of carrots, peas and a few cabbages. Underneath the table were sacks of potatoes and on a shelf above the table were a couple of wooden boxes that looked to contain straw but on further investigation he discovered layers of apples between the straw.

There were several hand carts, shovels and barrows parked by the door. Buckets hung on hooks along the walls and scoops of every size hung beside them. He guessed this would be the feed store.

The next building held a couple of large carts one of which he recognised as his transport from yesterday. There was also a smaller cart parked near the door of the barn. At the back of the barn was a big metal contraption that he thought might be a plough but he wasn't sure. A host of spades, shovels, wooden rakes, metal rakes, pitch forks, hoes, scythes and so many other tools stood to attention along the walls. Shelves held boxes of smaller hand tools and an old chest of drawers held boxes of hammers, screwdrivers etc. There were saws of every kind hung on another wall and several axes were propped up by wooden rails. A stack of shelving contained tins and bottle jars full of nails and screws. This must be the tool shed he thought feeling quite proud of himself.

Outside and to the side of this building was a large log store. He was just about to investigate the track running towards the back when he heard the clatter of hob nail boots enter the yard. He looked up to see a large, hefty man wearing work clothes and a cloth cap approaching the side of the stables. The man raised an arm in greeting. Jack raised his hand in return.

"Good morning young sire" the man said "C'mon lad ya may as well gi me a 'and" as he turned and walked behind the stables. Jack quickly followed and caught up with the man as he was striding up the track that led behind the barns.

"I'm Jed" he informed Jack, "You must be Jack if I'm not mistaken. Gud to see thee up bright an early. Tuthers will be up afore long. I 'elp wi cattle. It's my job to bring in cows for milking an get 'em 'arnested up and feed prepared afore lassies arrive to 'elp wi milking."

He stopped at the back of the parlour and opened up the large doors.

"Cows are in't top pasture just nar," he said opening the gate to a field. The two of them continued across the field until they reached another gate. Jed opened the gate and began to shout. "Cush, cush cush." The cows at the far end began to lumber down the field towards them.

"Stand to one side lad the girls na the way."

The two of them followed the cows down to the open doors of the parlour where the cows obediently made their way to the rails and troughs. Jack was amazed that they knew what to do!

"Girls na routine," Jed explained to Jack, "they have their own trough in't barn they return to every time. I'll start 'arnessing em up. Is that somebody shouting for thee lad?"

Jack heard Jacob's voice calling his name. Jacob was relieved when he saw Jack emerge from the parlour. He had been worried when he found the room above the stables empty. He and Grace thought the lad would need a lie in after the excitement and long journey the day before, yet here he was with Jed.

"Mornin boss. Jack 'ere's been giving me 'and ta get girls in. Grand little werker an all. Dunt nar what I'd dun wi out 'im," he laughed.

"Thanks Jed," smiled Jacob, "reckon he'll be running the farm afore we know it!"

Jack was aware of the amusement shared by the two men at his expense and joined them in their laughter.

"Give me a week at least gentlemen," he retorted and they laughed even harder.

The cottage door opened and Grace's head popped out. "There you are!" C'mon in before the brew gets cold."

In the kitchen all except Agnes were sitting around the big table sipping at their hot drinks. Jacob and Jack went in to join them.

“Jacks made a start without us,” Jacob informed the company, “helping Jed bring the girls in.”

Grace looked surprised, “I didn’t say anything to you last night Jack as I thought we would give you a lie in on your first day. We usually rise at five and have a brew before we start on the morning chores. We have breakfast between seven thirty and eight o’clock.”

There was the sound of women’s chatter coming from outside, “That will be Flo and Nell arriving for milking.”

She went to the door, “Good morning girls, I’ll be with you shortly.

” “Righty oh,” responded the girls, “see ya later.”

Grace returned to the table to finish her drink.

“Maude if you see to the pigs and the hens, seeing as Agnes seems to be indisposed at the moment,” Grace instructed, “and if she does decide to join us today she can finish off and you can give us a hand in the parlour. What are your plans for the morning Jacob?”

“I’ll check the sheep as usual and I want to make a start on the ploughing,” he answered.

Gerald piped up “I’ve still got the repairs ta the wall in bottom field ta finish. I’ll take the lad with me if ya want, cud do wi a bit a company down there an he can watch a master craftsman at werk.”

"Thanks for the offer," said Jacob, "I'll not argue with your skills for dyking, you always make an excellent job but I'll take Jack with me today. He needs to learn the lay of the land and now if we've all finished we better get on."

Jack and Jacob walked up a track that ran by the gable end of the house. Here Jacob pointed out the vegetable patch and drying green at the rear of the house. On the other side of the track fields ran down to the river below. They went through a gate to one of the fields where lots of sheep and lambs were grazing contently. Jacob informed Jack that this field and the adjoining field were where the sheep were kept during the winter and that the barns at the top of the fields not only provided shelter but individual pens could be erected inside to house a sickly ewe, a weak lamb or pet lambs that needed to be hand fed with a bottle if need be. Prior to the winter taking hold these barns were stocked with hay and chopped beets and turnips.

"It's easier to have them ready on site rather than trail back and forth to the yard for supplies. On a day like today Jack it's hard for you to imagine deep snow and gale force winds battering you from every direction, yet we still have to care for and feed the sheep. They'd starve or perish in deep snow otherwise."

They entered the next field where a similar scene met them. Jacob pointed out a ewe standing by herself against the far wall.

"See her Jack, she's about to lamb. Notice how she's hunched up? That's a sign that she's ready to push. It won't be long now before the lamb is born. We'll wait quietly here and watch."

Jack couldn't take his eyes from the sheep. He felt excited with anticipation whilst he watched with bated breath. Jacob continued to tell him that they'd had a good year this year with no complicated births that needed any intervention from themselves and only one pet lamb whose mother didn't provide enough milk. Mother and lamb were kept in the barn and its feed had at first been supplemented by the bottle every two hours. Then as it got stronger only every four hours.

"It's now almost weaned and is growing fine and healthy so it only gets a bottle twice a day now. I did the first feed earlier so you can do the next."

"I'd really like that," said Jack whilst not taking his eyes off the sheep.

"Here we go lad," said Jacob as the sheep hunched up even further, "you can just see the little hooves emerging from her rear end."

Jack watched, thrilled as the legs and head of the lamb came in to view and then with a final push the lamb flopped on to the ground. The mother immediately began to lick the lambs face.

“She’s doing this to clean his nostrils to allow it to breath,” informed Jacob. They held their breath until a faint bleat could be heard.

“Good girl!” exclaimed Jacob and turned to Jack who was grinning from ear to ear!

” Congratulations Jack! You’ve witnessed your first miracle of birth.”

“Look!” said Jack, “it’s trying to stand up already!”

“Yes” said Jacob “it’ll soon be up and suckling from its mum.”

After a few failed attempts to stand it finally made it on to wobbly legs and was having its first feed within minutes of making an entry in to the world.

“We’ll check on the rest Jack but I think that was the last lamb for this year.”

They returned to the track via the barn where the pet lamb and its mum were sleeping curled up together in the corner of a pen. “We won’t disturb them,” Jacob said.

Back on the track Jacob pointed out where this track formed a circular route by winding its way right up and around the hill in front of them before descending in the distance and finishing at the top of the yard.

“Did you get as far as the pigs this morning Jack?”

"No" said Jack as they retraced their steps to the yard. He told Jacob what he had already discovered in the buildings. When they reached the lane above the log store they walked a little way on its length when Jack said, "I guess this lane runs all the way back behind the buildings?"

"That's right, you see you are getting your bearings already!"

On the right of the track they came upon a paved pen with a wooden shelter enclosed within a stonewall. There was a gate leading from the track and another gate sited on the left-hand wall. They entered the pen.

"The girls must be having a lie in this morning" said Jacob.

He pointed to a heap of straw in the corner of the wall, "That's where they do the toilet" he said, "pigs have really good toilet habits and always use the same area. It makes caring for them much easier and we only have to spread clean straw over the area every day and clean the whole lot up about every three or four days. It's important that they always have access to water Jack as they can dehydrate very quickly. They also need somewhere to shelter out of the sun because believe it or not they can get sunburn."

Jack was taking it all in and relishing in his new found knowledge. They went through the other gate that led into a small, enclosed field. Jack could hear running water as they crossed the space and saw a stream that was flowing from the hill in the distance behind. Its bank had been dug out and widened to form a small shallow pool.

"This is where the girls can go and wallow. My father and I dug out the bank there a lot of years ago. It's ideal for the pigs and saves a lot of work as we don't need to fetch and carry water for them. This stream runs right down past the top two fields where you fetched the cows from this morning. There's another stream runs down the other side of the farm. Water's very important on a farm Jack."

Jacob pointed out more fields in that direction.

"There are four top fields where we grow our crops. The stream runs at the far side of them and past down the other side of the wall where the lamb was born this morning."

They returned to the pig pen and as they were about to leave they heard a shuffling and grunting sound as an extremely large pig plodded through the door of the sty.

"Good morning Gertie!" Jacob said as he gave her a good scratch behind the ears, "I thought you'd be too nosy to let us pass in peace. Give her a rub Jack and you'll have a friend for life."

Jack rubbed and scratched the hide of the pig who seemed to smile with satisfaction!

"Doesn't look as if Josie is going to say hello this morning."

Jacob looked at his pocket watch and said it was almost time to head back for breakfast. They could hear the lowing of the cattle as they made their way back to the pasture and as they both made their way back down the yard Jacob pointed out the orchard at the back of the hen run which was surrounded with a high fence and held two coups. The hens were scratching about the area oblivious to the two watchers.

"We usually open the gate for them sometime in the morning and make sure they are all back in the run before nightfall. The eggs are collected at the same time. You'll soon get to know the other places around the farm where some of them prefer to lay."

They passed two smaller stone buildings nearer the house.

"These are Grace's domain," he said "so I'll let her show you round. The first is where she keeps her stock and the other is the dairy where the butter and cheese are made. It always remains cool in these building as they don't really get any sun and the milk from the late milking is kept in the dairy to be taken down to the road end with the morning milk. The large dairy wagons with the dray horses collect the milk and take it to the big dairy where it is processed and delivered to the shops."

Jed appeared leading Elda from the stable.

"Just goin' ta 'arness 'er to cart and I'll get milk darn ta end of road. Tuther 'orses are in paddock."

“Grand, Thanks Jed, then let’s all go for some breakfast.”

As they entered the porch Jacob began to take off his boots, “Better take off your boots Jack or you’ll have Grace after you!”

They entered the kitchen in their stocking feet. Grace and Maude had laid the table and were about to serve up the hot porridge.

“Come on in then, there’s warm water in the scullery to wash then sit yourself down,” Grace said to them.

“Have you had a good morning then Jack?” Grace asked as he was eating his porridge.

“The best,” answered Jack and he began to tell her about the birth of the lamb and the tour of the farm. She listened while she was pouring tea in to their mugs.

“Oh I’m so pleased you got to see the birth of the last lamb. It’s always special no matter how many times you see it. Isn’t that right Flo?”

She turned to a lady dressed in working clothes who was pouring cream onto her porridge.

“It certainly is. Hi Jack, I’m Flo an I ‘elp with t’milking and mekin pies. Me an me sister are ‘ere most days so ya’ll see a lot of us.”

“Pleased to meet you Flo,” acknowledged Jack.

"Nay lad, pleased to meet thee an allus glad ta get anuther pair of 'elping 'ands. You'll meet me sister Nell in a minute, she's just tecking cows back ta field. I think you'll fit in just fine lad."

Agnes entered the kitchen, "Did you finish off your chores?" Jacob asked her. She looked sheepish, "Don't tell me that you're just out of bed?" her face reddened as she turned and nodded. "Well, I hope you'll make up for it the rest of the day! The hen coups need cleaning out and fresh straw put down."

"I was going to help auntie Grace with her delivery to Pateley this morning," she said.

"Well you had better get a move on then with the coups!" Said Jacob pointedly.

She looked abashed then grabbed a slice of buttered toast off the pile on a plate and rushed through the door to the hen run.

"You were a bit t'ard on the lass," said Gerald.

"I'm sorry if you think so Gerald but she needs to learn that she has responsibilities around the farm as we all do. We have to work as a team to get through the work and she's not a child anymore. We ask very little of her really."

Just at that moment Nell entered the kitchen, "Mornin' folks, I'm starving, budge up" she nudged Flo, "Can't wait ta get me choppers round that toast. Yuv dun us proud agin Grace, oh an Maude too." She said as she reached for another slice of toast. The atmosphere in the kitchen lightened with her cheerfulness, "What's plan foh after?" she asked.

"I'm going to make the custard tarts for todays delivery and then load up the cart," Grace answered.

"If you and Flo make a start on the butter and get another cheese on the go as the orders are picking up now with the Inns getting busier again. At some point we need to get together to assess future sales and any changes we may need to make to ensure we can cope with the extra demand. The cheese and onion pasties aren't doing as well as I hoped so we might have to drop them from our menu. It would save making the flaky pastry which is more time consuming".

"Ohhhh" no!" said Nell, "there me favourite."

"Well I'll see how they go this week. Shall we say next Wednesday after work for a meeting?" They all agreed that would be fine.

"Jack you can come with me and Agnes, if Jacob and Gerald are going to be busy in the fields," she looked up at the sound of the cart returning to the yard. "That's Jed back, I'll get his breakfast. Likely he'll want it on the bench outside so he can light that smelly pipe of his."

Jack watched Jacob harness Tilda to the plough. They were in one of the top fields where Jacob would be ploughing for the rest of the day. A pungent smell sought Jack's nostrils.

"Cor! What's that?" asked Jack.

Jacob laughed, "That's the smell of the midden where all the mucking out and waste goes." He pointed to a festering heap at the other side of the wall.

"We spread it over the fields before we plant the crops. You're lucky that me and Jed finished that last week. It's hard going and you stink for a week. We grow a field of barley and a field of oats. The grain is used for animal feed and the stalks left are used as straw for the bedding. The other two crops are beets and turnip and they are essential during winter to keep the animals fed. There's no nourishment in the grass in winter. We rotate the growth of the crops every year. It helps the nutrient balance in the soil and gives a better yield. Different crops take different things out of the soil but they also put back different nutrients too."

"There's a lot to learn!" Jack said.

"Don't worry you'll know it all off by heart before too long" Jacob smiled, "in fact that's not quite right because new ways and methods are being introduced all the time. We'll have to learn together Jack. Now you better get back and give Jed a hand. He'll be mucking out in the parlour or the stables. Make sure you have a good wash and change out of your overalls before you meet Grace. She'll keep you right though. If you are back from deliveries in time for dinner bring something up for the both of us and you can see how the plough works, although I reckon it'll be a year or two before you are strong enough to handle it. Right, see you later and enjoy your trip."

Jack returned to the yard and as he approached the hen run he smiled at the sight of Agnes's behind sticking out of the door of one of the coups where she was laying fresh straw. She emerged just as Jack was passing and her face was like thunder when she saw Jack smiling.

"Don't know what you find so amusing" she said, "you'll have it to do when I'm gone."

"Maybe," he responded, "but my backside will fit in to the coup!" he laughed.

"You cheeky little bugger!" she said amazed at his impudence.

"Better get that straw out of your hair before we make those deliveries," he shouted over his shoulder, "Don't want you showing me up" he said as he continued down the yard whistling whilst leaving Agnes staring after him dumfounded by his cheek.

He found Jed in the parlour and worked alongside him until the parlour and stables were immaculate. He took a pale of cold water up to his loft and had a good wash and changed out of his overalls. He scraped a comb through his hair and admired his new outfit in the mirror before going in search of Grace.

He found Grace in the kitchen. She was packing the fresh custard pies on to clean wooden trays ready to be transported.

"Just in time Jack," she said, "grab one of these trays and we'll get them loaded up."

Jack gingerly picked up a tray, it wasn't heavy but he was terrified of dropping it and smashing all of the pies. Carefully he negotiated the tray through the open door. He was glad when Grace took it off him and expertly stacked it securely on the back of the cart.

"Right! Climb up Jack. Where's that girl? She's never there when you want her. If you're not here in one minute we're off without you!", Grace shouted through the open door of the house. In seconds Agnes came running out of the house and jumped on the cart.

They made their way slowly down the farm track and over the river and turned towards the village passing the cottages. Grace pointed out where Flo and Nell lived. She said that Jed lived in a cottage behind the next row of dwellings. In daylight, Jack could make out the layout of the village better. As they passed the village green Jack noticed that the shop was much bigger than he remembered when he first saw it in the dark. It had tables outside full of all kinds of domestic utensils.

"The shop is owned by Johnny Rudd," Grace told him, "It acts as a post office as well. We'll stop on the way back as I've got to buy a few things."

They turned left on to the main road passing the school. Jack was looking with interest. He thought it looked very small.

"The school is run by two sisters," Grace told him, "there's only two classrooms. I think the children aged five to ten are in one class and the older children in the other. You'll be in the younger class Jack for a year. Your teacher will be Miss Lewis. She's very nice I've heard. We'll take you down to introduce yourself before you start so you can get a better idea of what to expect. Did you like the lessons at the orphanage?" she asked him.

"Yes, and I got to help the younger boys with their reading."

They travelled in silence for a while. Jack could now see the vast but wild scenery better in the daylight. It seemed to go on forever but in the light of day it wasn't as intimidating as it seemed in the dark.

"Did you manage to sleep alright in the loft?" Agnes asked him.

"Yes thanks," he replied wondering why she was being nice.

"Weren't you scared all by yourself in the dark?" she asked and Jack thought he knew where this was going.

"No, not at all," he said.

"Oh, you don't know about Howling Harry then. He wonders across the moor at night dressed in black and carrying a big scythe. He howls and moans as he makes his way across the moor looking for young boys to chop off their heads. Then he eats them!"

Grace glowered angrily at Agnes and had just opened her mouth to tell Jack not to take any notice when Jack piped up.

"Oh! Would Howling Harry be the brother of Screaming Susan who wonders around isolated farm yards in the dead of night carrying a giant axe? Her bright orange, glaring eyes can see through walls. She's looking for young women who try to frighten young boys! When she finds one she silently creeps up the stairs and chops off their head then throws it in the midden!"

He turned to Agnes and gave her a cheeky grin, "You can't kid a kidder" he laughed. Both women looked at one another and burst out laughing.

Agnes gave Jack a nudge with her elbow, "I think you're alright after all sprat!" she said.

"Why thank you Marm," he replied.

The two of them bantered all the way to Pateley and they seemed to be enjoying themselves with each wanting to get the last word in. Grace listened in amusement. She wasn't used to having young ones around and this was a new side to Jack she thought. From the polite young boy she met the night before to the conscientious lad this morning to the joker now she liked this side of his personality. As did Agnes by the sound of the chatter and giggles coming from them.

Their first delivery was at an Inn sitting on the banks of the river just as they crossed the bridge at Pateley. Grace pulled the cart in to the yard.

“Agnes take Jack with you to get the order and I’ll have a quick chat with Pearl” she nodded towards a woman sitting on a bench outside. “I want to know how her mother is getting on.”

Agnes armed with a notebook and pencil entered into the back door of the building with Jack on her heels.

“Good morning Mrs. Evans” she said to a lady cleaning the floor, “is it alright to go through to the bar to get the order?”

“Aye lass, ‘elp yersen” the lady answered.

Jack was mesmerised when he entered the large dimly lit room. It had a long, polished bar that ran along the whole length of the room. The tables and chairs were also gleaming with polish. A fire had just been lit in the large stone fireplace its flames reflecting in the mirrors and bottles behind the bar. Old copper jugs hung from the beams and paintings of country scenes hung on every available wall space. He wasn’t so keen on the sour smell of the place though.

"Jack, this is Master Bowles, he is the landlord" Agnes told him "Good morning sir" said Jack.

"And who might you be young man?"

"He's my new cousin." Agnes replied.

Jack felt an odd sense of pride at Agnes's comment, maybe she's not so bad after all he thought.

The order was taken and given to Grace who placed the items in to either trays or baskets then the three of them carried them in to the kitchen of the Inn. They delivered to another smaller Inn further up the steep road. Grace expertly manoeuvred the cart through a narrow alley to reach the yard at the back of the Inn. Grace left the youngsters to get the order again whilst she went to the butchers next door to get some minced pork for her pies. The order here wasn't as big as the one from the large Inn so Agnes let Jack write it on to the pad. He felt so important as he painstakingly entered each item neatly in to the order book. Grace returned just as the youngsters had finished delivering the order. Grace checked the order and tallied the payment due.

"I'll not be a minute" she told them, "Do you two want to get the order from the shop while I have a quick chat in here?"

The two of them scurried off down the street. It was only three doors down so it didn't take long for them to get the order.

"They want the usual" Agnes told Grace.

"I thought so, they nearly always do but it's better to ask anyway, right Jack, can you count out four dozen eggs. Agnes take this basket with the butter and cheese and I'll catch you up with this tray of pies."

Agnes looked at Jack with a grin, "Can you count up to four dozen then sprat?"

"Does that mean I count to twelve four times then? Don't worry if you don't know the answer I've already worked it out." He grinned.

"You cheeky sprat!" retorted Agnes "Best keep you in your place from now on!"

Jack carefully carried the eggs to the shop. He breathed a sigh of relief as he placed them safely on to the shop counter.

"We'll be back with the rest in a minute" Grace told the shop keeper.

This time Jack carried a basket of curd tarts while Agnes and Grace carried a tray of pies each. Agnes was sent back for the last tray of two dozen custard pies while the shopkeeper paid Grace for the goods. He asked Grace to include half a dozen jars each of pickled onions, chutney and pickled beetroot on his order for the following week.

“I certainly will” she told him and asked Jack to write it in the order book, “I can read your writing Jack” she said with a wink.

“We’ve made good time today”, Grace told them as they were making their way back home, “When I’m on my own it takes twice as long. We’ll stop and say hello to Beth at the Inn before we go to Rudd’s.”

They pulled up outside the big coaching Inn opposite the school. This place was much larger than the two in Pateley. It had several stables at the rear of the building and a large barn with room for several carriages.

“It’s their quiet time just now” Grace informed them, “in the morning and the evening it’s a hive of activity with travellers coming and going and stable hands seeing to the horses.”

They entered a long bar area and Grace rang the bell on the counter, “Service please!” she shouted.

A woman came running through from the back, “Oh its only you Grace!” she smiled, “How are you doing?”

“Just finished the deliveries to Pateley,” answered Grace “and I think my two little workers here and myself deserve a glass of lemonade before we go back to the graft of the farm. How are you Beth?”

The two women caught up with news whilst Jack and Agnes sipped their drinks. Jack had never had lemonade before and loved the refreshing taste. He told Agnes expecting a jibe at his innocence but she admitted it was a special treat for her too. Before they left, Beth asked if it was possible to get an extra two dozen eggs added on to the order for Friday and did Grace have another dozen pork pies on her now? "I think I can manage that" she said and asked Agnes to run and fetch them.

The next stop was at Rudd's the village store. Once more Jack was introduced before Grace gave her order to Johnny. Jack was astounded by the variety of goods on sale and he was particularly drawn to a corner displaying all kinds of stationery. He had never been in a store like this before. Grace noticed Jack's interest and remembered what Jacob had told her about Jack wanting to write to his friends back at the orphanage. She walked across to him and asked him if he would like some writing paper to write to his friends at the orphanage.

"We've got plenty of pens, ink and pencils in the bureau back home but we could do with some more paper and envelopes."

Jack hesitated, "Thank you, but would it be alright if I got a couple of these note books instead? They are cheaper and would make good diaries. That way I can write in them every day and I won't forget anything when I write to Tom and Archie."

Grace was touched by Jack's consideration, "I think that's an excellent idea" she said as she picked up half a dozen books, "But we'll get some paper as well for your letters."

She placed the items on the counter where Johnny was gathering her food order. Johnny asked her if she had any custard pies and pork pies left. He could do with a dozen of each if she had.

"I'll just go get them for you, won't be a minute," she returned with the goods, "and there's a curd tart in there for you and Alice for your cuppa this afternoon. My treat."

"Thanks Grace, you're a love, now let me give you a hand to the cart with this lot. I'll see you on Friday if not before," he called as he waved them off.

As they turned up the track to the farm they could see a line of washing drying in the gentle breeze. "Brilliant" said Grace, "looks as if your mum has been busy Agnes."

Grace pulled the cart to a halt outside her dairy and store, "We'll put the unsold stock back in the store before returning the cart to the barn."

Jack carried the basket of pickles etc. in to Graces's store. The walls, ceilings and shelves of this spacious room were painted white. A small window deeply inset in to the far wall allowed light in to the space. Every surface was spotlessly clean. A set of shelving held an array of jars labelled clearly with a date and their contents. Jack emptied the basket making sure that each jar was placed in the correct position on the shelves. Agnes stacked the unsold tray of eggs on top of the few trays that were already on the counter. Grace explained the system of keeping each day’s eggs separate from each other so they would know which trays to use first.

Grace returned with a tray of pies. She put all the unsold pies on to one tray.

“We’ve not done too bad today,” she told them, “Only got six meat and potato left. Put them in a basket Agnes and we’ll take them in to the house to use up. We’ve still got a dozen cheese and onion though. Guess what we’ll be having for dinner tomorrow?” she laughed, “Right let’s get the cheese and butter to the dairy next door and that’s us.”

Flo and Nell were in the dairy when they entered.

“Owd it go?” Nell asked Grace.

“We’ve still got cheese and onion left,” she said, “take a couple home with you when you leave and well done girls you’ve churned all that butter.”

“Aye, we’ll finish off packing it afore dinner, it won’t tek long.” Nell said.

This room like the other one was all white and pristine. The layout was similar to the room next door but the shelving held large round cheeses and pats of butter. Grace had brought in the custard pies that had been unsold, “They’ll keep better in here Jack” she said as they left the girls to finish off.

Grace took the cart back to the barn and unhitched Elda. She asked Jack to lead her back to the paddock. He felt so proud as he led the horse down the farm yard towards the paddock. Once he was safely through the gate he had to stand on tip toe to release the halter but his determination won in the end. He thanked Elda for getting them back safely and gently stroked her velvet nose. She responded as usual by nuzzling his neck and it made him giggle. It also made him feel good.

"Jack", Agnes shouted down to him, "You've got the pet lamb to feed! Auntie Grace 'as asked me to show ya what to do you being just a sprat an all."

Jack was grinning as he followed Agnes in to the kitchen and through to the scullery. Agnes opened the door of a large dresser.

"This is where the bottles, measuring jugs and formula are kept" she said. She scooped some powder in to a jug. Four scoops she instructed. Then we mix in one pint of tepid water. That means only very slightly warm Jack. She picked up another jug with water she got from the kettle earlier.

"Always get your water ready before you start," she mixed the water with the powder. "Do it gradual so you don't get lumps, if you get a lump it blocks the hole in the teat". She then poured the mixture in to the bottle and showed Jack how to put on the teat.

"Right Jack, ready to go!"

When the two of them entered the barn the little lamb ran to the front of the pen bleating. They climbed over and the lamb started nudging at them looking for its food.

"Well done Jack," Agnes said when he got the hang of it, "remember to keep the bottle upright and keep the teat full so that air doesn't enter or it will give the lamb a sore belly."

The process only took a few minutes as the lamb guzzled down the mixture. Jack thought that this was one of the most enjoyable things he had ever experienced.

Back in the scullery they thoroughly cleaned all the utensils they had used and stored them back in the cupboard. Agnes explained the importance of keeping all of the equipment spotlessly clean to prevent giving the lamb an infection. She also went on to tell Jack that new born lambs wouldn't be given the formula if it could be helped. Milk would be given from another ewe if its mother wasn't able to provide the milk because the first milk the lamb takes from the mother is the most important. It has all the nutrients the lamb needs to help it grow and fight infection. Jack thanked Agnes for showing him what to do.

"You were very good! You could be a teacher if you put your mind to it." Said Jack.

"Oh no chance!" she laughed, "I want to work in a dress shop if I can."

Jack just rolled his eyes and they both laughed.

They heard the sound of the kitchen door opening and the voices of Flo, Nell and Jed deep in conversation.

"Dinner time," said Agnes, "Come on."

Chapter Thirteen.

Grace and Maude were serving up bowls of broth with thick slices of bread and dripping.

"Jack and Agnes get yourselves a good bowl of broth before you take the packing up to Jacob and Gerald", Grace said to them, "I've made up a bag each with a jug of tea and slices of bread and dripping. Put in a couple of meat pies before you go. Agnes if you make a start on the ironing when you get back and Jack if you give Jed a hand cleaning out the pigs. The girls and I will be in the veg patch if you need us."

Jack hiked up to the field where Jacob was ploughing. Several deep furrows ran along the full length of the field in an almost perfectly straight line. The soil was dark and moist where it had been turned over and birds were having a feast on the worms that were uncovered from their dark home.

When Jacob saw Jack waiting at the top of the field he beckoned for him to come down and join him. He unhitched Tilda so she could nibble on the grass yet to be ploughed. He took a seat resting his back against the wall.

"I'm ready for this lad," he said to Jack as he helped himself to the contents of the bag handing Jack a pie.

"Well how's your morning been Jack?"

Jack chatted away relating all the mornings events finishing with Agnes teaching him how to feed the lamb.

"Agnes did?" Jacob said surprised, "What did she tell you?"

Jack went through everything that Agnes had taught him.

"She was very good explaining everything," he ended.

"Well she was certainly thorough I'll give her that! Maybe she's turning over a new leaf. Must be your influence Jack."

"Oh she's alright when you get to know her," Jack said. Jacob raised his eyebrows and smiled to himself.

They remained chatting for a while longer until Jacob said that he would have to crack on.

"Yes and I've got to help Jed clean out the pig sty now", Jack said, "See you later."

Jacob watched him make his way back up to the gate with the empty bag swinging over his shoulder. That boy is wise beyond his years he thought. We'll be in for a few more surprises yet if I'm not mistaken as he smiled to himself again.

Jack and Jed finished the last touches to the sty with all the dirty straw bedding and the waste from the pig's midden piled up in the barrow ready to be taken to the main midden.

“I’ll get ridda the barrow Jack if you top up water in’t trough then we’ll see if the lasses ‘ave kettle on.”

As they entered the kitchen the smell of freshly baked bread made their mouths water. Maude had just taken six loaves out of the oven to cool where they temptingly sat on the work table.

“You’ll be after a cup of tea then lads!” Maude said, “kettles just boiled.”

Poor Agnes was sweating at the back of the kitchen, a hot iron in her hand.

“I hate this job,” she said, “I’ve done one basket load and there’s still another basket full on the line.” She turned to see Jack grinning at her.

“Pack it in for now love, I’ll fetch rest in once its dry and iron it after tea tonight” said Maude.

Agnes didn’t have to be told twice and soon had it all cleared away and joined them for a cuppa with a big smile on her face.

“You’re quite pretty when you smile,” Jack said to her, “pity you’ve got a sulk on most of the time!”

“Cheeky sprat!” she said but continued to smile both outwardly and inwardly.

The door opened and Grace and the girls came in for their cuppa.

“I’m ready for this” said Nell as she poured them all a mug of tea, “I allus forget ‘ow ‘ard it is forking over’t soil.”

“Don’t we all” agreed Grace, “But I’d like for us to start planting start of next week if possible.”

“I’ll be able to give you a ‘and between tuther jobs” Jed offered, “but this afternoon I was planning for me ant lad to groom Elda and Briney afore milking starts agin. Lad’ll ‘ave to teck a buffet ta reach!” he laughed.

Grace noticed the sparkle in Jack’s eyes at this news.

“Just do that then Jed, that’ll be fine.”

Jed gathered up everything they would need from the tack room.

“We’ll start with Briney first afore milkin’ starts agin,” he said as he slowly approached the horse to fit on the halter. He calmly spoke softly to her as he gently stroked her neck and shoulders. It reminded Jack of when Joe had showed them how to groom the ladies. Jed continued whispering gently to her as his hands made long smooth strokes over her back and down each leg without ever making a sudden movement. He finished grooming her and stood back. Elda’s turn now.

“Reet, your turn lad,” as Elda stood ready.

Jack followed Jed’s instructions trying to mimic the long slow movements that Jed had used but not always possible when he was balanced on the buffet.

"Well done lad," praised Jed when they had finished.

"Elda and Tilda are so biddable you'd manage them yersen but Briney 'ere needs a bit more reassurance and patience and she can tell when sum ones nervous around 'er. She's a grand 'orse though 'aving said that". He looked at his pocket watch, "Time ta bring tha girls darn from't pasture. Ya comin lad?"

Jack followed Jed to the top pasture. The cows were already waiting at the gate as if they knew that it was time for them to be milked. They headed down and made their way to their places in the parlour as they had done that morning. Jed allowed Jack to halter a couple of the older cows to their rail.

"Tuther lasses need to get ta know ya lad, all in gud time. Ya can 'ave a go at milkin' this un when Flo an Nell gets 'ere."

Right at that very moment the two of them arrived in the parlour.

"Speak o' the devil" Jed laughed.

"Grace has gone to teck Jacob anuther brew", Flo said, "an Gerald must a finished, ees mecking 'is way back up field".

"I said lad cud 'ave a go at milking" Jed said, "Flo do ya want ta show 'im ropes wi old Maggie 'ere?"

After several failed attempts Jack got the hang of it with Flo's expert tuition. She told Jack the cows were very sensitive and knew when it was a different milker doing the job.

"Mind an tell 'im ta get out of road if cow lifts 'er tail" shouted Nell, "else he'll get shat on!"

"It'll only 'appen once" laughed Jed.

"That's true" said Flo as she explained to Jack what they meant. They all laughed at the look on Jack's face.

"Don't worry" he told them, "I'll never take my eyes off the back end!"

It was much later and almost getting dark before Jacob entered the kitchen. Jed had checked on the pigs and got the two horses back in to their stable before leaving for home. The girls had left once the milking was finished. Jack and Agnes had got the hens safely back in to their pen for the night. Grace and Maude prepared the evening meal and Gerald had gone for a lie down after finishing the wall.

Agnes and Jack were sitting playing dominoes at the small table in the kitchen when Jacob entered looking exhausted.

"Hi love, you look shattered" said Grace, "dinner won't be long now, I'll get you a brew to put you on."

“No thanks love, I’ll freshen up first. Tilda’s settled down for the night. She did me proud today. She got a treat with her food for all her hard work.”

“Everything’s been done out there, just the sheep to check on last thing”, said Grace.

“Thank you everyone”, he said to them all, “we’ve made a good team today.”

They all enjoyed the meal of stew and dumplings followed by curd tart and custard. Jack and Agnes cleared away and washed the dishes while the adults sat talking around the table. Maude stood up to make a start on the last of the ironing whilst Gerald and Jacob left to check on the sheep and Gerald wanted to show Jacob the finished wall. They left with a lantern in hand in to the night.

“Gerald’s like a child sometimes,” Maude said, “he always seems to need praise for his endeavours.”

“Well Jacob had to check on the sheep anyhow so no harm done,” said Grace as she left the table.

“Come with me Jack,” and they left through the door in the kitchen that led upstairs. They entered a small L shaped hallway and turned through a door on the right.

“This is the front parlour Jack, we very rarely use this room.”

Jack looked about him and saw the polished wooden dresser that held fancy decorated plates and dishes.

There was a long couch and two chairs made from soft fabric and in front of the stone fireplace was a thick colourful rug. A polished bureau stood next to the window and it was this that Grace approached and dropped down the hinged door. Inside, besides several stacked ledgers, was every stationary item you could think of.

"Help yourself Jack to what you want for your diary and letters. Just come in here any time you need anything."

"Thank you!" said Jack. Grace noticed his eyes on the books in the tall bookcase.

"Take a couple of books if you want, I'll leave you to browse," she told him as she took out paper and a couple of pencils from the bureau before she left.

Jack was in his element sifting through the books and chose a couple that roused his interest. He helped himself to paper, pencils, pens, ink and envelopes. Balancing his chosen items he returned to the kitchen. The men were back and everyone was having another brew.

"See you've found something," said Grace.

Agnes looked up seeing Jack struggling to keep hold of all the items. She disappeared in to the scullery and came back with an empty basket for him to carry all of his collection.

"Thanks sprat." said Jack.

"Do you want another game of dominoes or are you frightened I'll thrash you again?" grinned Agnes.

"Go on then, seeing as I let you win the last time."
"Huh!" Agnes muttered as she set up the table.

Maude and Grace gave one another a look and smiled. They were pleased that the youngsters were getting along together. Maude couldn't remember Agnes being so friendly before and so relaxed. She rose and got Jack a brew from the pot.

"Here you are Jack. You'll need a drink before you go in to battle with this one," she winked at him.

Grace was intently scribbling something on the paper that she had got from the bureau. Gerald excused himself and said he was going to have an early night. His back was aching after lugging heavy stones all day he told them. Jacob began to read his farming journal and the only sound in the kitchen for a while was the crackling of the logs burning on the fire until Agnes suddenly shouted.

"Yes! I've got you sprat!"

"Third time lucky!" said Jack.

I've got something for you Jack," Grace announced and showed him what she had been doing. He couldn't believe his eyes. Grace had drawn the likeness of himself down to the tuft of hair that always stuck up at the back of his head. His mouth was wide open as he tried to bite on a pork pie!

"Thought you could include this in your diary," she said.

"Thank you so much! It's amazing! You are so talented Grace. I can't believe it. Thank you I will treasure this forever."

Jack proudly placed it in to his basket of goods. Shortly afterwards Jacob accompanied Jack back to his loft, Jack carrying the basket and Jacob carrying a lantern and a pale of hot water.

"You've made it really cosy up here Jack. Are you sure you don't mind not being in the house?"

"No! I love it up here," answered Jack, "in fact I'd like to stay up here all the time if that's alright with you?"

"We'll have to run it past Grace, Jack. You might change your mind come winter but we'll wait and see. What did you think of your first day on the farm Jack?"

"It was brilliant!" Jack answered, "I learned a lot of new things and met loads of new people. I can't really believe that this will be part of my life from now on. It all seems too good to be true!"

"Well, you better believe it lad. You're part of our family now. Don't get me wrong there will be days that nothing seems to go right but we all pull together to support each other through any adversity. That's the beauty of having a good team that you can trust and respect. There's still lots for you to learn Jack but we'll do it together."

"Thank you sir." Jack said.

"Oh I think we can dispense with formalities Jack, just call me Jacob like everyone else. I know that Grace would like to be called by her name too. Only strangers call her Mistress or Marm and you are not a stranger Jack."

Thank you Jacob." Jack grinned at him feeling happy inside.

After Jacob left Jack set out his books and writing materials and then washed and put on his night shirt. He intended writing up the day's events in his diary but he was only half way through when his eyes began to close. The days toil and the fresh air had caught up with him. He jumped in to bed and once more he was sound asleep in minutes.

Jack woke up with a start. What had woken him? He could hear rain beating down on the roof and then all of a sudden a flash of lightening lit up the loft space followed by a clap of thunder. Jack cuddled down under the bed covers feeling safe and warm.

A few minutes later he heard one of the horses below pacing around her stall and whinnying in fright. Must be Briney he thought as he jumped out of bed and climbed down the ladder to the stable below. He lit one of the lanterns and in the soft light he discovered that indeed it was Briney who was very frightened and seemed to get worse with every clap of thunder. Her eyes were wide and saliva was running from her mouth as she paced up and down her stall.

Jack was frightened that she would injure herself if he didn't try to calm her down. He approached the half door of her stall and with his back to her he began to speak calmly and softly. He lost track of the time but continued standing like that until she seemed to take some comfort from the sound of his soothing tone. He continued for a little longer and eventually she slowly approached his shoulder. He very slowly turned to face her and gently stroked her shoulder. She nickered and rubbed his neck with the side of her head. The storm seemed to have passed but the rain was still pelting down outside beating a rhythm on the roof.

He didn't want to leave her so he slowly entered her stall. He began stroking her soothingly as he had seen Jed do. He'd stay here all night he thought if it meant that she wasn't scared.

As Jed approached the yard the following morning he wondered why a light was showing from the stable. He entered to investigate. Nothing seemed untoward.

Elda and Tilda approached their doors in greeting. He gave them a nuzzle and then moved on to Briney's stall and couldn't believe his eyes. Briney was laid on the floor with Jack fast asleep by her side with one arm reaching up across her back as if she was a giant teddy bear!

"Jack, Jack" he whispered. Jack stirred and rubbed the sleep from his eyes.

"What on earth are thee doin' lad?" Jed asked angrily. Jack gave Briney a rub and then left her stall.

"She was frightened in the storm," Jack told Jed, "I had to try and do something to calm her down she was going to hurt herself!"

"Dus tha no ya cud 'ave bin killed? Ya shud 'ave got Jacob!"

"I'm sorry Jed, I didn't think."

"What exactly did thee do lad?" Jed asked.

Jack told him. "An ow did thee know ta do that Jack?"

"I did what I've seen you and Joe do."

"But how did thee no to turn ya back to the 'orse and let 'er cum to you?" Jed continued.

"I didn't know, I just did. It seemed like the right thing to do at the time," Jack told him.

"Well thank the lord no 'arms bin dun. Go get thee sen dressed lad."

Jack climbed back to his loft. Jed made is way up the track to bring down the cows. There's something about that lad he thought. He had sensed it the day before but couldn't put his finger on what it was. The lad had a natural way with the animals, there was no doubt of that. It was the way they responded to him that got Jed thinking that the lad had a special gift. He had heard of folk who had the ability to communicate with animals, especially horses, but he had never met one until now. Jack was young yet but Jed was certain that he would become what folk called a horse whisperer. Well mighty be!

Two months later.....

It was Saturday afternoon and Jack had returned to his loft after dinner to get washed and changed.

The Inspector from the orphanage was due to visit the farm in a couple of hours' time. Jack was apprehensive. What if the Inspector said he had to go back to the orphanage for some reason. Surely not he thought. He loved it here and he was sure Jacob and Grace wanted him to stay.

His innate suspicion of those in authority made him doubt the facts obvious to everyone else. Don't be silly he told himself. Just be yourself and try to relax.

He picked up his diary and began to flick through the pages whilst waiting for the Inspector to arrive. He couldn't believe that two months had elapsed already. So much had happened within that time. Agnes, Maude and Gerald were now in their new home near Skipton. In fact, Grace had just received a letter from Maude who wrote that she wasn't keen on the cottage that came with Gerald's job. It was cold and damp. There were other families staying close by and she got on well with the other wives although they were all a bit younger than her. One of them was expecting a baby and the other had three small children. Maude having no such commitments helped with the milking and earned a small income of her own.

Gerald wasn't too keen working solely with the cattle and he hadn't made friends yet with the other men, surprise, surprise she had written. Agnes had got a job in a lady's wear shop in Skipton. She now lives in a small room above the shop that she shares with another young girl. The owner of the shop is an elderly widow who seems pleased with Agnes's work so far. She wrote that she was missing Agnes dreadfully but she was glad that Agnes was happy. She went on to say that she was missing all of them and was glad that she got to meet Jack before she left. Jack was glad too and he was pleased Agnes was following her dream.

He was now attending the village school and already helping Miss Lewis with the younger children in his class. There were only eleven children in the class, five girls and six boys. Three of the girls and four of the boys were much younger, aged between five and six. One of the girls the same age as Jack was almost blind. She had to use a strong magnifying glass to read and had difficulty writing but Miss Lewis was so kind and patient with her and was often coming up with new ideas that might help her.

He had made friends with the other two boys in his class. They were the same age and had joined the village cricket team together.

One was Joshua Rudd, the shop keeper's youngest son. Joshua was a studious boy, slight in stature. His two older brothers who were in Mrs. Greens class were also in the cricket team. His other friend Jimmy was a miner's son. He was tall and lanky and more outgoing than Jack and Joshua but the friendship worked well.

Grace had streamlined her business but her customers in Pateley still required her famous pies and tarts and dairy goods as did the local coaching Inn who was busier than ever. She now only supplied dairy products to Rudd's and the pasties had been dropped from the menu. Jack liked the pasties though so she would make a batch for themselves every now and then and Jack often took them to school for the break because Joshua missed them too.

There had been several new additions to the farm, fifteen chickens, four calves with another four due in six weeks and ten piglets. Jacob, Jed and himself had built another hen coup and pig shelter to accommodate the new arrivals. The fields were now ploughed, sown and planted and showing signs of healthy shoots of the crops to come and the sheep were all back on the hill.

Jack now had daily chores to do and before he went to school he would lead the horses to their paddock and then muck out and prepare the stable for their return before dark. He fed the hens and collected the eggs, fed the pigs and watered the veg patch. He then got washed and changed for school before breakfast. He had got it down to a fine art now and was often finished with time to spare to chat with Grace as she prepared breakfast.

It only took him about twenty minutes to walk to school and a little longer to get back up the steep hill. Sometimes he got a lift if the weather was bad but it depended on what the rest were doing. Grace had taken him to Pateley market one day and got him kitted out with new boots and an oilskin coat. His pride and joy though were the black jacket and hat she had bought him for church on a Sunday. He looked really smart and a miniature version of Jacob. He felt really proud walking in to the church with the two of them by his side.

After school his tasks varied. Certain days he would have to clean out the hen coups and pig sties, others he would have to weed the vegetable plot, fetch water and carry wood. Sometimes he would sit and churn butter, reading a book as he did so. His favourite task though was to groom the horses and most of their care now was left to Jack and that suited him just fine. He would help with the milking sometimes if he had time.

The highlight of his day though was riding up the hill with Jacob and Bob after tea to check on the sheep. He delighted being on horseback and being as one with this majestic animal surrounded by the wild yet beautiful scenery and spending time alone with Jacob. The two of them were often silent and yet at home with each other and their own thoughts.

He once was able to accompany Jacob on his trip to see Ruth. He liked Ruth as she was always full of news on what was happening at the big House. He found the way she spoke to Jacob quite amusing as at times she would chastise Jacob as if he were still a small boy.

When they were saying goodbye to her she gave Jack another gift and this time it was a knitted pullover. When he tried to thank her she waved her hand at him, "You're welcome Jack" she said, "I enjoyed knitting it as much as I hope you will enjoy wearing it! Besides, it gives me a chance to try out new patterns. Now be off with you!"

Jack smiled as he remembered the bossy little lady waving them out of sight.

It was now time to return to the house and he felt the nerves returning. As he crossed the yard he realised that the others were also apprehensive about the meeting. Why else would Jed have swept the yard as clean as a whistle and also placed the planters that he had been making all week at each side of the porch. They looked lovely with their beautiful blue and yellow blooms adding a mass of colour and sweet scent to the yard. The girls and Grace had scrubbed the inside of the house until it shone with not a thing out of place.

Jacob had also been busy and he had repaired the broken latch on the door and even painted Bob's kennel! Yes he thought, they were nervous too. This realisation made Jack feel grateful that they cared so much for him and that they too wanted to make a good impression for the Inspector's visit.

Grace and Jacob were waiting for him when he entered the kitchen. They were both dressed in their Sunday best.

"How are you feeling Jack?" Grace asked him.

"A bit nervous." he answered.

"Nay lad," Jacob said, "there's no way we'll let him take you back. There's no reason why he should want to anyhow. I think we are letting our imaginations run riot. Grace let's have a cuppa whilst we wait. Do you want a glass of milk Jack?"

"Yes, I'll get it." Jack answered.

Grace had just brewed the pot of tea and reached for her best cups and saucers from the dresser when Bob started barking outside and there was the clatter of a carriage entering the yard.

The three of them hurried out of the house to see a gentleman alight from the carriage. He didn't look anything like Jack expected.

He was a small portly man with a ruddy complexion. His clothes were mismatched, his brown checked trousers clashed with his brown striped jacket in a garish way and a black checked hat finished off this ensemble. He removed his hat as he walked towards them.

"Good afternoon folks!" he said with a big smile, "I'm Cecil Sefton and I believe you are expecting me. I'm the inspector from Bartholomew's Orphanage in York."

"Indeed we are," said Jacob, "If you would like to come in, Jed here will see to your horse." Jed had been hanging about in the stables specially to do this hoping it would give another good impression.

"Thank you so much," replied Mr. Sefton, "that's very kind and I shouldn't be too long!"

Grace busied herself setting the table with another cup and saucer and brought out a sponge cake layered with homemade jam and fresh cream.

"You'll be ready for a bite to eat," she said as she served them, "have you travelled all the way from York?"

"No, no", he replied, "I had a couple of homes to visit in Harrogate yesterday and stayed there overnight and I visited two more homes on the way to your good selves. You're the last visit today. I have a room booked in Pateley Bridge tonight. I've several more homes to visit over the next two days as I make my way back to York."

"You're a lot busier than I thought." Jacob said.

"Yes, my area covers all the outlying farms and hamlets and it's not unusual for me to be away a week at a time but I enjoy the variety of places I get to visit. Some of my colleagues never get out of the town! This cake is delicious Mrs. Smithson and that's another good reason why I enjoy being based in the countryside. The kind hospitality of country folk never disappoints." he said as he patted his paunch with a smile.

He turned to Jack, "Now young sir, you must be Jack?"

"Yes sir." Jack answered.

"Well Jack don't look so worried! I've got a bit of paperwork to fill out then maybe you'll show me round. Is that alright Jack?"

"Yes sir." Jack answered.

He opened his brown leather case and retrieved a bundle of papers and began to ask them questions marking each question with a tick or a cross depending on their answers. The questions were straightforward enough. Did Jack attend school? Did he like the school? Did he have any friends at school? Who else lived in the house? What chores was Jack expected to do and what was his favourite? Jack began to relax as he could answer the questions easily and in depth.

All was going well until Jack was asked if he had a bedroom to himself to which Jack answered truthfully that he had the loft over the stable to himself.

Mr. Sefton looked taken aback. "So you don't stay in the house Jack?"

Jack shook his head and said, "No. sir."

Jacob interrupted and explained the reason why Jack had been first temporarily accommodated in the loft and when their relatives had left Jack asked if he could remain in the loft and not move in to a room in the house that was set aside for him. Grace and himself saw no reason why he shouldn't and Jack knew that he could move in to the house at any time he wanted. Jacob voiced that time might occur when winter arrived.

Mr. Sefton nodded, "And why do you want to stay in the loft Jack?" Jack thought for a moment before he answered.

"I like being near the horses. The horses feel like family. The first time I stroked Elda it was like I belonged to something special. I felt safe with them and could tell them anything and they wouldn't feel bad about me. I'm not lonely when I am with them". He paused for a moment, "Now I feel the same about Grace and Jacob just like I feel about the horses."

Tears began to fall down Grace's cheeks and Jacob swallowed hard and tried to clear the lump in his throat.

Jack continued, "I like lying in bed and listening to the sounds the horses make. I like everything about them. I never knew what it was like to have a family. For years at the orphanage I was just another one of the boys to be looked after and not special to anyone. Sometimes I felt invisible. If I took ill and died there was no one in the whole world that would care until Tom and Archie came and I felt a connection to them but then I lost them when I came here. I thought that I would become invisible again but of course I haven't. I am part of this family and I belong here. I won't go back sir."

Mr. Sefton bundled up his papers and put them away in his case.

"I've heard enough Jack and I am very satisfied that this arrangement has been a complete success for all parties concerned. There is no way Jack that you will have to go back."

He turned to Grace who was still wiping her eyes, "Now Mrs. Smithson, I see that there's still some of that lovely cake left." he said with a warm smile.

"You made an excellent speech Jack, and, speaking of Tom and Archie I have a note from them addressed to you."

Jack's eyes lit up! He read the note whilst the adults chatted over another cup of tea and a slice of cake.

Excitedly Jack informed them some of what was in his letter.

"They miss me but are glad that I like it here and love hearing everything about the farm in my letters. They even read my letters out to the other boys on an evening! They are not able to write back to me due to the cost of postage but they want me to continue to write to them."

Mr. Sefton added that this would be correct as Matron has a very tight budget that she has to stick to and every farthing had to be accounted for in her accounts. She was due to retire soon and would be sorely missed he told them.

Jack continued excitedly, "Good news! Tom and Archie's father has recovered after being in hospital for nearly a year. He had a short visit with the boys! He told them he couldn't go back to his old job at the quarry as he wasn't fit enough anymore but had managed to get a job working in the kitchen at one of the big hotels in York. The pay wasn't too good but it covered his rent for a room in a hostel. He hoped to get a job there as a night porter that he knew would be coming up shortly. With the extra money he would earn he would be able to afford something bigger and they could all be back together."

Jack couldn't stop grinning at his friend's good news.

Mr. Sefton stood up to leave. "If you want to show me around Jack and then I'll be on my way."

He was very impressed with the cleanliness and order of the farm. The animals looked to be well cared for and the lad certainly seemed to be happy. When he went up the ladder in to Jack's loft he noticed the writing material set out on the table and the collection of books on the window sill. It might be above a stable but it was very impressive he thought compared to some of the rooms that he visited that held only the bare essentials.

It was obvious Jack was taking pride in showing him around. His knowledge after just a few months living on the farm was quite intensive. As he was waiting in the yard for Jed to bring round his horse and cart he told the three of them that it had been lovely meeting them all. He was just thanking Grace for her lovely cake when Jed arrived with the horse and cart.

When Jed saw Grace's red eyes and tear stained face he immediately jumped to the wrong conclusion.

"What's going on!" he shouted angrily, "Yall not teck the lad awa over ma deed body!"

"It's alright Jed" Jacob calmed him, "Everything couldn't be better! Mr. Sefton is just leaving."

"That's alreet then, I'll get cows darn foh milkin'."

Mr. Sefton smiled to himself as he made his way down the track. Young Jack won't ever feel invisible ever again he thought with so many good people watching over him.

Five years later.....

Grace and Jack were sitting at the kitchen table. Grace had a ledger open in front of her. She was completing her monthly audit, updating her accounts and customer orders. A task she didn't particularly enjoy.

Jack was updating his diary. He no longer made notes on a daily basis, sometimes a couple of weeks could elapse before he updated his entries, mainly due to the routine of tasks around the farm and at school and often he had nothing new to write about. Also four years ago he received a package from the orphanage returning eight of the letters he had sent to Tom and Archie. There was a curt note saying, "Tom and Archie were no longer in residence and were both apprenticed out and would he refrain from writing as the mail would not be forwarded on to them."

He was so upset. There was no way now he could keep in touch with his friends. For a while he laid awake at nights puzzling why they had been apprenticed out and had they been separated? What had happened with their father?

Jacob and Grace were worried about him. He had lost his usual cheerfulness and became distracted and withdrawn. A few weeks later Jacob called him in to the kitchen.

"I've just received a letter you might be interested in," he told Jack.

He went on to explain that because they had been worried about him, Jacob had taken the liberty to write to Mr. Sefton the Inspector directly. He told him what had happened and asked if there was any way he could find out where the boys had been placed. He had got the reply that morning and he handed the letter to Jack.

He saw a smile cross Jack's face as he read.

"It's not too bad," he told them, "they are both together and working for an engineering firm in York. Mr.

Sefton says that he had a chat with his colleague who carried out their inspection and he said that both boys were doing well and the owner, a Mr. Ackroyd was pleased with their progress. They are living in staff accommodation and have occasional visits to their father on their afternoon off. Best of all he has included a forwarding address so I can continue writing to them!"

Jack was pleased, at least there was still hope that there was a chance to meet again.

It was pitch black outside. The wind was whistling through the rafters. The rain earlier had now turned to sleet splattering hard against the window panes.

"I hope Jacob got to Ruth's before this started," Grace said to Jack.

Jack heard the concern in her voice and answered, "Don't worry, he set off in good time this morning, he's bound to be there by now. He'll be warming his feet by the fire listening to the latest stories from the big House!"

Jack's voice croaked. His voice hadn't quite broken yet and it annoyed him when it went from squeaky to gravelly without any warning.

"Don't worry Jack it'll settle down before too long and you'll have your voice. I can't believe that you are already becoming a young man! How the time has flown."

Jack flicked back to the beginning of his fourth diary.

He smiled, “Do you remember the summer when the travelling gypsies asked for permission to camp on our bottom field by the river? They said they were looking for work in the area.”

“That was a good summer,”, Grace said, “they helped with the hay making and we got it done in record time. Jacob was so pleased to have it all safely stacked in the barns. Remember he suggested we celebrate with them by having a meal on the banks of the river next to their camp? That was a good night that was. Everyone sitting around the campfire, tables bowing under the weight of food that had taken me and the girls most of the day to prepare. What a surprise when Jed got out his mouth organ to play along with the chap on the fiddle! Flo and Nell were up dancing with the gypsy women. I believe you joined them for a while too!”

Jack laughed, “Yes that was a good night although I spent most of the night around their horses. Do you remember the old chap with the brown trilby who kept mistaking me for one of his cousin’s sons? He kept calling me Patrick!”

“Yes I remember that! In the end they all started calling you Patrick! It’s a shame they didn’t return last year but you never know we might see them this spring or summer if they are in the area again.” she sighed and returned to her ledgers and accounts.

Jack continued to flick through the diary. He read about the winter before when they had lost five sheep buried in the snow drifts. He had insisted in accompanying Jacob every time he went out in the storm. It lasted for days on end. Jed had battled up the hill to reach them and afterwards stayed in the farmhouse until the storm was spent.

Grace closed the ledger. “That’s that done for this month. Would you like some hot milk Jack? Be a love and put some more logs on the fire.”

Jack fed the fire with a couple of logs, “I’ll just nip out and check on the sheep,” he told her, “I won’t be long.”

Jack braced himself against the elements as he left the house. It took him all of his time to remain upright. The light from the lantern did little to illuminate his way. Bob kept low to the ground at his heel trying to dodge the worst of the weather. Jack checked the two barns and all seemed well but he sent Bob to check the two fields for any sheep that were daft enough not to have taken shelter. Bob returned alone so Jack then knew that all the sheep were safe inside.

He was glad to get back to the warmth of the kitchen after checking the sheep. There was a mug of hot milk and a plate of homemade biscuits waiting for him by the fireside.

“It’s wild out there,” he told Grace, “but the sheep are all hunkered down in the barns. Is it alright if I bring Bob in for the night?”

"Aye, bring the old boy in, he deserves it now he's getting on."

The three of them sat basking in the warmth of the fire. Jack always took pleasure in evenings like this. It wasn't often that he and Grace were able to just sit and chat.

"Grace," he asked, "Why have Jed and the girls never married?"

She sighed, "It's a sad story Jack."

She told him that Jed had been married and had a young daughter. He had not long worked on the farm at that time and was intending getting a tenancy of his own. Unfortunately during the winter of that year his poor wife contracted a disease of the lungs that spread to their six-year-old daughter. They both passed away within three days of each other. Jed, as you can imagine was devastated and I don't think he's ever gotten over it to this day. He threw himself in to his work at the time and shut himself off from the folk in the village. He hasn't set foot in the church since their deaths. He still carries a lot of anger inside against God and the church. That's why he always works on a Sunday and has Saturday off. He would still work seven days a week mind if we let him.

"The girl's story is just as tragic. They were both married to two brothers that were miners. They lived in the miner's village at the end of the road. Flo was expecting a baby when the news came down from the hill that a seam in the mine had collapsed. Both brothers and another young man had been buried alive. It is still their resting place because it was too dangerous for the men to be recovered. Afterwards Flo and Nell moved back in to the village to live with their widowed mother and sadly not long after Flo lost her baby. They thought it was due to the trauma she had experienced with the death of her husband."

"That's awful," said Jack, "you would never know that they have been through so much grief in their lives."

"Well it all happened a long time ago now Jack but I doubt they ever forget it. They've had to learn to move on with their lives."

"Grace," he enquired, "how did you and Jacob get together?"

"Well that's quite a story! First I better tell you about Jacob's childhood. Jacob's father had got the tenancy of this farm when Jacob was a small boy. Jacob has an older sister Ruth who you know and he also had an older brother Joseph. Jacob's father was very religious and very strict. His mother was a sweet little woman but was very subservient to her husband. The children had to work hard on the farm with no time for leisure. His father really did believe that idle hands did the devil's work. He would thrash them if he found them laughing or playing. They had to stand for hours at a time whilst he recited passages from the Bible to them. After Jacob's mother passed away it got much worse. Ruth had to run the house and she was only thirteen at the time. Her father wouldn't pay anyone to help on the farm so all the work had to be done by himself and the boys. Jacob would have been eleven and Joseph fifteen when their mother died."

"They worked for years without a break and then one harvest when Jacob was twenty years old, he and his father and Joseph were getting in the hay from the bottom field and their father ignored his sons concerns regarding the overloaded cart. He began to drive the cart back to the yard and on the way across the field a wheel hit a rut and the cart keeled over crushing Joseph who was walking alongside. Jacob ran to the village to get help but by the time the men arrived to lift the cart it was too late. Jacob had to carry the battered body of his brother back to the house. Jacob's father never got over the tragedy and locked himself away in his room and he refused to eat or drink for days. He turned in to a recluse and refused to leave the house from that day on."

"Jacob had to try and run the farm on his own with the little help that Ruth could give him. Eventually word got out about Jacob's plight and everyone who was able would try and help out at the farm."

"At that time, my family had the dairy farm above the miner's village so Maude and I were sent down to help. Although I was younger than Jacob, I took charge organising the work load and eventually insisting that he stood up to his father and apply for the transfer of the tenancy in to his own name or otherwise they would end up losing the tenancy and their home. Jacob took my advice and he employed two men from the village and turned the fortunes of the farm around. During this time I had fallen head over heels in love with the quiet, respectful hard-working Jacob and we were married two years later. Jacob's father died the year after our marriage. Ruth had already met her husband by this time and had moved to Harrogate."

"Poor Jacob", said Jack, "I had no idea that his childhood was so bad. Seeing his brother die like that must have been horrendous."

"Yes," agreed Grace, "it's testament to Jacob's strength of character that he has turned out the gentle soul that he is."

"I think you have helped then in that respect," Jack told her.

"Maybe Jack," she said with a far away look in her eyes as she looked back on that time, she gave herself a shake, "Right, time to say goodnight we can't sit here all night. I hope you get some sleep with that wind howling like a banshee! Leave Bob here, I'll see you in the morning."

She stood and gently kissed the top of his head before making her way up to bed.

Jack couldn't settle and laid awake listening to the wind battering the roof and for some reason he didn't feel tired. His thoughts drifted to Jacob's childhood and the tragedies of Jed, Nell and Flo, and he realised he wasn't the only one to have been dealt a poor hand in life. It just goes to show that everyone has their own story to tell in one way or another. It was how you dealt with it that mattered he thought. In a strange way it made him feel better about his own past.

Chapter Fourteen.

The following year brought changes with some expected and others not. Jack left school as planned and was now working on the farm full time although his teachers had wanted him to carry on with his studies and become a teacher like themselves. They were disappointed at his decision to work on the farm but they also knew the vast majority of young farmers did just that.

His two friends from school had also got jobs, Joshua as an office boy in the mill at Pateley and Jimmy worked at the Inn helping out wherever he was needed.

Jacob had invested in another plough and this meant that ploughing the top fields now took half the time with Jack and Jed taking the majority of the workload from Jacob. Jack was pleased that he could now take away some of the burden of ploughing from Jacob has Jack had become genuinely concerned over the past couple of years on how much the ploughing took out of Jacob.

Jack's extra pair of hands meant an easing of the work load for the others too. Flo and Nell now took it in turns to have an extra day off on a Wednesday as well as their usual Sunday.

Jed who always had a Saturday off didn't want another day off. He said he wouldn't know what to do with himself. Instead he preferred to finish earlier on the days that the farm was less busy. On such days he would be found on the banks of the river by the bottom field fishing and drawing on his pipe. Sometimes Jacob and Jack would join him for a couple of hours. Only the occasional trout was caught for tea but the men enjoyed the banter and their restful time together.

A new dog had arrived at the farm. She was a black and white furry ball of fluff, the cutest little thing and full of mischief. Jack named her Becky and initially she slept in the loft with Jack in a wooden box at the side of his bed but after several sleepless nights with Jack being the one not sleeping, a kennel was built next to Bob's. This proved a fruitless task as she would crawl in to Bob's kennel to cuddle up with him. Bob was very taken with his new little pal and put up with his ears being chewed and his bones going missing. It was early days yet but she had all the signs of becoming a good worker.

Just after Easter, as they were sitting on the bench in the yard having a quick cuppa, they heard the sound of an approaching cart making its way slowly up the track. The dogs as usual went to greet the newcomer with a chorus of barks.

It was Maude with her Briney pulling a cart that was loaded with several boxes. She jumped down from the cart and the two sisters embraced each other.

With a mug of tea in her hand Maude explained that Gerald had gone off to Scotland to earn his fortune with a gang of other men to work on the big sheep farms that were being created up there. He had expected Maude to just pack up and go with him but she refused but he left anyway. So would it be alright if she stayed them for a while?

"Of course it is." said Grace and Jacob in unison.

She told them that Agnes was now betrothed to a butcher's son called Ted. He was a bit older than her but seemed a fine enough lad that doted on her. She was now running the dress shop in Skipton since the owner had retired and she was still enjoying her work.

Jack thought that Maude herself seemed younger, happier and more relaxed than he last remembered her.

Jack was delighted to be reacquainted with Briney who recognised him instantly and allowed him to unharness her from the cart and lead her in to the paddock to join Elda and Tilda. Good! Another horse to look after, the more the merrier he thought to himself.

With Maude now at the farm and taking over most of the household chores and Jack taking over the deliveries for Grace it meant that Grace could now take it a bit easier.

Jack knew that the Doctor had advised her to slow down a while ago but being as stubborn as she was she chose to ignore the advice. Jack had overheard her and Jacob arguing one evening which was something they never did. Jacob had wanted her to either give up her business or get in someone to help. Keeping the business meant she was working seven days a week cooking and making the produce but she was adamant she would carry on for a while longer.

The arrival of Maude was a Godsend, no doubt about it. Grace and Jacob would often go together now to visit Ruth and would stay over for a few nights. Ruth was still well and was always delighted when Grace went to stay. The two of them would spend a day going round the shops and visiting the tearooms in Harrogate. Jacob said they never stopped talking from the moment they arrived to the moment Ruth waved them off. He said he was glad to get back home for some peace and quiet but Jack knew he was happy to have seen his sister again.

The dairy herd had expanded and there were so many hens now that Jack and Jed had to expand their run and build another two coups.

The following three years passed without drama or mishap. Warm summers and mild winters and all was well at the farm. Looking back Jack thought it was a blissful time. Even the village cricket team won a few matches.

Looking back at those happy times Jack thought it would last forever.

Chapter Fifteen

Reading back in his diaries Jack realised that the destiny of them all began a downward spiral when Maude left the farm to live with Agnes and her husband.

Agnes was near the end of her pregnancy with her first child. She and her husband Ted had bought their own house on the outskirts of Skipton. Although modest it had several bedrooms and its own garden with plenty of room for Maude and the new baby. Maude would care for the baby while Agnes continued to work. The Dress shop had now expanded to twice its original size thanks to Agnes's forward planning and the owner giving her free reign on all business decisions as it was obvious to her that Agnes was honest and knew what she was doing.

It was bitter sweet to see Maude leave. She had become integral to the smooth running of the farm but most of all they would miss her cheerfulness as she carried out her chores. She was like a mother hen to them all and always there to offer advice or a helping hand. Even so, everyone was pleased for her and knew that her new role as a grandmother would suit her down to the ground.

Jack himself had become a bit restless. He now knew the workings of the farm inside out although there was always the occasional problem to solve or unexpected dilemma with the livestock. He still loved the work but felt that something was missing. He wondered if this feeling was due to his friends Joshua and Jimmy making tentative plans to find work away from the area.

Joshua hated his job as office clerk at the mill in Pateley and Jimmy was getting itchy feet too. He liked his job at the Inn but like Jack, he felt he wasn't challenged anymore.

One evening at the Inn he got speaking to one of the guests who told him that he was looking for several young men to work for him during the summer season at his fairground in Blackpool. He told Jimmy he could earn more than twice as much money in one season than for a years work elsewhere. Board and lodgings were provided at a minimal rate so most of their earnings would go straight in to their pockets.

He gave Jimmy a business card. "Mr. Elijah Bates, Showman of Bates Entertainment" with an address in Blackpool printed on it. Keep this he told Jimmy and if ever you or any of your pals are interested just turn up any time after the end of April.

Jimmy was full of enthusiasm about the job when he was telling Jack and Joshua about his encounter with Mr. Bates, Showman!

"What about it?" he said to them, "the three of us working through the summer earning good money and most importantly having a good laugh! We might not ever have a chance like this again. Surely we deserve this opportunity to experience something else in life and to get away from this village and spend some time by the sea. None of us have even seen the sea before and after all, even if we hate it, it's only for a few months and then we'll be back. I'm sure I'll get my job back at the Inn. Joshua you hate your job anyhow and are looking for something different and Jack the farm will still be waiting here when you get back. What do you think lads?"

It certainly sounded a good opportunity to try something different. Joshua was all for the plan and would discuss it with his parents.

However, Jack said that there was no way he could leave the farm in summer when the shearing and haymaking took place but he wished his friends well. It would be a while yet before they set off anyhow. Jack mentioned his pals plans to Grace and Jacob that evening while having their meal.

Grace was a bit dubious. "They don't know anything about that fellow and what if they get stranded in Blackpool and can't get back? What if when they get there and find that all the jobs are taken or non-existent and how do they know the wages will be as good as he makes out?" Grace thought it was all too good to be true.

Jacob's opinion however was more positive. He understood, they were both young and eager for something different.

"Blackpool is not the end of the world away and if it doesn't work out for them they'll easily get back somehow. If the wages are as good as they have been told though they'll be worked hard morning till night if I'm not mistaken. Will the two of them be able to handle that do you think?"

Jack thought that maybe Jimmy would but Joshua wasn't used to physical labour and might struggle.

Jack didn't have much time to dwell on his friends upcoming plans as he was too worried about Grace. Her health seemed to be deteriorating again since Maude had left. She was now on her feet from morning to night. He'd noticed that her feet were swollen to almost double the size by the time she rested in the evening. She had also become breathless if she had to hurry along or climb the stairs. Jacob had insisted that she visit the Doctor again and this time she came away with pills to take but she still ignored the Doctor's advice to take things easier.

The week after Grace had been to the Doctors Nell arrived for work alone. Solemnly she told them that their mother had taken unwell in the night and the Doctor had been sent for. She had suffered a stroke that had left her paralysed down one side and unable to talk. The Doctor explained to them that it would be unlikely for her to recover and she would require constant nursing from now on. Nell sat down and wept. She looked dreadful.

"Get yourself back home," Grace told her, "and get some sleep. We'll sort something out tomorrow and don't you be worrying about us."

The girls ended up taking it in turns to come up to the farm. This was beneficial for the two of them as it allowed the burden of responsibility for caring for their mother and all that it entailed to be shared equally and for both of them to still have input at the farm.

Grace had asked in the village if anyone was interested in a part time post at the farm but all the females were either too young, too old or busy with young children.

Everyone was working flat out. The men taking on all of the milking to allow the women to concentrate on getting their orders out on time. Jack would often sit on an evening churning butter. It wasn't hard work but it was time consuming but it saved the ladies a lot of time through the day. Grace was still hopeful that they would manage to get more help now that she had broadened her search to Pateley and offered accommodation with the job. She was now, at Jacob's request, looking for someone fulltime. Hopefully someone would be interested before too long.

The sheep were now back on the hill. In order to free a pair of hands for milking either Jacob or Jack with the aid of Becky would go alone to check on them.

One evening Grace rushed in to the milking parlour where Jack and Jed were just finishing the milking.

She was breathless and extremely distraught. Becky had returned home alone with no sign of Jacob. The dog was agitated and wouldn't settle. Grace was worried something had happened to Jacob. Jack ran to the paddock and without bothering to saddle the horse he jumped on to Elda's back and galloped up the hill. Jed followed as quick as he could on foot.

Flo got Grace back to the house and tried to calm her down. She put the kettle on because she said they would all need a cuppa once they all got back.

"Maybe nothing untoward has happened as Becky is a young dog still and just might have made her way home unbidden. Wait and see," she said to Grace, "Jacob will be back soon calling the dog all the names under the sun!"

Jack crested the hill and could see Tilda tethered to a bush in the distance. He made his way over but couldn't at first see any sign of Jacob.

Then he spotted Jacob lying beside the stream where they often stopped for a drink.

Puzzled, Jack made his way across to him. Was he sleeping he thought?

Jacob was lying by the water, a ray of sun brushing his face. His expression so serene and still.

"Jacob!" Jack cried and rushed to his side, "No.... No....." he screamed. Dear God no. Please no.....this can't be happening".

He laid down next to Jacob and sobbed holding Jacob so tight as if his will alone would breathe life back in to Jacob's body.

This is how Jed eventually found them as the sun slowly lowered over the horizon.

The weeks that followed Jacob's death were shrouded in a haze for Jack. He moved in to the house to be with Grace.

He continued working with Jed but couldn't concentrate and it was hard to keep his mind busy. He lived his life in a perpetual numbness. He was just going through the motions. Nothing seemed real to him and he felt empty inside with no motivation.

Often he would wake in the night and hear Grace sobbing. He would go and try to comfort her but it felt as if he wasn't really there. Even when he was standing by Jacob's graveside he couldn't believe it was real. He just hoped that he would wake up and it had all been a nightmare.

Grace had lost all interest in the farm and her business. Like Jack she was in a state of shock. Jed and the girls were trying their best to keep things going but were fighting a losing battle.

The heart had gone out of the farm since Jacob had passed and the light out of their lives. Not long after and early one morning Grace and Jack entered the kitchen to find Bob curled up by the fireside unresponsive. He had passed away in his sleep to join his master.

This was the last straw for Grace. She owed it to Jacob not to let the farm go under but knew that she hadn't the will anymore to continue.

That evening she asked Jed and Nell to stay behind and the four of them discussed the future of the farm. They could no longer remain in limbo she told them. It was time for her to move on. They already knew her health wasn't good and without Jacob she no longer wanted to stay on the farm.

The tenancy still had fifteen years to run and Jack still had almost two years to work through his apprenticeship so he wouldn't be able to take it on. So the best solution all round she suggested was to transfer the tenancy to Jed, after all he knew the farm as much as Jacob did. Jed was silent for a while but before accepting this plan he wanted to know what Grace intended to do.

She had written to Ruth she told them and intended to live with Ruth. They had always got on well together and she knew it would be what Jacob would have wanted for her.

She turned to Jack and reached for his hand. He could stay on at the farm or come with her and find work there it was whatever he wanted to do as long as he was happy it was alright with her. The girls would continue as they were and it would be up to Jed to continue the pie business or not. Jed accepted the plan as long as Grace was sure that this is what she wanted. Grace assured them that it was.

Every one of them was surprised at her decision but knew she was right and Jack knew it had taken Grace great courage and strength to come to it because by leaving the farm she was leaving the biggest part of her life behind. Things had to change to ensure the future of the farm and Jacob's legacy.

Later that evening Grace took Jack in to her arms.

"We've got to be strong now Jack. We have to make a new life for ourselves because it is what Jacob would want. I love this farm. The happiest days of my life have been spent here but realistically we are only custodians of the land for a short time. We have done a good job and we are leaving it in a better condition than it was before but now it's time for someone else to take over the reins. That's how it should be and will continue to be for generations to come. Each one of us leaves our own mark on the land and surrounding environment in our own way and then we pass it on for others to continue it in their way."

Jack decided that he would stay on at the farm until Jed could get another couple of farm hands and then Jack would join Grace.

It was a joint decision that the pie business would not continue, after all it was Grace's name and recipes that had made the pies famous in the first place. It wouldn't be right to continue it without her. A lot of locals would be disappointed but it couldn't be helped. They would now only supply butter, cheese and eggs to their regular customers.

New homes would be found for the pigs and the pig field would become an extra pasture for the cows. This would allow for the dairy herd to expand further. The sheep farming would continue as before. Elda would go with Grace and would enjoy an early retirement in Ruth's paddock. Tilda and Becky would continue their work at the farm.

Now that the plan for the future of the farm had been settled it seemed to make the situation slightly easier for Grace and Jack.

Grace was busy packing the bits and pieces she wanted to take with her. Jed had informed all the businesses that they supplied of the changes and had obtained a new home for the pigs at a farm outside of Grassington.

Jack had finished the ploughing and made a start on the sowing. It was back breaking work and he wondered how Jacob had done it for so many years.

He thought about Jacob all of the time and at times he felt that Jacob was beside him as he toiled in the fields alone. He would silently talk to Jacob telling him of his uncertainties for the future or just the general running of the farm. He often found himself asking Jacob's advice about something or other. This didn't sadden him in any way, in fact he found it somehow reassuring.

One morning Jack found himself wondering how long it would be before Jed managed to get more help for the farm. He felt in limbo and although part of him was happy to stay for as long as it took the other half of him wanted his own future to be settled.

Jed had planned to put an advert in the local paper in Skipton the following day as it had quite a widespread circulation. However that afternoon as Jed was about to collect the cows for milking a young man entered the yard.

“Ow do” said Jed, “wot can I do foh thee?”

The man introduced himself as Michael Haywood. He had heard in the village that there might be work going on the farm. He and his wife had been living and working up at the big dairy farm by the mine at the end of the road for the last four years but because the farmers lad was now leaving school at the end of the month, and his daughter had recently married a stockman, he no longer needed Michael.

He had given Michael plenty of time to find another job but Michael decided to move forward right away.

Jed had seen the lad in the village from time to time and he always thought he seemed a quiet sort of lad and seemed to be well liked.

“Well” he said, “I’m just abart to get coos darn ta milk. Ya can giv us a ‘and we’ll talk abart it”.

Jack couldn’t believe it when he entered the kitchen later and Grace introduced him to Michael their new farm hand. Jack shook his hand warmly and welcomed him to the farm.

Grace told Jack later that Michael's wife would visit the farm the next day and she would show her around the house and farm and go over the work routine.

That night as Jack lay in bed he thought that perhaps everything was falling in to place after all. He couldn't help but wonder if Jacob had a hand in it somehow. He smiled to himself as he closed his eyes and drifted off to sleep.

Chapter Sixteen

Grace was very taken with Bridget, Michael's wife, she seemed a very capable young woman who had grown up on a farm. She had milked her first cow at the age of seven and helped her mother make butter and cheese even younger than that.

Bridget loved the house, it was much bigger than the cottage they were leaving although she was slightly concerned that their bits and pieces would be lost in the large rooms here. Grace told her that apart from a few items most of the furniture would be staying and there would be just the two of them living there for now as Jed owned his own house in the village and intended to stay there. However, they may have to accommodate another farmhand in the future if the workload at the farm demanded it.

Bridget was impressed on how the farm and buildings were kept. They were in good repair with no muck or clutter scattered around the yard. She liked the routine that Grace had of meeting with the staff each morning at breakfast to discuss the plans of the day. They weren't used to that and it seemed a friendly way of keeping up morale and involving everyone in the running of the farm.

Jed would continue with this way of working but of course it would be up to Bridget to provide breakfast.

"Was she alright about that," asked Grace.

Bridget said of course and she couldn't wait to get started. Grace noticed she seemed to be as keen as she was at that age and thought she would fit in with no bother.

It was decided that Michael and Bridget were to move to the farm in three week's time which would be two days after Grace had left. Jack was going to see Grace settled in at Ruth's then return to the farm for a while until Jed managed to get more help.

The following few weeks were a whirl of activity for Grace. Packing and repacking what she wanted to take with her, visiting her friends and clients to say her farewells and of course her usual work in the house and farm still had to be done. She didn't have the time to dwell on leaving her old life behind or worry of what her future may hold.

As Grace laid in bed the morning she was due to leave it suddenly hit her. A wave of sheer panic swept over her and she had never experienced anything like it in her life before. Her hands trembled, she began to sweat and she began to gasp for breath. She managed to swing her legs over the side of the bed and holding on to the top of a chest of drawers to steady herself she stood up. A rush of nausea overwhelmed her. She forced herself to take slow, deep breaths until the feeling passed. Slowly she made her way downstairs to the kitchen. She needed a mug of strong tea.

Jack looked up from stoking the fire. "Grace, what's wrong?" he said, his voice full of concern. Her face was as white as a sheet and she was still in her nightdress which was unheard of.

"I'll be alright Jack", she said "I just need a mug of tea and then I'll be as right as rain."

He handed her a mug of tea and wanted to know exactly what had happened. Grace tried to explain to him about her feelings of doubt that she had been having about doing the right thing. She realised that she had kept brushing these concerns to one side instead of dealing with them and this morning they had overwhelmed her and she had panicked.

"Right!" Jack said, "let's put this in to perspective. First and foremost you are still grieving for Jacob, and it has hit me hard too, and there is nothing we can do about that and only the passing of time will help ease these feelings. Secondly, you've had to make enormous decisions that affect not just your own life but all of our lives too and I'm proud of the way you have managed to do that. The farm couldn't be in better hands than Jed's and remember you will still have connections to the farm, you still own the beasts, the equipment and all of the sheds. You can come back at anytime if you want but would you really want to do that? Jed can buy the stock and equipment over time if that's what you want too."

Grace thought for a few seconds before shaking her head.

"No," she said, "If I'm honest with myself I'm not fit enough anymore," She smiled at him, "and don't you dare repeat that statement to anyone else!"

Jack laughed at her, "I wouldn't dare!"

"Thank you Jack, I feel much better now we've had a chat. Well we can't sit here all day we've got a busy day ahead of us. Are you nipping down to the village this morning to wave off your pals as they leave on their big Blackpool adventure?"

"Yes I'd better get down there," Jack said, "Are you sure you are alright Grace?"

"Never better," she smiled as she waved him through the door.

Later that morning following a tearful farewell and promises to come back for frequent visits, Grace and Jack set off on their journey and waved goodbye.

It was perfect weather for travelling and they chatted away as they went. Grace asked him if his friends had managed to get off on time and Jack said they had. He said that at the last minute Joshua and Jimmy had decided to hitch lifts to Blackpool. It would take them a couple of days they thought but would save them a lot of money that they might need as their wages wouldn't be paid to them until the end of the season. They were both in good spirits as they set off from the Inn where one of the coaches was going to take them in to Skipton. From there the main road would follow the Aire valley west. It was a busy road and they shouldn't have too many problems getting a lift. They hoped.

Grace couldn't help but notice the wistful look Jack had on his face when he talked about his friends' venture.

They made steady progress and reached Ruth late afternoon. Ruth greeted them both with open arms and ushered them inside where she had prepared a meal for them. After they had eaten Jack had seen to Elda and left her contently grazing in the bottom paddock and then he began to unload some of the boxes from the cart and the two women began to put some of the items away into what would be Grace's bedroom at the back of the cottage. The single bed had been removed from the room and Jack had to get Grace's double bed from the cart and rebuild it in the room. With this done the ladies made up the bed ready for the night.

Jack continued carrying in boxes that Ruth told him to stack in the corner of the kitchen for now. He was just wondering how he was going to manage the chest of drawers, the bureau and the bookcase by himself when suddenly a head appeared through the door.

"Da ya need 'and lad?" said a tall dark-haired man. "I'm Joseph, Ruth's neighbour next door but one. I've just finished werk an I saw the cart pullup an I sed ta wife I better giv 'im 'and afore I sit down ta eat. Looks as if I'm reet on time anall."

Jack gratefully accepted Joseph's offer of help and it didn't take the two of them long before the furniture was installed and the cart was empty.

"I'd normally stay fer a chat" said Joseph, "but ma teas waitin'. I'll bid thee gud night an let us naw if ya need a 'and we owt tomorra it's me day off so it'll be no bother. Lovely ta meet ya".

He nodded to Jack and Grace before he went through the front door.

Ruth explained to them whilst they were having their supper that Joseph was a general handyman at the big House and his wife Mary was a kitchen maid. They had not been married long and they and the rest of the neighbours were friendly and always ready to lend a hand if need be.

"Jack" she said, "you'll be wanting an early start in the morning to get back to the farm so I'll make up a bed for you in front of the fire then I think we all deserve an early night.

Grace did her best not to shed a tear when saying goodbye to Jack the following morning.

She took him in her arms and told him how she couldn't be more proud of him. He was a lovely, gentle caring young man who always put others first. He got quite embarrassed and gave her a tight squeeze. He realised that was almost the way Ruth had described Jacob to him when they had first met.

He looked at Ruth and she smiled and gave him a wink, she had remembered too.

"Now be off with you!" Ruth said, "and no galivanting with loose women!"

"Chance would be a fine thing!" laughed Jack as he pulled away.

The farm was a hive of activity when he arrived back later that day. Michael and Bridget were removing the last of their belongings from a cart in the yard and Jed and Flo were finishing off the milking.

Jack reunited Elda with her pal Tilda in the paddock then shouted out to them that he was taking Becky up the hill to check on the sheep.

He needed some time alone to think. It was strange watching someone else making the house in to their home. He knew he was being foolish but he felt almost the same as when he left the orphanage, that everything was out of his control.

He hiked up the hill with Becky at his heels. She had turned out to be a first-rate worker but then she'd had the privilege of two excellent trainers, Jacob and Bob.

He watched her as she ran in front always alert to her surroundings. Not for the first time he wondered what she had witnessed on the hill that evening when Jacob died. The Doctor had told them that Jacob had suffered a massive stroke and would have died instantly with no pain.

Jack had seen with his own eyes how peaceful Jacob had looked as he lay there but only Becky would know for sure as she was the only witness to Jacob's last moments. How he wished that she could tell him he thought as he circled around the hill thoroughly checking all the crags and inlets just as Jacob had taught him all those years ago.

He sent Becky off to gather in a group of ewes and lambs that were perilously close to a steep crag then he made his way to the bank of the stream where he had found Jacob.

He always felt closer to Jacob here than anywhere else. He knew that here on the hillside was Jacob's favourite place to be, alone watching the sheep, his beloved Bob at his side. It was here, he had told Jack, that he did most of his thinking. Often he would find a solution to a problem as he sat quietly contemplating the vastness of nature before his eyes. It was here that he felt most at peace away from the hustle and bustle of the farm where there was always another job to attend to.

Jack felt honoured to have shared this place with Jacob. He too found peace here and the ability to clear his mind from the worries of the day.

Feeling thirsty he cupped his hands and bent over the clear water to take a drink.

As he did so he caught a glimpse of a reflection in the water but it wasn't himself. It was Jacob with a big smile upon his face. Jack gasped and instantly the reflection was replaced by his own.

What had just happened? He knew what he had seen but couldn't make sense of it. Just then Becky came splashing in to the water wanting his attention and the moment was gone.

He sat quietly on the bank for a while with his arm around Becky deep in thought. What if Jacob had just stopped for a drink and the stroke took him just as he made his way from the bank Jack thought and then he heard Jacob's voice in his head.

"By that's just grand!" while he smacked his lips.

Jack laughed out loud as this was a standing joke between the two of them every time they took a drink from the cold clear water they would perform this ritual of smacking their lips and echoing those words.

He had no idea or understanding of what he had just experienced other than Jacob had somehow communicated to him what had happened to confirm his speculations.

He did know that it was real and he felt a warmth and a feeling of euphoria that Jacob was still with him somehow. He knew he couldn't tell anyone about this as they would think he was crazy and maybe he was but his heart was gladdened non the less and it was with a lighter step that he returned to the farm.

The next few days Jack did what he could to help Michael and Bridget settle in to the farm.

He had moved back in to his loft to give them more privacy while they sorted out their own belongings.

He particularly liked the way that both of them treated the animals, especially Bridget who would chatter away to them as she performed her tasks. She would even ask them questions and answer herself in a different voice. Sometimes it was hilarious listening to her conversations with different animals. She told them that she had done this from being a child working on her parent's farm and it had become second nature to her now. The rest of them urged her to continue as they enjoyed listening to her dialogues as she did it so naturally without any self-consciousness.

One evening Bridget asked Jack if she could accompany him whilst he went up the hill to check on the sheep. They took the horses and rode up the track with Becky at their heel. Jack pointed out certain landmarks as they came in to view and gave her their names. Bridget told him that she loved the wide-open space of the moor and the breeze flowing through her hair.

They sat for a while and chatted by the stream, she wanted to know all about Jacob and what kind of man he was. Jack was able to open up to her, more so than he could with the men and was only too happy to tell her about Jacob and how much he cared for him. She sat listening quietly while he finished talking.

"You know what you should do Jack?"

He looked questioningly at her.

"You should build a cairn right here, in memory of Jacob. It would be a tribute to him and all he did to turn the farm around against all the odds. It would be a place for future generations of tenants to pay their respects and enjoy the peace and solitude as he had done."

Jack loved her idea and was excited and he could not think of a better tribute to Jacob. The two of them started making plans on how it could be done whilst they made their way back to the house.

Everyone back at the farm was as keen as Jack on the idea and would help in any way they could. They would start by gathering as many rocks as they could and place them at the foot of the track. Every time Jack went up the hill to check on the sheep he would carry as many as he could in bags attached to the saddle of the horse. It would be a slow process but they couldn't think of anything better than a permanent tribute to a good man.

Jed announced one evening that it was time to get another horse. They would need another when Jack eventually left and took Elda with him.

He had heard of a sale coming up in Skipton and thought that he and Jack should take a look. Jack was thrilled at the prospect of attending a horse sale as he had never had the chance before.

Jack and Jed set off at first light on the day of the sale in the hope that they would arrive before all the best horses had been sold. As it turned out they were too early so they decided to pay Maude a quick visit before the sale started.

Maude was so pleased to see them. She loved being at Agnes's but most days she only had the company of her little four month old grandson as Agnes and her husband Ted were out working all day. On hearing that they were on their way to maybe buying a horse at the sale she looked thoughtful and smiled.

"What about Briney?" she said to them, "I have no use for her now and Ted has his own horses for deliveries. I have thought for a while now that I should find a new home for her and where better than at a farm she already knows? Free of charge of course." She laughed.

"Well we'll not get a better deal than that yon. Job dun!" Jed said has he shook her hand.

They stayed with Maude for a bite to eat then went to collect Briney from the paddock. She remembered them straight away and whinnied in greeting. Once they had tethered Briney to the rear of the cart and they had said their farewell and thanks to Maude they still had plenty of time to spare.

“Why don’t we take a look at the sale while we are here anyhow,” said Jack as he wanted to see what it was like.

“Yeah might aswell.” Jed agreed.

Jack was in his element amongst the horses most of them had already been sold but Jack enjoyed walking around the pens and stroking their necks anyway. Jed was in deep conversation with one of the farmers he knew so he was quite happy wandering around on his own.

He noticed a small sturdy cart parked by the side of a pen that held a little Sheltie pony.

He looked at the cart and pony and a plan started to form in his head. While he pondered this plan he made acquaintance with the pony. He was a calm biddable little chap who was probably about seven years old.

His owner noticed Jack taking an interest and came across to see if Jack wanted to make an offer. Jack said that he might be interested but would have to run it past his boss. Jed approached them just at that moment to tell Jack that they should be on their way back to the farm. Jack took him to one side and told Jed what was on his mind.

“Mmmmm,” Jed thought, “That might just work Jack.” and began to barter with the owner for the pony and the cart and eventually a deal was struck on the shake of a hand.

Jed laughed at the sight of Jack sitting in the little cart.

"Ya'll be lucky ta be back afore midnight!" he called to Jack as he set off for home with Elda and Briney.

Jack had plenty of time to think about their purchase as Paddy the little pony trotted back to the farm. He had no doubt that Paddy with the little sturdy cart would be ideal for transporting the rocks up the narrow track to the moor to build Jacob's cairn.

It was dark by the time he arrived back but Bridget had a meal ready for him. She laughed, "Jed said not to expect you until tomorrow!"

She and Michael would get to know Paddy as they got him settled in to his new home while Jack enjoyed the chicken stew and dumplings she had made earlier.

The next morning Jack took Paddy with the cart for a trial run up the hill as he went to check the sheep. It could not have gone any better as the little pony hauled up the cart that was half full of rocks as if it wasn't there and he was content to graze and drink from the stream whilst Jack unloaded the cart and then checked on the sheep.

Whilst having their meal at mid-day the five of them discussed other ways that Paddy could become useful around the farm. Bridget said she could use him to make the deliveries to the village. Jed said he would come in handy to transport rocks unearthed during the ploughing instead of using the barrow and Nell said an extra pony and cart would always be useful during hay making no matter how small. Yes, Jack thought, they had all taken to the little fellow!

Two weeks later Jack was in Rudd's shop posting a letter to Grace and another to his old friends Tom and Archie. He felt a bit guilty posting the last letter as it had been over three months since he had last written to them. He'd found it hard to write to them about Jacob's death at the time. He still hadn't had any word back from them but remained hopeful that they were both still well and enjoying their work.

He was hoping that Mr. Rudd would have heard by now how Joshua and Jimmy were getting on, however, there had been no word. Johnny Rudd couldn't understand why because Joshua had promised them he would write to them as soon as he arrived at Blackpool.

"It's been nearly four weeks now since they set off and his mother is getting really worried," he told Jack.

"I'm sure they will both be fine," Jack tried to reassure him, "they are probably really busy and might not get much free time. They would be back by now if anything had gone wrong or they didn't like it there."

"Aye, your right lad," Johnny agreed, "there's a letter here for you Jack, it looks as if it's another one from Grace. Hope she's getting on alright in her new home?"

"Yes she seems to be," answered Jack as he took the letter, "she's already made friends with Ruth's neighbours. One of them is delivering Ruth's knitwear to

Harrogate for her until I arrive with Elda. Grace has been going along for the ride and has enjoyed going around the shops. She still misses the farm and everyone here though."

"Any idea yet Jack when you will be leaving us?" Johnny asked him.

"No," Jack answered, "there's been no response as yet to Jed's advert in the local paper. I want to finish off the cairn before I leave so there's no rush."

"Aye, I heard about that. What a smashing idea, he was well liked around here. Good luck with it Jack."

Two women entered the shop and Jack made his escape. Johnny Rudd meant well but sometimes he'd have you there talking all day if he wasn't busy.

Jack sat by the river to read Graces's letter before he walked back up to the farm. She was busy trimming and weeding the garden at the front of the cottage. The veg patch at the back was maintained by Ruth's next door neighbour Ronnie who was the head gardener at the big House and his son Harry who was an under gardener. They had been doing this for Ruth since her husband passed away. Ronnies wife Edith had become a good friend to Grace and the two of them would go for walks in the grounds of the estate when the weather permitted. Like Grace, Edith was a good cook and would help out at the big House when a large event was planned.

Grace had started sketching again, often in the evening while Ruth was either spinning or knitting.

Grace herself had, at Ruth's suggestion, began to knit colourful tea cosies that Ruth was going to try to sell along with her usual goods to the shop in Harrogate.

Grace expressed her delight of Jack's mission to build a cairn in Jacob's memory. She'd shed a tear when she read of it in Jack's last letter she told him. If possible she would like a simple inscription engraved on it when it was finished. What did Jack think? She was glad that Michael and Bridget had settled in well and everyone else was hail and hearty. She missed them all terribly, especially Jack, but if he changed his mind and decided to stay at the farm she would understand. She sent her love to everyone and signed off.

Jack was glad that Grace seemed happier and settling in to her new life. He missed her more than he could have ever imagined and knew that he wouldn't change his mind about joining her.

He related Grace's news to the others when they gathered for dinner.

"It's good news," Nell said, "now that she's able to go for walks. Her health must be improving. Before she left here she'd struggle to walk up yard."

"That's true," agreed Jed, "and long may it continue."

Suddenly there was a loud knock on the door and Bridget went to answer it.

A tall well built young man stood on the step with his cap in his hand.

"Is Jed abart?" he asked her, "I've cum abart job advertised in last week's paper."

Jed and Jack recognised the lad as Seth, the Blacksmiths youngest son. They went out to the yard to have a word with him.

Seth explained that he had left school at Easter a few weeks back. He thought that he would work with his dad and two brothers at the Smithy but there just wasn't enough work for the four of them. He was bored sitting about most of the day but his dad and brothers didn't want to say anything and would invent work to give him something to do. So this morning he had made the decision to do something about it and look for another job and here he was. He wasn't afraid of hard work he told them and he could handle horses of course but didn't know much about farming apart from helping out at hay time.

Jed remembered that he had helped them out from time to time and always seemed a willing worker.

"What if we giv yer a few weeks trial" Jed said, "an we can see 'ow ya get on an if ya like it."

"Nay bother. That sarns fair enuff," Seth replied, "I can start nar if ya want?"

Jed laughed, "Cum on then lad, follow me tha seems keen 'enuff."

Seth in his own way proved to be an asset to the farm. He couldn't get the hang of milking, his large hands being too cumbersome for the job but he could muck out the barns, stables and sweep the yard in record time. He was excellent with the horses, his gentleness with them in contrast to his strength. He had picked up the delivery schedule with ease and now he was learning from Jack about the sheep.

He had started accompanying Jack on an evening when he went up the hill even when he should have finished work for the day. He had learned the lay of the land and what to watch out for in the behaviour of the sheep though it would take some time yet to be comfortable with it. Like everyone else he loved it up there. He had lived in the village all of his life and didn't realise all of this was on his doorstep. Most people don't Jack told him.

Of course when they were upon the hill the two of them would work on the cairn for a couple of hours. It would soon be finished Jack thought as he stood back to admire their work.

It stood just over five feet high with its large round girth about five feet in diameter, tapering as it rose up from the ground. The rocks knitted together mirroring the stone walls that criss crossed over the moor behind. The stones locked together like the dykes around it to withstand the heavy winter weather. Just over halfway up the cairn a large flat surfaced stone was in place ready for the inscription that Grace would choose. It had taken three of them to get it in position.

"We shud get it finished tomorra night," Seth said, "just got tha top ta round off."

Jack felt proud that he had managed with the help of his friends to have built such a wonderful memorial for Jacob. Their involvement would mean that they too would appreciate it every time they were on the hill.

"Thanks' for all your help Seth," he said to his friend, "but if you don't mind I'd like to come up here alone tomorrow."

Seth nodded, he understood perfectly.

The following evening Jack rode up the hill on Elda with Becky leading the way. The three of them had done this hundreds of times before but Jack knew that this time it was different. This was going to be his last trek up the hill with his trusty companions.

He would be leaving the farm the following day. He hadn't told the others yet. He would tell Jed tomorrow after breakfast because he knew he wasn't strong enough to face a long emotional farewell with everyone.

It started to rain as he was traversing the hill checking on the sheep. Blast he thought, I should have brought an oilskin jacket. The heavens opened and he became quickly drenched. He made his way back to the cairn and brushing the rain out of his eyes began to lay the last of the stones to finish off the rounded cap of the cairn. It didn't take him long. As he stood back to admire his handiwork a beautiful rainbow appeared in the sky. It seemed to form a perfect arch above the cairn and a celebration to the finished monument.

"Wow!" Jack said out loud. He spread his arms wide and looking up to the sky he shouted at the top of his voice.

"Thank you! Thank you! Thank you!" he would treasure this moment forever.

The next morning after breakfast when every one had left to do their allotted tasks Jack joined Jed in the paddock.

"Jed, I've something to tell you." he said.

Jed turned to him, "Ya leaving today am I reet?" Jack nodded.

"I felt it in me bones. I knew when yon cairn wa dun tha wud be off an ya dunt want a big palaver wi lasses in tears, am I reet?" Jack nodded again.

"Reet lad get ya stuff int cart an I'll 'arness up Elda foh ya. I'll explain ta others later."

Jack was ready to leave.

“I’m sorry Jed,” he said, “I’m really going to miss you.”

“Nay lad, tha’s nowt to be sorry abart. It’s bin a pleasure ‘aving ya ‘ere. I’ve cum ta think of thee as me own an I cudn’t be more proud of ya. Grace an thee will be back loadsa times ta visit. We’ll probably be sick o sight of ya! Nar bugger off afore tuthers ‘now summat’s up!”

Jed watched the cart until it was out of sight and wiped the tears streaming down his face with the back of his sleeve.

“Ya daft bugger,” he said to himself as he made his way across the yard to tell the others.

Chapter Seventeen.

It was early evening when Jack pulled into the side of Ruth's cottage. As he opened the gate behind the stable he heard voices and laughter coming from the top of the garden. He would investigate once he had the cart safely in the paddock and Elda unharnessed. However, before he could begin Grace came running down the path and ran in to his outstretched arms and welcomed the bear hug he gave her.

"I can't believe it!" she said to him, "What a lovely surprise. We didn't think that you would be here so soon! In your last letter Jed had not got anyone to replace you. Oh it's lovely to see you!"

She gave him a hand to settle Elda. "I've missed you too", she told the horse as she rubbed its neck.

"Come on I'll introduce you to everybody!"

She took hold of his hand and led him up the path to the cottage. There was a trestle table set out with all manner of delectable treats and a group of people sitting around it chatting sociably. They stopped talking when Grace, her arm linked in Jack's, approached the table.

Ruth stood and gave him a hug and a peck on the cheek.

"Everyone, this is Jack!" Grace said, "Jack you've already met Joseph and this is his lovely wife Mary".

"Welcome back lad", Joseph said as he stood to shake Jack's hand. Mary gave him a big smile.

"This is Ronnie and his wife Edith who live in the cottage next door," as Grace continued the introductions.

Jack went to shake Ronnie's hand and he could now put faces to the head gardener and Grace's friend that she had written about in her letters.

"Pleased to meet you," Jack said, "thank you for making Grace feel so at home here."

"Nay lad," Edith said, "It's bin a pleasure. Our 'arry might join us later. He's just walkin' is young lady 'ome. She lives int village darn road."

Cum an sit thee sen darn 'ere lad", said an elderly man sitting on the garden bench, "Me names Noah an it's me that's bin teking stuff inta 'arrogate foh Ruth." Jack went and shook his hand and sat down beside him.

"Nah that ya 'ere wi us, me services won't be needed nar", he continued, "That's a reet shame as I've enjoyed me sen driving along wi a pretty young woman foh company". He gave Grace a toothless grin.

"Behave yourself!" Grace laughed at him, "now everybody help yourselves to something to eat while I make another brew for us all."

Jack asked the group in general if this gathering was a celebration of some kind. Ruth explained that it was Noah's ninetieth birthday and everyone had made something to bring along to celebrate.

Jack turned to Noah, "Many happy returns! I'm glad I arrived in time to share it with you."

"We've 'eard so much abart thee Jack" Noah told him, "that we feel we know you already."

Everyone nodded in agreement before helping themselves to the copious amount of food.

Ruth took a loaded plate over to Noah who began to tuck in to the contents with relish and in between mouthfuls he told Jack that he had been a coachman at the big House until he was forced to retire twelve years past. Now he only got out on the road when he was running an errand or two for one of his neighbours. He began to recount to Jack some of his many exploits and adventures that he had encountered during his travels.

Jack was in awe of this old man's knowledge and expertise. The two of them were still rapt in conversation an hour later when Harry arrived. He was a tall lanky youth with a shock of red hair, a few years older than Jack. Introductions were made and then after a few minutes Jack excused himself to check on Elda and fetch his belongings from the cart. Harry went with him to give him a hand and Noah hobbled slowly after them leaning heavily on his stick as he wanted to make acquaintance with Elda.

"I'm so relieved that Grace seems happy here," Jack told them both, "I was worried that she wouldn't settle but she looks really well. I can see why though, it's down to the friendliness of all of you. I can't thank you enough."

"Well it were touch an go for a while," Noah told him, "but we all played ar part. Keeping 'er busy an encouraging er ta try new things 'elped. 'Arry an 'is dad showed 'er ow to use a cold frame int veg plot an fetched cuttings fromt estate garden's for er ta plant. Edith swapped recipes wi 'er an went foh afternoon walks wi 'er rand the estate woods. Joseph asked 'er to mek a list o what needed fixin rand place", Noah laughed, "I think 'es lived ta regret that as she gi 'im a list to keep 'im busy til Christmas! Mary asked 'er if she would teach er ow ta mek er famous pies an I ad the pleasure of teking er ta 'arrogate an showing er the sights."

"We all luk after one anuther ere," Harry told Jack, "I suppose it stems from all of us werking at the big House at sum point or t'other. We're all int same boat so ta speak an it creates a bond between us I suppose."

"It's a bit like that at the farm," Jack said, "we were like one big family."

"Yeah jus like that." Harry agreed.

They left Noah nuzzling Elda and carried Jack's bags up to the cottage. It was getting dark now and someone had lit a couple of lanterns. The friends continued to chat happily surrounded by the golden light. Grace and Ruth excused themselves and took Jack in to the cottage. There was a ladder in the back hall that he had not seen before. It stretched up to an open hatch in the roof. The two women exchanged conspiratory looks.

"Up you go Jack!" Ruth said.

Jack gave them a puzzled look but climbed the ladder and by the soft light of a lantern placed on a small table he saw the bed with a colourful quilt similar to what he had at the farm. There was a sturdy chest of drawers, a bureau, two chairs and a bookcase full of books, all of which he recognised from the farm. The whole room had been white washed and a large new rug was placed on the scrubbed wooden floor. He looked down on the two smiling faces.

"Welcome home Jack!" they chorused.

That night as Jack was lying in his new bed gazing at the stars visible through the window in the sloping roof above his bed, he thought of what an emotional day it had been. He had been devastated leaving the farm and his friends that morning and had cried almost all the way to Pateley and acquired some funny looks from some of the people he passed.

He had journeyed in a solemn mood until mid-day when he stopped to buy a couple of pies from a roadside Inn and to get Elda a pale of water from the trough in the Inn's yard. As always Elda nuzzled him with thanks. He buried his face in to her neck and immediately felt better.

What was wrong with him? He had thought. He should take after Grace and accept the changes in his life. Likely there would be many more ups and downs in the future and he would just have to make the best of things as Grace had done.

Meeting Ruth and Grace's kind neighbours this evening proved to him that there was truth in the saying, as one door closes another door opens. He was still to discover what this particular open door held for him and with that thought he closed his eyes and snuggled down to sleep.

As usual he was up early the next morning. He had the range cleaned out and a fire burning in the grate before Grace and Ruth made an appearance to make breakfast.

The morning was spent clearing up from the night before and Grace catching up with all the news from the farm. Ruth sat spinning her wool whilst she listened to his stories. The latest news Grace had for him was that the tea cosies she had been making were accepted for sale at the shop in Harrogate. She laughed at the image of them gracing the tables of the more influential homes there. Grace stood and reached down her sketch book from the dresser for him to have a look at.

On the first couple of pages she had captured the likeness of Ruth's front garden to the smallest detail. Another was of the view leading down the paddock to the river at the bottom and the trees on the far bank were expertly mirrored in the clear water. It always amazed him how Grace could capture so much beauty in her sketches.

He turned over to the next page and his heart stopped. A lump formed in his throat and with a cracked voice he exclaimed this was absolutely amazing.

He tenderly looked down on a perfect likeness of Jacob standing on the top of the hill at the farm. He was staring in to the distance with Bob sitting faithfully at his side. Jack had witnessed this scene hundreds of times and to see it replicated so beautifully brought a tear to his eye.

He stood and gave Grace a long embrace. She smiled tenderly at him also moved by his strong reaction to her favourite sketch.

The next few pages showed sketches of Jack carrying out various jobs around the farm. He especially liked the one of him stood between the two horses as he led them across the yard.

Her last sketch was yet to be finished. It was of Noah sitting up on his cart sucking on his pipe. That was meant for his birthday Grace had said but it would have to be a little bit late. She went on to tell Jack that she was wanting to try her hand at water colours. She had bought everything she would need the last time she was in Harrogate. Grace wanted to capture the colour of the flowers in the garden while they were still at their best.

He was pleased to see how animated Grace was at the idea of trying something new. He told her how well she was looking now. Life was much easier and simpler nowadays and she had finally realised that she should have taken Jacob's advice when he wanted her to cut down on the pie business. It had been sheer stubbornness that had made her continue she confessed!

His afternoon was spent with old Noah. Grace had sent him with some food that had been left over from the gathering the night before. Noah kept him talking about the old times but Jack didn't mind as he found it all so interesting. They swapped horse related stories and Jack was mesmerised by the old man's knowledge and listened with rapt attention.

Whilst the three of them were having their meal that evening Jack announced that he would have to start looking for a job. He thought that he would take Elda around some of the neighbouring farms the following day to see if any were taking on hands.

Grace and Ruth exchanged one of their looks that Jack had now come to recognise that meant they had been conspiring together.

There's no rush Grace had said as she rose from the table. She opened the drawer of the dresser and removed an envelope and handed it to him. His name was printed on the envelope with Grace's neat hand writing. The two women watched his reaction as with a puzzled look he opened the envelope.

He couldn't believe it! There sitting in his hand was a return train ticket to Blackpool and three silver florins. He was speechless. He looked at the two of them open mouthed. They were grinning back at him and Grace explained that they had decided a while back that when he eventually joined them over here they wanted him to take some time to himself and not rush in to the first job that came along. They thought the perfect solution was for him to spend some time with his friends over the summer and to have some fun.

"You deserve this Jack for all you've been through over the last few months. It's our thank you to you for all you have done recently for us and for the farm." Grace said.

"Thank you so much!" Jack told them, "This is a wonderful surprise," he smiled, "I can't wait to see Joshua and Jimmy's faces when I turn up!"

Chapter Eighteen.

Two days later Jack thought he was going to burst with excitement. The train that he had boarded early that morning was to arrive in Blackpool within the next few minutes.

He had shared the compartment with a family with two young children who were now jumping up and down at the window waiting for their first sight of the sea. He felt like joining them and he couldn't ever remember feeling as thrilled as this before!

The train pulled in to the station and there was a rush of bodies spilling from the train and pouring down the platform. He joined in with them and was carried along in the torrent of people streaming from the open doors.

He left the Station and there it was across the road, the sea!

A vast expanse of water rolling on to the shore in front of him. He slowly made his way across the road to the railings that divided the beach below from the promenade where he stood. He looked upon the scene with wonder. The undulating pulse of the waves rolling landward before cresting and rippling to shore in gentle rhythmic vibrations. He had always thought of the sea as being blue in colour but its actual greyness did not take away from its splendour.

He watched as children ran in and out of the waves crying with glee as the sea almost caught up with them. Adults walked hand in hand bare footed in the shallows and dogs dived fearlessly in to the waves to retrieve sticks. As he breathed in the salty air he thought he could just stay there the whole day watching the scene before him. He was tempted to pay for the hire of one of the colourful striped chairs that adorned the beach like confetti but instead, eager to find his friends, he joined the throng of people making their way down the promenade.

Everyone seemed to be in good spirits, groups of mill workers, factory hands, miners, shop workers and a host of other professions enjoying their new found freedom. It seemed to Jack that he was surrounded by the whole of humanity. Even the busiest market days in Pateley were nothing like this.

He passed by numerous stalls selling all manner of souvenirs and foodstuffs and he couldn't resist the smell of the fried dough and purchased two slices dipped in sugar. He basked in the sweet taste sensation as he continued on his way to find his friends.

Eventually he reached the Fairground. A mass of colourful tents of all shapes and sizes with billboards advertising the delights within. He meandered between the stalls, some selling food but mostly there were a variety of coconut shy's, hoopla stalls, rifle ranges, tombola booths, puppet theatres, boxing rings and photograph booths. There were horse drawn roundabouts and boat swings and clowns and tall men on stilts interweaving amongst the crowd selling balloons to excited children, their eyes wide with wonder.

He wondered how on earth he could find his friends in this maze of confusion but just as he had lost hope of ever finding them he heard a familiar voice shouting out in to the crowds to.

"Come an have ago, everyone a winner!"

Jack knew it was Jimmy calling and he smiled as he approached the booth that had all kinds of toys on display. Each toy had a number next to it and the object of the game was to pick a number from a cloth bag that Jimmy was offering to the people passing by. They would retrieve a numbered wooden disc and their prize would be whatever toy corresponded with that number.

Jimmy was reaching over the counter to allow a small boy to reach in to the bag and as he looked up he caught sight of Jack standing grinning at him. He looked quickly away ignoring Jack.

He handed the boy his prize of a peg soldier then turned and said something to the old man who sat smoking at the back of the booth. The man scowled and spat on the ground.

Jimmy left through the side door of the booth and once out of sight of the man within he beckoned Jack to join him. Jack couldn't understand what was going on as his friend seemed dismayed at his arrival.

“What are you doing here?” Jimmy said to him as he indicated for Jack to follow him. He led Jack to the back of several large tents. Jimmy opened the door flap of one of the tents and ushered Jack inside.

“I’ve come to join you and Joshua!” Jack told him, “I’m hoping to get a job with you and Joshua until the end of the season.”

“No. No. No!” said Jimmy distressingly, “You can’t do that Jack. You’ve no idea what it’s like here! I don’t have time to go in to details but me and Joshua are planning to up sticks and leave shortly but we have to be careful. Anyone caught trying to leave are given a good beating to deter others from doing the same. We’ve witnessed it first hand when a lad that shared our tent had his face smashed in with a cricket bat and his arm broken. Bates has his spies everywhere. We can’t trust anyone. We had all our money stolen on the first night we were here. Someone crept in to the tent in the middle of the night and took the lot, not just ours but other lads as well. We’re worked eighteen to nineteen hours a day every day. It’s relentless and unfortunately it’s having a bad effect on Joshua. He was never as strong as the two of us and he’s throwing up nearly every night and having dizzy spells. He’s too weak now to be able to hitch back home and if he doesn’t turn up for work he’ll be thrown out over the fence in the middle of the night and left to his own devices. We’ve seen that happen a couple of times already. This place is all locked up tight at night and Bates’s men patrol with dogs just to make sure no one can get in or do a runner. In two days’ time Joshua and I are due to work a spell outside on one of the booths selling cheap souvenirs next to the wax works. That's our only chance of getting out of here together and having a bit of breathing space before someone raises the alarm."

Jack was shocked at his friend's revelation. "I want to help somehow Jimmy," he said.

"How?" Jimmy answered.

"For a start," Jack said as he reached in to his pocket and handed the return ticket to Jimmy.

"Give this to Joshua, if he's thrown out before you plan to leave this will get him to Harrogate and from there he can make his way to Ruth's place."

Jack quickly jotted down her address on a piece of paper taken from his diary.

"It's about six or seven miles from the station but there's plenty of traffic on that road and he should easily get a lift. Grace and Ruth will look after him once he gets there."

Jimmy stuffed the ticket and the address down to the bottom of his sock for safe keeping.

"I'll meet you on Monday by the souvenir booth Jimmy. If Joshua is still with you we'll get him on a train then and the two of us can hitch back together. What time will be best to meet?"

"Late morning," said Jimmy. He took a deep breath, "You've no idea what a relief it is now I know Joshua can get away from all of this. I've been so scared that he wasn't going to make it and of course I couldn't leave him here. What are you going to do in the meantime Jack?" he asked.

"I've no idea but I'll think of something," Jack answered him.

"I'd better get back to the booth or old Bart will be thinking I've taken too long to go to the privy." He gave Jack a big hug. "Thank the Lord for you Jack!" he said as he rushed out the door.

Jack's head was full of confusion as he made his way through the revelling crowd. The euphoria he felt earlier totally drained as reality kicked in. He no longer gazed around with wonder but realised it was all an elaborate illusion. He wanted to get as far away as possible from the sham of the fairground. As he neared the exit gate he got a glimpse of Joshua. He watched his friend from a distance and he was shocked by the change he saw in him. Joshua had never been heavy but now he was just skin and bone and his face was as white as a sheet, his sunken eyes rimmed with dark shadows. He looked really ill. He was half heartedly giving out flyers outside the circus tent and lethargically moved from one side of the large tent to the other. Jack understood why Jimmy was so worried.

Back on the sea front Jack found a shelter to sit in and gather his thoughts. He watched the families enjoying the simple treats of paddling in the sea, collecting sea shells or building sand castles. He took a couple of deep breaths of the salty air to calm himself down and he felt better for it.

He needed a plan. He would find somewhere cheap to stay for the next few nights so he crossed the busy road thronged with carts and went to investigate the numerous lodging houses that were situated in the back streets of Blackpool.

He finally found one that looked a little more run down than the rest. He entered the scuffed door to ask the cost for two nights stay. There didn't seem to be anyone about.

"Hello, hello!" he called but nobody came to answer.

He ventured down the dark hallway and opened a door to a kitchen. The doors were hanging off of several cupboards, the sink was cracked and plaster was hanging from the ceiling. This was obviously not lived in and empty he thought and was just about to retreat back down the hallway when the outside door opened and a young couple dressed in work clothes entered the room. They looked at him in surprise.

"I'm sorry" said Jack, "I did shout out but you were obviously busy outside. I'm looking for somewhere to stay for a couple of nights and didn't realise that you weren't open."

"That's alright", the young man said, "but you'll be lucky to get anywhere to stay this weekend, it's the

Manchester holiday week and everywhere will be chock o block."

They both noticed Jack's crest fallen face, "So sorry to disturb you," Jack said and turned to leave.

"Not so fast!" the young woman stopped him, "If you are willing to help out here for a few hours each day we've got a room upstairs that might suit you. That'll be alright won't it Ron?"

"Aye if the lads wants", Ron answered her.

Jack couldn't believe his luck, "Thank you that'll be grand, " he answered gratefully.

"I'm Sally and I'm just about to get kettle on so sit yourself down."

Ron explained to Jack that Sally had been born and brought up in Blackpool but because of his job as a mason and having to travel where the work was, they had not lived here for several years. Sally had inherited the house from her great aunt who Sally had helped to nurse when she became ill and unable to look after herself. That had been five years ago and the house had stood empty until last month when they had eventually saved up enough money to start renovations. They hoped to get the place in shape again to catch the last few months of the season and would be really glad of any help Jack could give them.

Sally took Jack up a dark stairway to show him his room. He entered a spacious, bright and nicely furnished room. It was spotlessly clean but smelled a little of fresh paint. This is lovely he told her.

"We've already finished all of the six guest rooms," she told him, "and we live in the two rooms in the attic space. We started renovating from the top and have worked our way down to the ground floor."

"This room is more than perfect for me," Jack reassured her. "I'll do all I can to give you a hand as I am so grateful for helping me out."

"We'll talk about that later I have to get back to give Ron a hand in the back yard, he's just finishing off some new cupboard doors for the kitchen. You get settled in and we'll see you later."

Jack left his knapsack in his room then left the house to return to the station where he made a couple of notes of train times. He then strolled down the street on the sea front and was pleased to discover that the waxworks were only a ten minute walk from the station. All he had to do now was bide his time until Monday morning.

When he returned to the house he found Ron removing all the old cupboard doors in the kitchen and Sally was stirring a pot of stew on the range. She turned to Jack with a smile.

"I wasn't sure if you wanted to eat with us Jack", she said, "or if you would prefer to eat out. You're quite welcome to join us but I warn you that it's just plain fare or cold cuts as I don't always have the time to cook."

"I'd love to join you," Jack said, "but only if you let me pay my way."

"No, no," said Ron, "it's more useful to us if you work for your board. Our deadline to get finished is getting shorter and the list of jobs is getting longer, but we appreciate your offer none the less."

"Right then!" said Jack, rolling up his sleeves, "let's get these cupboards sorted."

The two men worked well together and had all the new doors attached to the cupboards in no time.

"What a difference it has made already," Sally said as she dished up the stew.

She told Jack that her father's friend Frank was coming in the morning to replace the sink and that Ron's pals were coming at the end of the week to fix the ceiling and then the whole of the kitchen could be painted.

"Aye", Ron said, "and they're going to put scaffolding up so we can get all the outside paintwork and pointing done. Hopefully by the end of next weekend all the outside will be looking posh! Tomorrow I want to finish the stairs and the entrance hall." Ron told them.

"In that case I'll make a start in the front dining room. My mum has already got the curtains finished for in there and dad has almost finished the three tables he is making for us." She explained to Jack that her father was a carpenter and was happy to help out.

Jack enjoyed listening to the two of them enthusiastically making their plans. Although he was a stranger to them both he felt very relaxed in their company.

"Hello," he interrupted them, "and what would you like me to do?" They both laughed. "I'm a dab hand with a paint brush, why don't I finish off the stairs and hallway while you two paint the dining room? Together you'll get it done in half the time."

"That could take you most of the day," Sally said, "surely you want some time to discover the delights that Blackpool has to offer!"

"Oh I'll probably go out for a couple of walks down the front, but to be honest, I'm not that keen on all the crowds. I was supposed to be meeting a couple of my pals here but they couldn't make it at the last minute. So here I am at a loose end for a couple of days."

"Lucky for us," said Ron, "It's funny how life turns out sometimes."

Jack was up at first light the next morning. He slipped quietly from the house and made his way to the end of the road to the sea front. The sight of the great expanse of water still gave him a thrill. He made his way down to the waters edge and removed his shoes and socks and rolled up his trousers. He gasped as the first ice cold wave rolled over his feet and laughed as the sand rippled through his toes. He paddled along in the shallows enjoying the sensation of the gentle pull of the tide. It was like walking on a living, breathing magic carpet he thought and was glad that he was alone to indulge himself in this new experience. He felt so calm and yet invigorated at the same time and lost in another world.

Abruptly he was shocked back to reality as a large black dog bounded in to the waves splashing up the cold water which soaked Jack's trousers, its apologetic owner shouting at the dog who took no notice whatsoever! Jack laughingly waved the irate owners' apologies away! After all, the dog was only keen to get in the water and who could blame it.

Back at the house Sally and Ron were just sitting down to a bowl of porridge when Jack joined them. They laughed as Jack related his encounter with the dog, all the more amusing especially when Jack added slight embellishments to the story. After breakfast the three of them set to work as planned.

It was late morning and already Jack had painted half way down the stairs and it was looking much brighter already. Ron and Sally were also making good progress in the dining room. Suddenly the front door burst open and a well built man dressed in overalls entered the hall. On seeing Jack he looked a bit puzzled.

"How do!" he said, "I'm Frank, I've come to replace the sink in the kitchen".

Jack introduced himself and told Frank that he was just helping out for a couple of days. On hearing men's voices

Sally appeared in the hall saving Jack from any further explanation.

"Sorry I'm a bit late", Frank said to her, "Got caught up down at our Sam's at the Fairground. He's been having problems with a leak on one of the pumps. It's all kicking off down there this morning!"

"Come and tell us all about it over a cuppa," Sally said to him, "I was just going to put the kettle on anyway." She looked up at Jack. "You're doing a great job and this looks better already, come and join us you'll be ready for a brew by now, I know I am."

Ron joined them in the kitchen a few minutes later and asked Frank what was going on down at the fair. Jack's heart missed a beat, he hoped it didn't involve his friends.

Frank, who loved to relate the latest gossip and news, told them that while he was down there fixing the leak, a massive trailer from one of the big travelling circuses had pulled up. It had come to collect the elephant and its keeper. It was the second attraction Bates had lost in as many weeks. The girl with the dancing horses was the first to go and also the father of the young lassie who had the dancing dogs was seen in negotiations with the chaps that had come to pick up the elephant. Bates was furious by all accounts. It looked like there was some truth in the rumour that he hadn't been paying the acts fairly for some time. Who would blame them for going elsewhere.

Our Sam also has it on good authority that Bates won't get the lease on the ground renewed at the end of this season. The council has had too many complaints from the locals about his ruffians beating up folk. There was that incident that was reported in the local paper about the chap that wanted his money back and got beaten to an inch of his life in full view of the women and children!

Sam said he wouldn't be surprised if that body of the young lad that was found on the beach last month had something to do with Bates and his gang. Trouble is, it reflects badly on all of the other fairground folk as well. According to Sam they can't wait to get rid of Bates with his bad crowd and shady dealings and apparently the fair folk have submitted their own plan to the council to take over the lease of the ground. They propose to build a boating lake and gardens with a miniature railway running around the perimeter.

"If that comes off," Sally said, "It will be a big boom for the area. It's a shame that Bates turned out to be such a rogue. I remember though when he first came everyone, including the fair folk, thought that his circus and side shows would also benefit the area."

"He got too greedy that's the problem when he decided to set up his own stalls and booths in competition with the fair folk and then couldn't get the local lads to work for him because of the way they were treated. I feel sorry for the poor buggers that he recruits from the country. Lambs to the slaughter every one of them. I heard that if they manage to make it to the end of the season he scarpers without paying them a penny piece! Well I'm glad to hear he's getting his come uppance at long last. Well I had better get your sink in. Thanks for the cuppa lass."

Jack returned to painting the stairs. He felt so angry listening to Frank and how his friends had been duped by Bates. It took him back to his own childhood when he and Tom had been taken by the Gooding gang. He knew his friends were now being treated the same way that he and Tom had been and he wished there were some way he could get revenge on his friends' behalf. He was glad though that the people running the fair were determined to get rid of Bates and hoped that their plans worked out. He wondered if Jimmy and Joshua were fully aware of what was going on but it was unlikely he thought.

By mid afternoon he had finished all of the painting and was cleaning the fanlight windows above the hallway doors. The main front door had a mosaic of coloured glass above the door with a matching central panel to the door itself. It had cleaned up beautifully with the afternoon sun casting colourful shadows on the newly painted white walls within. Sally was over the moon when she saw this effect.

"You should probably take a break now Jack," she told him, "you've done more than enough today."

"I'll probably go for a walk." he said.

She grinned at him saying, "I can't thank you enough Jack, you've no idea what a difference it makes having you help out!"

“That’s alright one good turn deserves another,” he told her.

Jack made his way along the beach towards the fairground. He wanted to make sure that his friends were still alright. He wasn’t going to risk approaching them but if he could just see them at a distance it would put his mind to rest.

The streets and fairground were busier than ever. He made his way around the stalls and found that Jimmy was in the same booth as before with the old man still keeping watch on the proceedings.

He made his way to the circus tent to find a notice pinned to the entrance of the tent informing the public that the evenings performance was cancelled. It seemed Frank was right after all and maybe more of Bates’s performers had jumped ship.

He stood for a while watching the kiddies riding on wooden horses on a small roundabout, each child with a big grin on their face. Since listening to Frank that morning he’d revised is opinion of fairgrounds. The excitement and happiness on the faces of the hard-working people passing by him was testament alone for a need for such places. It was bad luck that his friends had become involved with Bates.

As he made his way back to the house he noticed a shop selling fried fish. On impulse he entered and bought three pieces so he could treat Sally and Ron.

When he got back to the house he put the kettle on the range and buttered some bread. He went to see how they were getting on in the dining room.

He couldn't believe how much work they had achieved. The walls and the ceiling in the room were finished and the light cream colour chosen made the room look twice as big as before. Sally had polished up the fireplace and its surround. The large dining table that sat in splendour in the bay window also glistened with polish. Ron was just finishing painting the wood work.

Sally looked up, "I was just about to make something for tea," she said to him.

He laughed, "I've beaten you to it!" he said, "come on I've got us some fried fish, it's getting cold."

Late morning the next day Sally's mum and dad arrived to lend a hand. Mother and daughter worked on the finishing touches to the dining room and the men started painting the sitting room. Jack was delegated to working outside at the front of the house.

He cleared the overgrowth in the small, enclosed garden and discovered the most beautiful paving underneath. It was a blue grey in colour with white veins marbled through it. Once he'd brushed and rinsed it down it looked really petty. He painted the front door and the iron railings that surrounded the area a rich blue colour and the overall effect was beautiful. The house was fast becoming the prettiest on the street.

Jack enjoyed working outside. He could hear the sea as the waves rolled in to shore, the constant rhythm was hypnotic and lost in his own thoughts he was finished in no time.

When the five of them were sitting having their tea of fish pie and veg that Sally's mum had brought with her, Sally's dad asked Sally if they had decided on a name yet. He was going to make a wooden plaque for them to hang above the door and wanted to get started on it.

"Yes!" said Sally, "Ron and I discussed it last night and actually it was down to Jack really that we came up with the idea."

Jack looked puzzled and Sally laughed at him, "It was the effect of the rays from the sun shining through the clean fanlight window yesterday Jack. Do you remember?" Aye he nodded.

"Well, it inspired us to come up with the name of "Rainbows End," she told them and they all agreed it was a good choice.

There wasn't much more he could help with now so he went for another wander on the beach. He paddled in the shallows, lost in his own world as usual.

Would he change his life in the country for this he thought to himself as his mind drifted to the wind-swept moorland, the sound of the stream rushing down the hill, the calls of the birds and the bleating of the sheep. No, it was in the country where his heart belonged. He suddenly felt a wave of homesickness and he was glad that he was leaving in the morning. Despite the dilemma of his friends he had enjoyed his time with Ron and Sally but he couldn't wait to be on his way from Blackpool.

He turned and began retracing his steps along the shore and watched behind him as the sea removed any trace of his footsteps in the sand, cleansing the beach of any trace of mankind. He caught sight of something shining amongst the damp sand. It was a silver coin. A half crown. That was lucky he thought as he placed it in his pocket. A new plan started to formulate in his head and he began to hurry. He would have to make a quick visit to the station before he went back to the house.

Chapter Nineteen.

Jack had a little time to kill before he had to meet his friends at the booth where they should both be working.

He'd left the house straight after breakfast as he didn't want to hold Ron and Sally up from their work. He made his farewells promising them that he would be back one day and would look forward to seeing "Rainbow's End" in all its glory. They told him that they would love to see him again and he would be their guest of honour with not a paintbrush insight!

He strolled along the shore but couldn't settle his mind. He felt restless with nagging doubts that something was going to go wrong with their plans. He knew that he wouldn't rest until he joined Jimmy and Joshua and they were safely away from Blackpool.

The town was less crowded this morning as most of the holiday makers were on their way home after the holiday weekend. He watched as shopkeepers took advantage of the lull to clean their windows and sweep the pavements outside before the next onslaught of revellers arrived.

He found a seat sheltered from the breeze and taking a book from his knapsack he tried to settle down to read. An hour later Jack made his way slowly down the street. He noticed that the hatch was raised on the souvenir booth but it appeared to be empty.

Oh no, he didn't know what to do. His mind was racing and then Joshua who had been kneeling down in the booth to open a box full of souvenirs stood up in view. Jack breathed a sigh of relief. He crossed the road to join his friend and stood at the side door of the booth. Joshua gave him a tired smile and although he was pleased to see Jack he was very agitated.

"Jimmy's had to go work elsewhere because the few local lads that worked for Bates walked out yesterday. It's left Bates's so short of staff that the rest of us aren't able to double up. I don't know where Jimmy has been put to work as everything changed at the last minute. At least I won't have one of the Bates's men checking on me every hour or so to take the money as they've been put to work on the stalls as well."

"Right Joshua!" said Jack, "let's get you safely on the train and I promise to find Jimmy. Have you got the ticket?" Joshua nodded and went to close the hatch at the front of the booth.

Jack noticed an open drawer under the counter containing several coins and without thinking he quickly snatched a handful and stuffed them in his pocket. What had he just done? He wasn't thinking straight but it was too late to put them back now as Joshua had finished locking up and was waiting for instructions from Jack. He was shaking from what he had just done but managed to pull himself together for Joshua's sake.

"Right, let's get you to the station, it's only a ten-minute walk and the train leaves in fifteen minutes."

The boys hurried down the street but Joshua had to stop a couple of times to get his breath back and at one point had to stop to vomit in the gutter. Jack was more worried than ever about his friend's health and knew he had to get him on the train safely at all costs.

They were just about to enter the station when they heard a loud yell behind them! They both froze.

Jack slowly turned round in trepidation but was flooded with relief when he saw Jimmy sprinting towards them.

"There isn't time for explanations." Jack said and told them both to quickly get on the train standing on platform two, "I'll join you in a minute!"

With only seconds to spare Jack boarded the carriage his friends occupied, the guard blew his whistle and the train slowly pulled out of the station. The friends began to laugh hysterically with relief.

"Explain yourself!" Jimmy said to Jack as the train chugged along leaving the outskirts of the town behind.

Jack told them that he had come up with the idea the day before when he found some money on the beach. He had checked at the station and discovered that he had enough money to pay for two single tickets for himself and Jimmy that would get them a good part of the way home and meant that the three of them would instantly be away from the clutches of Bate's thugs.

Jimmy patted him on the back and said, "Good thinking Jack you were always the brainy one out of the three of us!"

Jack was too ashamed to tell them that some of the money he had stolen from the booth had got himself and Jimmy a little further down the track than he initially had planned.

Joshua smiled at him with thanks and lay down on the seat and was instantly asleep. Jack updated Jimmy on what he had been doing the last couple of days and what he had heard from Frank regarding Bates.

Jimmy told Jack that they knew something was going on when the circus performances had been cancelled. He had heard that a couple more acts had left and then this morning when the local lads had not turned in for work he knew that something was seriously wrong. He had been put to work on the hoopla stall that was luckily by the exit gate. When he thought the coast was clear he legged it for all he was worth. It was lucky that Joshua was still put in the booth on the street or he wouldn't have managed to make his escape.

Jack understood and told Jimmy it had taken Joshua all of his strength to manage the short distance to the station. Jimmy nodded and said Joshua had really struggled to get through the work the day before and he had been so worried about him. He continued to tell Jack how bad it had been from their very first day. They and the lads that had been recruited from other area's were called the goons. We had the dirtiest jobs and the longest hours to work. The worst job was emptying the portable lavvies in to the latrines at the back of the site.

The food they got was always cold and it was the same lumpy gruel for breakfast every day with thin watery broth and a slice of stale bread at dinner time and whatever was left over from the stalls the day before at tea time.

Three of the lads from their tent had got beaten up and thrown out and two became ill and were chucked out in the middle of the night. He and Joshua had intended to make a run for it earlier but when Joshua became ill everything changed. There only hope was to go when they were working together up the street. We thought Joshua could hide somewhere while I got help but to be honest it was too risky.

The train travelled on and they nodded off for a while waking up as the train entered a big station at Lancaster.

Joshua was still sleeping. Jack nudged him to wake up. He sat up with a start with a frightened look on his face but then smiled when he recognised his friends sitting opposite. Jack told him that he and Jimmy would have to leave him once they reached a small town called Bentham which was about an hour away at a guess. Joshua was to stay on the train until it reached Skipton then he would have about an hour to wait for the train to Harrogate. He reached in to his pocket and pulled out the last silver florin and gave it to Joshua.

"Get yourself something to eat and drink at Skipton, there's a lady selling pies just outside the station on the street. Once you get to Harrogate there will be a row of hackney cabs outside the station and you will have enough left to get yourself to Ruth's. Have you got the address?"

Joshua nodded, "That's brilliant Jack. I thought I had to hitch a lift to Ruth's."

"Change of plan, the sooner you get to Ruth's and have the two of them look after you the better, the hitching will be left to me and Jimmy here. We'll get back as soon as we can and then we can decide when to get you home."

Joshua's eyes filled with tears, "Thank you so much Jack. I just feel so ill and I don't know what's wrong with me, I just feel so weak and nauseous all of the time. I know I'm a liability to you both and I feel so useless."

"Don't ever say that again," Jack said to him, "you would do the same for us in a heartbeat. Just get to Ruth's safely."

The boys got off the train in a small pretty station.

"Where to now Jack?," Jimmy asked.

"I don't think we are that far from the main road to Skipton." Jack answered.

They walked up a hill to the junction of the road. A Public house stood on the corner and at the other side of the road was a butcher's shop with a window display of delicious looking pies amongst many cuts of meat. Jack rooted in his pocket for the few pennies he had left.

Two pies and a bottle of milk to share later the boys set off on their journey. Their first lift was with a farmer who had just bought several sheep from the Mart in Bentham and they were occupying the back of the cart as he made his way home to Settle. The bleating of the sheep in the back of the cart limited any chatting to the farmer and both boys were glad when he dropped them off at the side of the road. They were now well on their way to Skipton.

Their next lift took them to the outskirts of Skipton and the boys decided to split up there. Jimmy would take the road to Grassington and once he got there he could walk the six or so miles to his home village if need be. Jack would take the Harrogate road. Once he got to Harrogate he too could walk the distance to Ruth's if he had to.

Jimmy said he would call in to the shop and let Joshua's parents know what had happened and that Jack would bring him home as soon as he could.

Before going their separate ways they said their farewells, shook hands and wished each other luck.

Jacks first lift got him about half way to Harrogate. It was from a farmer and his wife returning home from Skipton market. They were a jolly couple and kept him amused with stories about their family. They wished him well as they dropped him by the side of the road. It was a while before he got the next lift and he had to cover several miles on foot before a cart carrying sacks of wool pulled over and the driver offered him a lift. Jack's luck was in. The haulier was staying overnight at his cousins who lived in the village just up the road from Ruth's cottage. He did this trip regularly and he knew Ruth's cottage well, it's the one with the pretty garden he said to Jack and the two of them chatted pleasantly most of the way.

After listening to the haulier's tales of being on the road Jack thought he wouldn't mind a similar job himself for a change.

It was late at night by the time Jack was eventually dropped off at Ruth's and he was surprised to see a light still burning in the window. He thanked the haulier for the lift and wished him well on his travels.

He entered the kitchen and Grace and Ruth, both in their nightdresses, ran to him and threw their arms around him. They had been so worried imagining all sorts of disasters that might have befallen him. The women fussed round him making him hot milk and warm buttered toast. They had just sat down by the fireside to hear Jack's story when the outside door opened and Noah popped his head around the door.

"Cudna get a wink o sleep till I knew lad were back safe. I 'eard cart pull up an thought I'd mek sure," he told them.

"Come in Noah," said Ruth as she poured more milk in to the pan. Jack told them all what had happened while they sat having their late supper the women tutting and shaking their heads as Jack narrated the story.

"Sarns as if thee 'ad a lucky escape lad," Noah commented, "main thing is thee is back nar, safe an sound."

He stood, "I'll wish thee all gud neet or is it gud mornin,'" he hobbled to the door, "Nay I nearly forgot, young Sid came ta see me this fore noon an e ses tha's a job goin' darn at big 'ouse for a coachman. I'd get me sen darn there tommora lad if thee's interested like. Ask foh Adam Jenkins, tell 'im old Noah sent thee." He left closing the door quietly behind him.

"What do you think Jack?", Grace asked him.

"It's worth a try," Jack said, "but I was planning on taking Joshua back home tomorrow."

"The lads in no fit state to travel yet," Grace said, "We got the shock of our lives when we saw him standing at our door leaning on the arm of the cab driver. He could barely stand poor love and the driver told us that he had stopped twice for the poor lad to wretch at the side of the road. We got him in and gave him a hot drink but he wouldn't take anything to eat. He tried to tell us what had happened but he wasn't making much sense and we were so worried that we got Noah to go to the village for the Doctor. The poor lad could hardly stay awake and he kept nodding off mid-sentence. We managed to get him undressed and in to one of your nightshirts then made him comfortable in my bed. When the Doctor arrived and examined him he told us that Joshua was severely malnourished and dehydrated and was suffering from a malady of the stomach and probably exhaustion. He left instructions for us to give him a drink of warm water every two hours for the rest of the day and through the night. Tomorrow we can give him small amounts of nourishing broth and if he tolerates that without vomiting, to give him coddled eggs or mashed potato with chicken stock and we've to let him sleep as much as possible. The Doctor was confident that with the prescribed care he should make a full recovery over time."

Jack was relieved to hear this. Ruth had put on the kettle to warm more water for Joshua.

"You can take it through for him Jack, he'll be pleased to see that you are safely back home."

"I'll stay up through the night to see to him, Grace are you in my bed?" Jack said.

She laughed out loud! "Nay Jack I might manage to scale the ladder but I don't think I'd be able to get back down! No, I'm in with Ruth. It won't be the first time we've had to share a bed, it'll take us back to being young girls again won't it Ruth?"

Ruth laughed and nodded her head in agreement, "That it will!" she said.

Jack gave Joshua a warm drink of water holding the mug for him as Grace had instructed. Joshua smiled feebly at him and then turned over and fell asleep again. This was how he was all through the night until Jack entered the room early in the morning. The first rays of daylight illuminated the bedroom and Joshua was already awake. He managed to sit up and take the mug from Jack.

"How are you feeling?" Jack asked him.

"My headache is not as bad and I feel a little hungry. It was a nightmare yesterday after you left. I fell asleep again and the guard on the train woke me up in Skipton thank goodness otherwise I would have ended up back in Blackpool!"

"Oh no!" Jack gasped he hadn't thought of that.

Joshua continued, "I managed to get a drink of water from the tap in the station but didn't want anything to eat. Then the headache started, it was really bad. The sickness got worse and my vision kept blurring. I felt dizzy when I stood up so I just sat on a bench with my head in my hands waiting for the Harrogate train to arrive. Once I was on the train I fell asleep again for a while but then woke up and began to wretch to the horror of the two ladies that shared my carriage. I had to stand with my head out of the window clutching on to the frame for the rest of the journey. I don't know how I got in the hackney carriage. I think the two ladies may have escorted me there. The only thing I do remember is giving your note to the driver and the next thing I was here with Ruth and Grace."

Joshua wanted to know how Jack and Jimmy had got on but Jack told him to try to go back to sleep and he would tell him later.

When Jack returned to the kitchen he could hear Grace and Ruth getting ready to rise so he put on the kettle and began to make some toast for them. Grace insisted that he went to lie down for a while because he looked shattered and she and Ruth would take care of Joshua.

Jack didn't think that he would get to sleep, he was tired but so much was going through his head. So many things could have gone wrong yesterday and he had been naïve to think that he had sorted everything out. Joshua had clearly been more ill than he and Jimmy realised and they shouldn't have left him alone but what else could they have done.

He pictured himself stealing the money from the booth and thought he should have taken the lot instead of being so timid then he would have had enough for the three of them to stay together. He dismissed this thought immediately because he felt so guilty as it was and deeply regretted his actions but if he had not acted on his impulse he would not have had the money for Joshua to get a cab and then Joshua would not have made it to Ruth's and then what would have happened to him? He was so confused but eventually fell in to a deep sleep.

Joshua improved gradually over the next few days, enough to accompany Grace on short walks down by the river. Other times he would sit in the garden chatting to

Noah or one of the other neighbours. The colour was slowly returning to his face and he was ravenously devouring all the good home cooked food that Grace and Ruth placed before him.

Jack applied for and was offered the job as coachman and would start at the end of the following week. He was thrilled!

There were so many horses of all sizes and pedigrees for him to get to know and care for and he was relishing the task. Part of his duties were to keep all of the different types of carriages, as well as the two coaches, in pristine condition. He would work on a shift pattern with the other six coachmen as two of them had to be available at any given time day or night in case they were required to transport members of the family at any given time. He would be trained to drive a team of horses and best of all, for the first time in his life, he would be earning a wage! He couldn't believe his luck.

In celebration the neighbours had planned another evening together and Sid, who Jack was to be teamed with, was also invited. Sid was not a young lad as Noah had described to him but a man in his forties with lots of experience. Jack supposed that anyone under seventy would seem young to Noah!

Grace had written to Joshua's parents informing them that they planned to take him home on the Tuesday of the following week. This would give Jack plenty of time to get back before starting his new job. Grace and Ruth had decided to accompany the boys on the journey as Bridget from the farm had written to Grace to let her know that the stonemason had completed the engraving on Jacob's stone for the cairn. Grace thought it was the perfect opportunity for Ruth and herself to visit the farm and go up the hill to see the memorial for Jacob. She had written back to Bridget to let her know when to expect them.

There was an air of excitement as Jack with Joshua sitting beside him flicked the reins to set Elda off on their journey to the farm. Grace and Ruth were comfortably sitting in the back of the cart on a bench that Joseph had erected for them. Noah and Edith waved them off and wished them a safe and speedy journey.

The women chatted and giggled like young girls and called out greetings to passers-by. Both of them had been busy the day before baking and making all sorts of savoury treats to take to the farm so they wouldn't be arriving empty handed!

It was a lovely sunny day with just a hint of breeze that made the journey quite pleasant. They stopped for a while and had a picnic at the side of the river allowing Elda to have a rest and quench her thirst. They seemed to reach Pateley in no time at all but in fact had been travelling for almost five hours. As they reached the top of the hill leading out of Pateley and the wildness of the moors came in sight Grace had an overwhelming feeling of joy. She was coming home. Unbeknown to her, both boys were experiencing similar emotions and they were eager to cover the last few miles to their destination.

As the cart pulled on to the village green Joshua's parents and brother came running out of the shop to greet them. Joshua jumped from the cart and could not hold back the tears of joy as he ran in to their arms. They could not thank Jack, Grace and Ruth enough for getting their son safely back to them. Jimmy had told them everything of the nightmare situation that they had endured for so long. They were so relieved to have their son back safely and they told Jack that Jimmy had got his old job back at the Inn and would pop up to the farm later to see him.

Chapter Twenty.

A welcoming party also greeted them at the farm.

Jed, Nell, Bridget, Michael and Seth stood cheering at their approach. However, the most enthusiastic welcome was from Becky who was so excited her tail was wagging ten to the dozen, her whole body in rhythm with her tail. Her tongue hung out of one side of her wide-open mouth giving the impression of an insane grin as she danced round the cart. Everyone couldn't help laughing and made a big fuss of her.

Bridget ushered Grace and Ruth in to the house where the kettle was on the boil and the table set for a meal. Michael and Jed carried in their belongings and the baskets of food whilst Seth and Jack saw to Elda who got a welcoming whiney from Tilda and Briney as she entered the paddock. Nell sat with the women whilst they had a cup of tea and then went to finish the evenings milking with the men.

Grace was impressed with the changes that Bridget had done to the house and told her so. Bridget was relieved, she had been a little worried about what Grace may think as she wanted to make a good impression. She relaxed and the three women were soon catching up with all the news.

The plan for the next day was for all of them to go up the hill after the late milking for the unveiling of the cairn and then they would have a celebratory meal back at the farm. Nell and Flo were able to attend together thanks to the help of a neighbour who would sit with their mother during the time they were away.

It was decided that the people walking up the hill on foot would set off early and Jack would drive Grace and Ruth up the hill in the back of Paddy's little cart that had been kitted out with lots of straw pillows to make the ride more comfortable. Bridget and Michael would take up the rear riding Elda and Tilda.

The next day everything was going well. The work on the farm had been completed in record time thanks to the extra help from Jack. The weather was perfect. Bridget, Grace and Ruth were in the kitchen making the last minute preparations to the food. The table was already groaning under the weight of all the dishes. Grace thought that Bridget had gone a little overboard with the food but better to have too much than too little she decided.

Jack gave them a shout. The cart was ready in the yard and with the help of Jack and Michael the ladies were safely ensconced in the back of the cart and little Paddy trotted off. They slowly made their way up the track with Jack doing his best to avoid the worst of the uneven ground.

It had been years since Grace had been up to the top of the hill, even longer for Ruth who had been just a slip of a girl when she had last accompanied both of her brothers while they checked on the flock. Both women travelled in silence reflecting on their own memories while the cart pulled slowly upwards and onwards.

As they neared the top of the hill Grace noticed a crowd of people making their way to the summit in front of them. She watched in puzzlement until she recognised all of the Rudd family from the shop, Seth's family from the Blacksmith's Forge, the teachers Miss Green and Mrs. Lewis, Beth and Jimmy from the Inn, several of her former customers from Pateley and Grassington and as they pulled onto the ridge of the hill, her sister Maude and niece Agnes stood grinning at her.

Grace was overcome with emotion. Jack turned to look at her and she could tell by his face that he was as surprised as she was. They both looked back at Bridget riding up behind them. She had a big grin on her face and winked at them both.

Grace was astounded at the majestic beauty of the cairn. It was crowned with a garland of wild flowers, another surprise of Bridget's.

Becky laid quietly at its foot. Etched neatly on the flat stone near the top of the cairn were the simple words:

Jacob

1802-1861

A Gentle Man who loved this Place.

Jack tried to make a speech to thank everyone for coming but his emotions got the better of him.

Jed took over.

"Fust of all ad like ta thank ye all on behalf o' Grace, Ruth and Jack foh trekking up 'ere ta pay thy respects ta Jacob. Ye all knew what a fine fella Jacob were. 'Ee want one foh fancy werds and neither am I so if we 'ave a quiet minute foh us all ta remember 'im in our own way. Dunt close thine eyes but cast them int distance to admire view that ee luved."

Everyone did as Jed suggested each lost in their own memories of Jacob. After several minutes silence Jed continued.

“Reet! Tha’s a load a grub darn int kitchen and yer all welcome ta fill yer boots! Anyone needing a lift int cart see Jack an he’ll ferry ye darn.”

Most people lingered for a while enjoying the scenery and the atmosphere it provoked but then slowly began to descend to the farm.

Bridget with Nell clinging on behind her rode down the hill first to be able to greet the others as they arrived and Michael went to check on the flock before leaving. Jack had to make several trips with the cart for some of the older guests before returning for Maude and Ruth.

Grace at her own request was left alone for a while to remember her beloved Jacob. Eventually when Jack arrived for her he could tell she had been crying but she welcomed him with a big smile. The two of them sat for a while hand in hand.

“You know Jack,” she said, “I feel so close to Jacob here. I think that he’s looking down on the two of us and smiling with pride that we are managing to move on with our lives. This place will always be my home in my heart. We’ve been so blessed Jack to share it for a little while with this gentle man.”

Jack squeezed her hand. He didn’t feel the need to speak as she knew already that he thought the same. As the light began to fade they bid Jacob farewell and made their way down the hill.

The gathering was in great spirits when they arrived back and continued in to the early hours of the morning. It couldn't have gone any better and it was lovely to see all their friends and family paying their respects to honour Jacob and the legacy he left behind.

There were a few tired folks the next morning at their respective work places but everyone agreed it had been well worth it. Everyone, including Grace, Ruth, Maude, and Agnes mucked in with the work on the farm with Jack and Agnes keeping them all amused with their light hearted banter. The party mood continued right in to the next day until it was time to make their farewells.

Jack always found it hard to leave the farm, his friends, the horses and Becky. He knew Grace felt the same so they decided to leave early right after breakfast to lessen the pain of leaving and also the others had the usual busy farm work ahead of them.

It was a sombre trio that made their way back down the farm track that morning leaving behind a group of subdued workers carrying out their allotted tasks.

Chapter Twenty-One.

Six years later........

The next six years passed in a blink of an eye, or so it seemed to Jack.

He and Sid were covering the nightshift down at the coach house. The loft above the large building contained several bunk rooms to accommodate the estate stable staff and the staff of visiting gentry. It had a good-sized room that contained a large table, chairs, an old oak dresser and several more comfortable chairs that were rejects from the main house. Sometimes the loft could be full to overflowing with coachmen and stable hands but not tonight.

Tonight there were just the two estate stable lads that lived in besides Sid and himself who only stayed over when they were on call. The other three had long ago retired for the night but Jack remained up for a while updating his diary. He wasn't feeling tired and he knew it would be a long night with the likelihood of being called out quite slim. He had finished reading his latest book the night before so he had come prepared this evening with several volumes of his old diaries to peruse.

He read about the first time that everyone had gone up the hill at the farm to Jacob's cairn. That was an amazing evening and the words that he had written brought back vivid memories for him.

Grace, Ruth and himself went every year on the anniversary of Jacob's death. It's more beautiful than ever now since Bridget planted daffodil bulbs around the foot of the cairn, the yellow blooms contrasting with the deep greens and brown foliage of the moor.

Bridget and Michael had a little girl the spit of her mother. She'll be about three years old now and has everyone at the farm wrapped around her little finger. She loves Paddy the Sheltie to death and would sleep in the stable with him given the chance.

Seth was still at the farm, he had just started to walk out with a girl from the village, it's early days yet so Jack didn't know how that would progress. The biggest event at the farm was last year when Jed and Nell got married! He would never have guessed that in a million years although Grace said she had seen it coming for a long time. They seemed really happy and Jack was pleased for his two friends.

Following the death of her mother Flo returned to work at the farm part time and she also works in the kitchen of the Inn in the afternoon making pies. The Inn had got busier than ever and had to extend the original building. Even with this added accommodation there were still times that they had to turn travellers away. Flo seeing the opportunity turned the empty rooms of her cottage in to guest accommodation and the rooms can be taken up to several nights a week she told them.

Jimmy continued to work at the Inn for a couple of years after his return from Blackpool and then he joined the military. Unfortunately, he hadn't kept in touch with his former friends but Jack hoped he was still well. Joshua also works at the Inn now. He started out helping in the kitchen but is now one of the main cooks and he loves his work, and by the size of him now, he loves the food he cooks too.

Maude is still living with Agnes, they moved to a bigger house but still in Skipton. Agnes is still running the ladies wear shop and there's been word that she has offered to buy it from the elderly owner.

Graces's water colour paintings are in great demand and selling well in Harrogate. Ruth continues with her business and they still have the same neighbours. Noah is a lot frailer now but his neighbours rally round to make sure he is alright. Jack still visits him on his day off as Noah still likes to keep abreast of what's happening on the estate.

Grace and Ruth visit the farm more regularly and stay with Flo when they are visiting there. They like to go to the local markets and catch up with old friends. Occasionally they travel on the train to York for the day and come back full of stories. Once they even visited Blackpool and stayed with Sally and Ron. They were really taken with the couple and their beautiful house and they were treated like gentry. Sally was so attentive to them and her other guests but unfortunately they weren't too keen on Blackpool itself. They were too old for that kind of place as it was best left for the younger ones to enjoy.

The biggest event in Jack's life had happened three years ago when he returned home from work and found two smartly dressed young men sitting in the kitchen waiting for him. The two of them sat there with huge grins across their faces as he opened the door to the kitchen. Jack stood for a second in puzzlement and then the light dawned and he rushed to envelop them in his arms.

Tears poured down all of their faces including Grace and Ruth who witnessed the meeting of Jack and his two friends Tom and Archie.

Jack could still remember the joy he felt as he held them in his arms. They had both finished their apprenticeship and were now both qualified journeymen. They still worked for Ackroyd Engineering. Mr. Ackroyd was a good boss and appreciated the hard work that they had put in over the years. He wanted them to set up another branch of his firm in Bradford and had enough confidence in them to know that they would make a success of this new venture.

They had a few weeks of free time before they moved to Bradford and the first thing on their list of things to do was to see Jack. The boys chatted all evening catching up with their news. Archie and Tom already knew most of what had been happening to Jack from his frequent letters to them. He had no idea, they told him, how much they looked forward to his letters arriving and they were so sorry they couldn't reply. Although they were well looked after with board and lodgings they never had access to money until now. Their father's health was much better and he was doing well at the hotel where he still worked. He now had a staff cottage that he rented and he lived with his mother and their young sister. It needed all the money he earned to look after them and didn't have anything spare for the boys but they understood that.

Archie and Tom were staying in a lodging house in the village up the road for a couple of nights and then planned to travel by train from York to Berwick on Tweed. They were going in search of Joe. They hoped Joe would be on the site where he stayed with his family for the winter somewhere in that area as it was their only chance of tracking him down. The boys were hoping that Jack would accompany them on their mission.

Chapter Twenty-Two.

Since their reunion two days ago the three of them had talked nonstop! They had a lot to catch up on and also plans to be made to find Joe. Jack was thrilled that he had been able to join them in their quest and hoped with all his heart that they would be successful.

According to the map that Archie carried they were to head south down the main road from the station. All that Tom and Jack could remember of what they heard Joe say about their destination was that it was situated between a forest and the shore and there was a small fishing village nearby bordering a country estate. The vital piece of information was that he could see Holy Island in the distance from the camp by the shore. Hence they knew to start their search near Berwick on Tweed.

This narrowed their search down considerably otherwise they would have had to trek the whole of Northumberland.

They cheered with pleasure when they spotted Holy Island from the window of the train on the way to Berwick. Eagerly they scanned the scenery, they caught glimpses of the sea crashing to shore between banks of sand dunes and copse's of trees and it felt like they could be in the right area. This feeling was verified when they saw a forest appear in the distance and it blocked the view of the shore for a couple of miles. The rail track then crossed over a bridge spanning a river.

"Yes!" cried Tom, "I remember now Joe did say his winter camp did have a river running past making its way to the sea!"

Jack agreed saying "That's right! Weren't there two rivers one on each edge of the camp?"

Just then the train crossed another bridge over the river and the two boys could hardly contain their excitement. When leaving Joe more than ten years ago they had dreamt that they would find him again one day, and now it looked as if that dream would become a reality.

The train pulled in to Berwick Sation. The three young men jumped down to the platform eager to continue their journey, each of them loaded down with large packs strapped to their backs.

"I hope we don't have too far to walk before we can set up camp," Tom muttered, "this is heavier than I remembered!"

"Don't be such a wimp Tom!" chided Archie good naturedly. Jack laughed at the way the two of them bantered at one another. It reminded him of himself and Agnes and how they couldn't help but wind each other up! Despite the weight of the packs the boys set off down the road with a spring in their step.

After walking for about two hours they came to the outskirts of a village.

“This could be the village that Joe spoke about,” Jack said as an elderly man was walking towards them with a sheep dog at his heel.

“Excuse me sir,” Archie approached him, “could you tell me if there is a winter camp for gypsies nearby?”

“Aye lad, you’ll be joining them by the looks of thee,” he said nodding at their packs.

“Maybe.” Archie replied with a grin.

“Carry on down the road for ten minutes then take a footpath through the field on your left, it’ll lead you to a wooden bridge over the river then take the left fork through the trees. It’ll bring you out right above the camp. That’ll save you a couple of miles at least on your journey.”

“Thank you so much for your help sir,” Archie replied and turned to grin at the other two.

They were tired, thirsty and ravenous by the time they made their way through the dense forest but the air of expectation surpassed all of these feelings. The light of the day was now fading with the path hardly visible under the canopy of the trees. They struggled on in single file, silent in their own thoughts.

Suddenly they heard voices and laughter in the distance and the yelp of a dog or two. Their heart beats quickened. Round the next bend they came to an abrupt stop, and there it was before them, the camp almost as Joe had described it.

There were several fields and paddocks with horses, a scattering of cottages and barns and beyond them several brightly coloured wagons surrounding a camp fire.

They continued down the track all tiredness forgotten in the anticipation of finding Joe. When they neared the paddock several barking dogs came running towards them alerting their owners of their presence. Two men came to meet them.

"What can we do for thee?", the older one asked the boys whilst standing to block their way down the track.

"Good evening sir, we are looking for someone called Joe. We believe he spends the winter in this camp is that right?" Archie answered him.

The two men looked at one another and shook their heads.

"No one called Joe here lad," he said to Archie. The boy's hearts sank.

"Do you know if he'll be back here for the winter?" Archie continued.

The man shook his head again. "Like I said we don't have any one here of that name or likely to have. All the family are already here for the winter. Now best be on your way lads."

“I’m sorry for the trouble,” Archie said and turned to leave. The boys downhearted began to retrace their steps that were sluggish now that their hopes were dashed. The men stood watching making sure they left.

They had almost reached the edge of the forest when suddenly one of the horses whinnied loudly and trotted to the fence towards the boys.

“Shannon!” Jack cried, “look Tom it’s Shannon!”

They ran back down the track and the horse nuzzled in to the two of them. They rubbed Shannon’s nose as tears poured down their cheeks. The two men looked at one another confused.

“How come you know yon horse?” the spokesman asked.

“It was Joe’s horse!” Jack told him, “Sheba as well”.

On hearing her name another horse trotted over and joined them at the fence. All three boys looked at the men.

“How come you’ve got Joe’s horses then?” Tom said angrily standing to face them square on.

“You had better tell us how you know yon horse’s lad and pretty sharp afore we set the dogs on thee!”

“No need for that!” Archie said pushing in front of Tom trying to calm the situation down.

“We knew Joe a long time ago,” Jack told them, “He looked after me and Tom when we had escaped the clutches of a gang of thieves that were after our blood. He got us safely back to our orphanage after we spent a couple of weeks with him on the road and we got to know the ladies here very well at that time.”

The men visibly relaxed.

“If he’s Tom, you’ll be Jack then,” he looked Jack in the eye “why didn’t you say that before lad?”

It was the turn of the boys to look confused now. “How did you know my name?” Jack asked,.

“Oh we know all about the two of you! Joe tells your story every year that we are here. It’s a favourite round the campfire! The young uns’ especially love it.”

“But what’s happened to Joe? Is he alright?” asked Jack dreading the answer.

“Nowt lad, nowt at all. We just don’t like strangers coming here in the dead of night asking questions.”

“Bloody hell!” Tom laughed and they all joined him.

The boys followed the two men towards the camp. The elder introduced himself as Sean as they walked. He was Joe’s cousin and the younger man was Marty who was Sean’s son. Joe’s away on an errand they explained. He was away to see his brother who is a keeper on the estate. He's gone to get some rabbits for the pot and should be back anytime now.

As they neared the camp Sean let out an ear-piercing whistle. Heads appeared over the doors of the wagons and everyone stopped what they were doing. Sean indicated for them to gather round.

"We've got important visitors!" he shouted.

The folk circled around the strangers wondering what all the fuss was about. Sean introduced Tom and Jack and Tom's brother Archie. A young girl gasped in surprise.

"Not *the* Tom and Jack that Joe tells us about?" she said.

"The very same!" Sean answered, "they've come looking for Joe."

"But they're not small boys!" the little girl said with confusion.

"No!" Jack assured her, "but we were the last time we saw Joe! It was a very long time ago though."

The little girl nodded accepting his explanation but still looked disappointed.

The mood of the camp came alive with expectation. Joe's going to be gobsmacked piped up a male voice.

"Let's get the lads settled in! Help them set up camp in the clearing of the dunes by Joe's wagon," said another voice.

"Better take them to meet Rosa, Joe's mother first!" Sean said.

The boys were led through to the far side of the camp. There was a narrow pathway that led in to the dunes. The path circled between two tall dunes until it reached a small clearing. There were two brightly painted wagons parked in the clearing and Jack and Tom immediately recognised Joe's wagon.

It was a little more battered and weather worn but they would have known it anywhere. They both stood quietly staring at it and it was obvious to those watching that the boys were struggling with their emotions that had been triggered at seeing Joe's wagon once again.

To give the boys a moment to collect themselves Sean turned to Archie. "How come *you* have come in search of Joe?" he asked.

"I have always wanted to meet Joe face to face so I can thank him for saving my brother and my friend. Without Joe's help the boys would not have survived on their own. We would never have seen them again and life would have been very different for me. The very least I can do is to shake his hand."

The door of the second wagon opened and an old, wizened lady stepped out with the aid of a stick.

“Is that you Joe?” she called in a shaky voice.

“No Rosa, it’s Sean and I have someone here to meet you.”

The boys stepped forward and Sean made the introductions. Rosa approached them one by one. She ran her hands gently over each of the boy’s faces and smiled.

“It’s a good day today, we have been blessed” she said to them, “time for a celebration Sean.”

“The folk in the main camp will be preparing food already,” Sean told her, “we’re going to set up the lads tents here with you and Joe. They’ll have a lot to catch up on and want a bit of privacy away from the hustle and bustle of the main camp.”

Rosa nodded. “Good thinking lad, now get someone to bring me and the lads a brew.”

The boy’s tents were set up in no time with the help of several eager and willing hands. A fire had been lit and lanterns swung from each wagon illuminating the clearing in a warm golden light. The boys sat around the fire on upturned logs and Rosa on a chair that one of the men had brought from her wagon. The men left them to chat with the promise that food would be brought to them shortly.

Rosa spoke gently to them. She told them that Joe had returned the year they had met a different person. That somehow what he had experienced with his time with the boys had helped him come to terms with his grief of losing his wife and daughter. Jack told her that they were never aware of Joe's loss and that he didn't talk much about himself.

"That's my Joe," she said.

Another ear-piercing whistle rang out. "That's Joe returning now," said Rosa, "the others won't have mentioned your presence to him. He'll get such a shock when he sees you! I wish I still had my sight to see his face."

Jack and Tom's hearts pounded. They both felt so nervous they held their breath.

When Joe walked in to the clearing he came to a sudden stop at the sight of his mother sitting with three young men that he didn't recognise.

Joe looked a little older but otherwise just the same as the boys remembered him. He carried a brace of rabbits and had a little dog at his heel. He took a step towards them with an enquiring look upon his face.

Why hadn't the others warned him there were strangers in the camp he thought and why did he sense such an electrifying atmosphere emanating from the camp he wondered as he neared the fire peering in to the dim light at the faces of the lads.

Another dog slowly entered the clearing catching up with his master.

“Pod!” shouted Tom and ran towards the dog. The little dog ran to Tom tail wagging frantically, licking the lads face as the boy stooped to gather him up in his arms.

Joe stood open mouthed and then something triggered his memory.

“No! It can’t be, surely not Tom?” he whispered.

The boy looked up at him and nodded, tears streaming down his face. Stunned, Joe looked across the fire at Jack who stood and began to walk towards him arms outstretched.

“Jack” Joe whispered.

Jack nodded unable to speak. Joe dropped the rabbits to the ground and ran to the young man and wrapped him in his arms. Tom joined them and the three of them stood holding on to one another as if their life depended on it with Pod dancing in glee around them.

A cheer rang out from the men, women and children who had silently watched the meeting from the top of the dunes.

“Celebration time!” shouted Rosa.

There was a sudden hive of activity. Young men carried in trestle tables, women laid them with platters of food. A barrel of ale arrived from nowhere and the clearing echoed with laughter and singing. Everyone wanted to pat Jack and Tom on the back and graciously included

Archie too. It was mayhem for a while until everyone had been fed. One of the men began to play his mouth organ and everyone began to sing and stamp their feet along with his tunes. Eventually Rosa signalled silently to one of the women and slowly the rest of the camp bid Joe and his friends goodnight and made their way back to the main camp.

Rosa also stood and wished them goodnight. She placed a gentle kiss on each of their heads and blessed them before slowly climbing the steps to the wagon.

Archie stayed up for a while listening to Tom, Jack and Joe catching up on each other's news until tiredness got the better of him and he crawled into his tent with the company of Tash, Joe's younger dog and the grandson of Pod. The little dog had for some reason taken a liking to Archie.

Joe told them he had worried so much about them after he dropped them off that he nearly turned around a couple of times to bring them back here with him but he forced himself to be strong.

"I knew deep down lad's that you had done the right thing and I'm proud of you and there wasn't a day passed by that I didn't think about you."

Joe told them that the following year he made a detour in to York and visited the orphanage. A young woman took him to the Matron's office where he hoped to get news of them both. However the Matron, a sour faced woman, said she had never heard of you and showed me the door. She told me if I didn't leave immediately she would send for a Constable.

I was devastated. I thought you had not made it back and the Gooding gang had caught up with you after all. I didn't know what to do or think. Luckily, the same young woman that had taken me to the Matron caught up with me just before I reached my wagon and told me that she couldn't help but over hear what had been said.

She told me that if the old Matron had still been there she would have given him a hero's welcome as would the rest of the staff who knew the story of Joe and the boys but this new Matron was a miserable bugger and wouldn't give anyone the time of day.

"So the boys did get back then?" he asked her.

"Indeed they did!" she answered, "I don't know the details but I know Jack has been placed in a foster home on a farm and Tom and his brother have been apprenticed somewhere in York but I'm sorry I don't know anymore."

He thanked her telling her he was so grateful for what she had told him and he left feeling happier that wherever they were they were safe and that was the main thing.

"It was beyond my wildest dreams and imagination that one day we would be sitting here round the fire like this. Now then gents put another log on the fire and we'll have another brew and guess what? I've got some slabs of rice pudding like Gabbie gave us that time. It's not quite as good as hers though as it lacks the dog hairs, not that there's anything wrong with an odd dog hair or two."

Jack laughed, "Yes I often chuckle at the sight of Gabbie crossing the farmyard in her hob nail boots with her leg flying out! A sight to behold was Gabbie, the most beautiful woman in the dale eh Joe? Sorry Tom you missed all that because you were fast asleep!"

"Don't worry Jack you've told me hundreds of times!"

They all laughed and Joe quipped.

"I often think of that woman down the dale who had her best sheets stolen from the washing line!"

"Best sheets my arse!" laughed Jack quoting Gabbie and once again laughter ensued.

The times they had shared were precious to each of them and would live in their hearts for the rest of their lives.

The next day Joe's brothers and their wives and family all wanted to get to know the boys and spend some time in the clearing with them.

Jack listened with interest to the stories of their travels and it reminded him of when the gypsies came to the farm every couple of years and helped with the shearing and haymaking. He told Joe's family of this and they were interested in where the farm was located.

They knew the area well and the folk that had camped and helped at the farm. In fact one of them was related to the husband of Joe's sister Maria. It was a pity that Maria and her husband were wintering further south that year as Maria would have loved to have met them. Her son Patrick was of similar age to the boys and they would have got on well.

"Patrick!" Jack said, "that's funny because one of the men that visited our farm always called me Patrick. He said I looked like one of his cousins' sons. In fact everyone of them started to call me by that name and carried on each time they visited us!"

Joe stared at Jack. "Now you come to mention it" he said, "you do have a look of our Patrick but your hair is much shorter but you have the same colouring and build".

Jack told him that his hair was much longer back then but now he had to keep it short because of his job.

"I thought that I knew you from somewhere when I first saw you but that'll be it," Joe had said.

Rosa listened to the conversation with interest.

Jack spent a lot of time in the paddock and stables getting to know the horses. He told Joe his love of horses had stemmed from his first contact with Shannon and Sheba. He and Joe took a couple of horses and rode them bare back along the beach amongst the surf. Jack loved this feeling of freedom it invoked deep within his soul.

On the morning they were due to leave Rosa clasped each boy's hand between her palms and blessed them wishing them good fortune and a speedy return.

When she took Jack's hand her sightless eyes stared deeply in to his own. She hesitated then gently squeezed his hand and whispered in his ear.

"You are blessed Jack for you have a powerful force watching over you. Sometimes you might experience things that you don't understand but don't be frightened of them. Embrace them and you will find the answers within your own intuition. Always have trust in your own thoughts Jack and listen to the sounds of nature and take wisdom from the beasts that walk this earth."

She then in her normal voice gave him the same blessing as the other two. Jack thanked her for the blessing and went to join the others deep in thought at her words. They had really touched him.

Joe dropped them off at the station. He wished them good fortune and cheerfully waved them off. He knew in his heart that the boys would return and each winter they did.

The boys reluctantly went their separate ways at York station. Tom and Archie returning to their lodgings to prepare for their move to Bradford and Jack onwards to Harrogate to continue with his job on the estate.

They all knew the parting wasn't a goodbye but a see you later.

Back at the coach house ....

Jack woke up with a jolt. He was still sitting in the chair with his diary that he had been reading across his lap. It was beginning to get light outside and he decided there was no point in going to bed now so he decided to take a walk around the stables.

He loved the atmosphere of the stables at this hour before the stable lads arrived with their barrows to start mucking out whilst shouting to each other or whistling tunelessly. He made his way slowly round the stalls stopping to rub a few noses and whisper words of endearment to his four-legged friends.

His thoughts turned to Bessie as they often did nowadays. He had first seen her a few years back when he had to take the Master and his wife to visit the Master's cousin who lived on a small estate at Langfell.

He and Sid had just entered the kitchen of the Hall for a bite to eat and the bonniest lass that he'd ever seen was sitting in a corner engrossed in a book.

The staff at the hall were all very friendly just as Sid had already told him, and it wasn't long before he had them all laughing at his stories.

Bessie however remained aloof. He could tell that she found some of his stories amusing by the little smile that would light up her face occasionally and he would tease her on purpose just to make her blush and he found her bashfulness very endearing.

At first she would try and avoid his company directly but he would try to seek her out or send one of the other maids to ask her to join them.

It took almost two full years of his relentless pursuit before she warmed to him enough to join in his banter. She was witty and funny and a good match for his good humour and they became good friends.

It took a chance encounter down by the lake, when Bessie had found him breaking his heart because he had to shoot a young mare and her foal that morning. She held him in her arms and tried to comfort him. He sensed then that her feelings towards him had grown deeper and beyond friendship after she witnessed his vulnerability. It wasn't the right time to explore this feeling further for either of them. He was still upset and felt a little embarrassed that she had found him in that sad state. He was a proud man and didn't want to appear weak even though he enjoyed the feeling of being comforted.

After his accident with the stallion and the months he spent laid in a hospital bed with nothing to do but reflect on his life he came to realise what he truly wanted for his future.

He had dalliances before with a couple of maids from the estate who had made it obvious they were interested in him. However, after a short while he realised they weren't meant to be long term and he lost interest. It wasn't through any fault of theirs but they would giggle and laugh at his stories and agree with all of his opinions but not offer any of their own. There was no substance in the relationships. He felt bad about this but for his own sake and theirs he wasn't willing to compromise and yet he didn't want to take advantage of their vulnerability.

However, before he met Bessie he did have a clandestine affair with a very pretty nursery maid.

She was four or five years older than him and already betrothed to a footman that worked at a neighbouring house. She had made it plain to him on several occasions that she was interested. She made a point of always sitting next to him at the big table in the kitchen and laugh a little too loudly at his banter. She would touch his arm and stroke it meaningfully as she leaned forward to whisper innuendos in his ear. He felt awkward and embarrassed but thrilled at the same time! He did nothing to encourage her advances yet enjoyed them just the same and she had a knack of seeking him out when he was alone.

One evening he had just finished cleaning one of the coaches when she crept up behind him. She placed a finger on her lips and took hold of his hand and stepped inside the coach and pulled him towards her. He tried to object, it was going beyond teasing, and he told her it was wrong and that she was betrothed. She laughed and told him not to worry! She only saw her young man once a month and it was not enough to satisfy her needs. She reckoned her and Jack could come to an arrangement that would benefit both.

He lost his virginity that night in the back of the plush interior of the coach.

For several weeks afterwards she sought him out at every opportunity. If he tried to object she would place a finger to her lips, place his hand on her breast, push her body hard against his and whisper in his ear how she wanted him to give her pleasure. He didn't stand a chance.

After each encounter she would kiss him gently on the forehead and walk away without a word. He would be left with the feeling of being used and riddled with guilt. He didn't fool himself in to believing that he had any feelings for her other than lust and knew it was the same for her.

It wasn't too long before their encounters became more infrequent. Then one evening she told him she was thinking of calling off her betrothal. She thought that her and Jack would make a better married couple and what did Jack think? His blood ran cold.

"Hell no!" he answered before he could think.

She smiled at him and walked away. Jack didn't miss her. He was relieved and wanted to put the whole sorry mistake behind him.

He did think afterwards that she had purposely contrived their last meeting as very soon afterwards the rumour from the house was that the Master's young son had been seen leaving her bedroom on several occasions. Good luck to him Jack thought!

If anyone from the house had found out or suspected about his dalliance with her they didn't say. He would have been mortified if Grace and Ruth had found out through gossip. He felt bad enough as it was but he knew he had a lucky escape, that's for sure.

The one good thing about that relationship Jack thought as he lay in the hospital bed, was that he knew his feelings for Bessie were totally different. Yes, he was attracted to her physically but he also respected her dignity, her family values and her kindness, her wit and sense of humour, her work ethic, her generosity and the list was endless. This hardened his resolve that he was right and his feelings towards her made him want to be with her.

He decided that first he had to be honest with Bessie and had to tell her of his deep feelings for her. If he was wrong and she didn't feel the same about him, or now that he was disabled she may have a change of heart, then he would have to move on with his life and try to forget her.

Although terrified he was determined that on his next visit to the Hall he would find the strength and courage to confront her with his feelings.

He was also aware that Bessie knew nothing about his past and who he shared his life with or what kind of person he had become and what his fears, strengths and weaknesses were. He wanted to be sure that she knew all about him before she committed to being in a relationship with him. Afterall, his deep sense of guilt at being abandoned and not even knowing his real last name or true birth date was always close to the surface.

It would not be easy and by being so honest with Bessie it would probably open old wounds within himself and he would have to be strong to face the emotions that he had strived to keep hidden all of his life.

Chapter Twenty-Three.

with Bessie at Langfell Hall ....

Bessie was abruptly brought out of her reverie by a particularly loud shriek of laughter from the nursery next door.

She smiled. She had been lost in thought for over an hour as she remembered the time that she and Jack had sat by the lake and he had told her all about his life.

She remembered the warm summer evenings as if they were yesterday. Jack had been so worried. He had thought that by revealing his past and his innermost fears to her she may change her mind about being with him. In fact, just the opposite was true and her feelings towards Jack became stronger. She respected him so much for being so honest with her even though she could tell that it was hard for him to reveal so much of himself and she sensed how his early childhood troubled him.

Over several evenings the couple had laughed and cried, had reflected and contemplated together until Jack had finished his story. She sensed a weight had been lifted from his inner being and she had taken him in to her arms and told him how much she loved and cherished him and wanted to be with him for the rest of her life.

She had known without a shadow of doubt that she didn't want to spend her life with anyone else but Jack.

Being with Jack enriched her life so much in the months that followed and he had taken her to meet Grace and Ruth which were his only family.

She had been so nervous at meeting them as she knew how important to him they were but she had no need to be. Within minutes of meeting them she had felt at home and so welcomed. She laughed at remembering the gathering of their neighbours at the big outside table and how they had all come to say hello to Jack's girl. Everyone contributed to the food and laughter echoed throughout the evening.

They had spent a few days on the farm and the two of them had helped with the chores and Bessie handled them with ease. She couldn't have felt more welcome as Jack's friends had all been really easy to get on with and she felt she had always known them.

Jack had taken her up the hill to see Jacob's cairn. She had held his hand as he told her how much he loved Jacob but had never told him and how he wished he could have had the chance to tell him whilst he was alive.

She had put her arms around him and hugged him tight and told him how much she would have loved to have met Jacob.

"He sounded as if he was a lovely man, well respected and loved just like you Jack," she had said.

She still recalled the gentle tremble and feeling of warmth that surrounded her heart as she envisaged a tall thin white-haired gentleman smiling and nodding at her in her mind's eye.

She didn't understand what had happened to her in that moment but she knew it would stay with her for the rest of her life.

Before they left the farm Jack's friend Joshua invited them down to the Inn. He wanted to cook a meal for them. She and Jack had never dined out before and didn't know what to expect. Jed and Nell joined them for moral support.

They were shown through to a private dining room where the staff treated them like gentry. The meal was delicious and she had told them she could very easily get used to it!

"You've no need to bother!" said Jack, "not on my wages!"

The four of them laughed. The evening had been a night to remember for all of them.

On another day they took the train and visited Tom and Archie in Bradford. The boys were really doing well with the new workshop and both of them had been given a small number of shares in the company as a reward for their great efforts. Most of Tom's time was now exploring and designing new ideas to promote the company's growth. Archie ran the workshop and was much happier on the shop floor. Tom had just begun stepping out with the owners youngest daughter but Archie was still single and fancy free.

Jack and Bessie had written frequently to each other whilst apart with Jack in Harrogate and Bessie at Langfell.

Jack's letters were full of stories of where he had travelled to with the Master and of the latest gossip and news from the big House and stables. She had loved to hear what Grace, Ruth and their neighbours were up to and how the farm was getting on as she felt very fond of them all. They had made her a part of their life and in return they were a part of her life too.

She was aware that her letters to Jack were not so interesting as the days at Langfell Hall were often much the same as the day before. The staff all got on well together and there were no scandals that she was aware of! She was sure that Jack wouldn't be interested in the latest fashion designs and accessories that she had created for Lady Celeste so she glossed over them.

She recollected how anxious she had felt regarding her and Jack's future. She loved this place but knew she would have to be prepared to move away eventually if she wanted to be with Jack. She was certain that Jack would find life here too tedious and too restricted compared to the comings and goings at the big House where landed gentry were always paying a visit. She knew he loved his job as a coachman and the not knowing where he would be travelling to from one day to the next and of course all of the horses he had to care for in the stables.

Langfell Hall could not compare to what Jack was used to.

One evening Watson, the butler, told her to expect a visit from Jack the next day. The family from the big House were visiting Langfell and were due to arrive the following afternoon. As usual she had made an extra effort with her appearance and she still got butterflies in her tummy whenever she knew Jack was coming to the Hall.

She had been surprised however when Sid entered the kitchen alone without Jack. Sid told her that Jack was busy with one of the horses. She had said she would nip down to the stables for a minute to see him but Sid became flustered and said she couldn't do that as the horse was very nervous. He turned to the cook with a pleading look on his face.

"Bessie," the cook had said to her, "can you give me a hand with these jellies if you have a minute they won't keep like this."

Bessie had given her a hand but had thought something was up but couldn't for the life of her think what it could be.

It was late afternoon before Jack made an appearance. He took Bessie by the hand and, ignoring her pleas of being too busy or Lady Celeste needing her, he led her down to the lakeside.

He sat her down on what they called “their” seat and then went down on one knee and reached out gently for her hand and clasped it tenderly in his own.

He asked Bessie to be his wife and she tearfully accepted as tears of joy ran down her cheeks.

“Why the subterfuge?” she asked.

“I’ve been busy all morning,” he told her, “first I went up to the farm to ask your dad for his permission to marry you and everyone up there are thrilled! Then I had to see Sir John” he said.

She looked puzzled, “Why ask to see Sir John?” she enquired.

“To ask for a job at Langfell” he told her, “You are now looking at the new assistant gardener!”

She gasped and shook her head.

“You can’t do that! You love your job with the horses!”

“I love you more,” he told her, “there’s no way I want you to leave your home and family to be with me.”

He placed a finger on her lips to stop her protests, “It’s all sorted” he said, “So let me finish, Sir John has proposed that I start in the garden just now and help with the horses if necessary and he would also negotiate with a few of the nearby racing stables where he says my natural expertise with the highly strung thoroughbreds might come in useful. A small fee will be charged for each visit that would be paid directly to me. I feel so honoured by this as it feels as if the little boy from the orphanage is now standing proud in his own achievements."

"Oh I nearly forgot!" he continued with a broad grin, "We are to live in Rose Cottage down by the river."

"Oh! Rose Cottage is my favourite!" she told him.

"Yes I know that!" he replied with an even bigger grin.

The news of the betrothal soon got around the estate and village.

A few days afterwards Lady Celeste presented her with the gift of a full roll of white satin for her bridal gown. It was beautiful and of very high quality. Bessie was lucky to be able to make her own wedding gown from this generous gift.

Jack and her brothers had worked hard in their spare time to bring Rose Cottage to its former glory. Arthur and Sam, the stable lads, had hauled the donated furniture from the Hall to make the cottage more homely.

Bessie had begun to make the house in to a home and made the wedding invitations to hand out to their friends and family. Everyone was so busy getting the cottage ready and the preparations for the wedding that the time since she said yes and the day arriving seemed to fly by.

In no time at all she found herself on her father's arm walking down the aisle of the church with the faces of her family and their friends smiling warmly at her.

Grace, Ruth, Tom, Archie, Ned, Nell and Joshua were able to attend but it was difficult for the others to leave the farm.

She couldn't help but shed a few tears as Jack said his vows to her in a trembling voice as he meant every word.

Her voice trembled too as she spoke her own vows and the gleam in her eyes showed she also meant every word.

It had been a beautiful autumn day with the leaves on the trees golden in the sunlight. The ceremony was in the village church and the reception was held afterwards in the barn of her parent's farm.

Bessie's mother and her family and staff from the Hall including Cook, Tess and Celia the housemaid, all helped to make it a great success. The tables groaned with the weight of food and even Watson the butler had provided a barrel of ale for the reception at his own expense!

It was a jolly affair with two of her brothers' pals providing entertainment on their fiddles and everyone at some point succumbed to the dance floor. Even Watson joined in and Grace and Ruth were in their element!

Initially Grace and Ruth were due to be staying at the Inn in the village but Lady Celeste would not hear of it and had sent them a formal invitation to stay at the Hall. They were a little overwhelmed at first but realised they couldn't refuse.

Sir John and Lady Celeste went out of their way to make them welcome with no airs or graces. Grace and Ruth both took fondly to Celeste as they were instructed to call her, and Grace was so happy knowing that Jack was going to be in a lovely job and living in a beautiful environment.

Unfortunately, Tom and Archie had to leave the reception early as they had to be back to see an important client later the next day.

The highlight of the day for Bessie though was when she and Jack were finally alone and he carried her over the threshold of their cottage in to their new home and a new life and closed the door.

Chapter Twenty-Four.

Two years later.........

Since their wedding almost two years ago Bessie and Jack had been so happy. They had yet to have a cross word and agreed on most aspects of life. Langfell Hall was now common ground to both of them and they would share news from the estate and village. They worked hard together to make their home comfortable and sat for hours planning their dream of one day owning their own home.

Jack had come to love his job in the gardens. He worked with Amos the head gardener who had been at the Hall for as long as Bessie could remember and, with the help of two young men from the village, the gardens flourished. Jack respected Amos's font of wisdom and knowledge. He learned something new every day he told Bessie. He still kept his hand in with the horses on the home farms on the estate and of course the Langfell stables as well as regular visits to the racing stables in the neighbourhood. The extra income this provided meant their savings were slowly mounting up.

Every morning the two of them walked together to the Hall before going to their separate places of work.

Jack waved Bessie good bye and went to collect the horse and cart from the stables. He was to meet Amos down by the lake. They were going to clear the weeds from the inlet and outlet of the lake to stop it choking up before the onset of winter. Amos had told him that the weeds were to be left to breakdown over the winter and would make good compost for the gardens in the spring.

Later that morning Bessie was to accompany Lady Celeste whilst she delivered the surplus fruit and veg from the Hall gardens. She did these deliveries to the sick or less privileged quite often.

Today they were heading up to the mining hamlet that was situated near the top of the Fell. A narrow steep lane weaved its way above Langfell village out past the quarry and up to the miner's village. Bessie always enjoyed these trips out with Lady Celeste as she was a good horsewoman and handled the small trap excellently.

Thankfully, it was a lovely sunny day compared to the constant rain they had endured for the last three days. They set off in good time and waved to Jack and Amos toiling by the lake.

Amos turned to Jack as the trap passed them.

"You're a lucky lad Jack," he said, "Bessie is a grand lass an 'as a 'eart of gold make no mistake."

"I am indeed," agreed Jack, "I don't know what I'd do without her."

They continued dredging the weed and throwing it in to the back of the cart. It was made all the harder as the inlet stream was swollen with water running off the fell. They worked in silence but making good progress until stopping for a brew of tea and a piece of sponge cake that Bessie had packed up for the two of them.

They were in deep conversation planning a new rockery for the following spring when suddenly there was a deafening boom followed by a long ricocheting roar that echoed down the dale.

"What the heck was that!" Jack shouted out.

"They must be blasting at the quarry," Amos answered, "but I've niver heard it as loud as that before."

Both men turned their attention towards the fell as a huge bellowing plume of dust swept the hillside and rolled down towards the village below.

"I hope everything is alright up there!" said Jack but no sooner were the words out of his mouth when they heard the sound of a bell tolling from the same direction.

"Oh no!" Amos exclaimed, "Summat's up at the quarry! Come on lad we'll best get up there to see if they need help!"

They threw the rakes on to the back of the cart and headed up the track and out towards the quarry.

As they were about to turn their cart up the narrow lane leading to the quarry another cart was racing down the lane towards them so they stopped at the lane end.

They noticed several men in the back of the cart were covered from head to foot in dust and they looked dazed, staring ahead with a blank expression on their faces.

A couple were bleeding and obviously in pain. The driver called out to them.

"I'm getting' these lads to the village to get medical attention. Sum of em 'ave broken bones I think!"

He told them there had been a massive land slide at the quarry. It was lucky that the blast had generated away from the workings of the quarry but it caused the huge overhang to break away from the fell or otherwise lives would have been lost. As a result of the outcrop of rock taking the blast the lane was now buried beneath tons of rock and rubble. They would need all the help they could get to get the lane cleared.

Jack began to panic. He told Amos that Bessie and Lady Celeste were up there somewhere and he hoped they had reached the mining village before the blast. His heart was pounding as he encouraged the horse to go as quickly as it could up the steep lane.

"Nay lad, I'm sure tha two of em will be alright." Amos tried to reassure Jack.

As they got near the thick cloud of dust they could make out the gigantic pile of rock blocking off the lane. There were men heaving heavy stones and yelling frantic commands at each other.

Jack spurred the horse on. He pulled the cart to a halt as near to the landslide as he could and jumped from the cart and began to run up towards the men. He was breathless and pouring with sweat by the time he reached the men and was just about to join in to help them when he froze at the sight of the twisted wreckage of Lady Celeste's cart buried under the rocks.

He fell to his knees.

"Please God no, no!" he yelled over and over.

One of the men came running over to him. Jack could hardly speak. He had never experienced so much pain. The blood was pounding in his head and he couldn't get his breath.

"It's my wife! It's my wife!" he stuttered and indicated to the remains of the cart. The man looked confused.

"No, no!" he cried. He was aware he wasn't making any sense but he couldn't get the right words to come out of his mouth.

He was still sitting there shaking and crying when Amos reached him. Amos was also white faced and in shock himself when he recognised the mangled trap but he knew he had to be strong for Jack whose body was going in to shock. He bent down and took Jack in to his strong arms and held on to him tightly as he didn't know what else to do. The two of them clung together for several minutes with Jack shivering and sobbing in to Amos's shoulder.

Suddenly there was the sound of a female voice shouting,

"Jack! Amos! Is that you?"

The two men looked up in confusion for appearing out of the thick cloud of dust were two bedraggled women leading a horse up towards them.

"Bessie? Bessie?" Jack whispered in disbelief.

He staggered towards her and picked her up in his arms and held on to her so tightly she could hardly breathe. He was still sobbing but now it was with relief and not anguish.

The two women noticed the mangled wreckage of the trap buried underneath the rocks and it became obvious to them why Jack was so distressed. They were shocked themselves as they realised what a lucky escape they had.

"It's alright Jack, everything is alright," Bessie said as she held and comforted him.

"We are both fine Jack, we're fine!"

The four of them sat out of the way of the quarrymen and the other men from the village that had come to help after they had heard the blast and the tolling of the bell. Jack still held tightly on to Bessie as she explained what had happened to them that morning.

Lady Celeste had been driving the trap up the lane and they had just reached the overhang of rock by the quarry when one of the wheels of the trap had got stuck in the mud from the previous heavy rain and would not budge!

Bessie had suggested that she go and get help from one of the men at the quarry who could ride down to the Hall for help and they could wait in the trap until the stable lads arrived.

Thankfully, Lady Celeste had another idea and unhitched the horse from the trap and using a coil of rope lashed the laden baskets to the horse's sides and the two of them set off to walk the remaining half mile or so to the hamlet.

They had not long reached the hamlet when the blast erupted and the dust cloud enveloped the hamlet where just moments before the children were playing happily.

There had been a second of stunned silence then everything seemed to happen at once. The children began to wail and their frightened mothers called them in to protect and comfort them.

Men who had been sleeping after the night shift at the mine came running out of their houses still fastening their breeches. The men's first instinct was to turn towards the mine above but when they saw the dust cloud below and the bell began to toll they abruptly changed direction and began to race down the hill to the quarry.

The two women were frightened and concerned but tried not to show it in front of the children and their panicking mothers.

They quickly left the baskets at the side of the road and began their descent not knowing what they were going to encounter. It wasn't long before the wall of rock emerged out of the cloud of dust in front of them.

The only way down was to make a circuitous route around the edge of the pile of rocks. This meant they had to head some way out on to boggy uneven ground that ran parallel to the side of the lane.

It was hard going but they managed to make sure and steady progress. Both of their dresses and footwear were saturated and caked in mud when they eventually made it back to the lane. Their shock at the sight of the devastation changed to total confusion when they saw Jack and Amos at the side of the lane in an obvious state of distress.

For the first time Jack noticed the state of the two bedraggled women but still thought they were the best thing he had ever seen.

Lady Celeste noticed that Jack was still shivering and thought it best to get him home as soon as possible.

“One good thing Bessie,” she announced, “Is that our carriage awaits to take us home!”

She indicated the weed laden cart and they all managed to smile.

Langfell Hall, 2015.

"Well girls!" Emma said to her nieces, "That's all of the story you are getting for tonight. This old girl is needing her bed and goodness knows I need my beauty sleep."

"I heard the men folk arrive back from the Pub over an hour ago and a little worse for wear by the sound of them! They'll be wondering where you are. It's still snowing outside so you will be needing your skis to get back to Rose Cottage if you're not careful."

The girls had sat wrapt with attention throughout the story of how their three times great grandparents had met and their link with Langfell Hall.

"What a wonderful story aunty Emm, and even more so knowing it's real! I can't wait to hear more." Sarah said.

"Yes and Lady Celeste seems an interesting character also," Laura commented.

"She certainly was!" said Emma, "and there's lots more yet to come, but as I said it's for another time my dears."

Both girls kissed her goodnight and left Emma alone to her own thoughts of the past and how history really did repeat itself.

Acknowledgements:

A special thank you to my proof writer and husband who hopefully has put all the dots in the right place!

Thank you.

Lynn Carter was born and brought up in Yorkshire before moving to the North East of Scotland with her husband and two sons. She is now a retired Nurse and this is her first novel and she hopes everyone enjoys reading it!

Printed in Great Britain
by Amazon

64537478R00210